Flytrap

By Mauro Azzano

© 2024

For Alison, who has always had my back, and will always have my love.

For our children, their spouses, and our grandchildren, who have our hearts.

Prologue:

The fog was thicker than usual tonight. The dirt road, rutted and weaving between tall pines in this remote park, would hide his headlights from anyone more than a hundred feet away. This late in the year all the summer campers had left the park anyway, and it was far too wet for the yuppie hikers to be out.

His van jostled, creaking over the ruts, its faded brown paint perfectly blending into the muddy ground. The name on the side, 'Custom Auto Upholstery', belonged to the previous owner, but it suited him to keep that name on it.

He blew cigarette smoke out the open window into the cold air, leaning against the steering wheel to keep the van headed straight. He had scouted out the road before—never in this van, of course. This was a perfect place to dump something, especially at this time of night, especially at this time of year.

His boots would be in a landfill next week, so footprints would not betray him. Logging trucks would drive this road in a few hours and cover the van's tracks, so that didn't worry him either. He opened the double back doors, slid out a long bundle wrapped in rough burlap, and dragged it fifty feet to the lake. The muddy water was not very deep, but the heavy bricks inside the burlap would keep the bundle under water until the contents had rotted or were eaten.

He walked back to his van, stood perfectly still for five minutes to be certain nobody had seen him, then he drove away.

Chapter 1: Roll Call

It was only twenty meters from his doorway to the next building. He could cover that in eight seconds. The best time to run was right after the next burst of gunfire, he thought.

There was a cacophony of rounds from the two or three AK-47s in the windows above, then silence. Bishop took a deep breath and sprinted across the open courtyard. He was two short steps from the other doorway when he felt a stabbing pain. He buckled and fell to the ground, flat onto his backpack. Looking down over his chest armor, he could see the gash in his thigh where the 7.62 round had gone through his leg. Someone ran towards him, holding an AK-47, his face wrapped in a scarf against the sand, wearing a quilted jacket over a shalwar kameez and sandals. The man aimed his AK-47 at Bishop, but Bishop already had his M 4 up and squeezed the trigger. The three-round burst hit the man squarely in the chest and he dropped to his knees, his weapon still pointing at Bishop. Bishop fired again. The man went down for good.

Bishop woke up.

In Seattle, it rains all the time. Everybody says so- especially if they're not from here.

Visitors complain about the rain, the gloom, the cold, the dark. They complain about it all.

Truth is, Seattle gets a bad rap. Houston is wetter. Most of Florida is wetter. Even Buffalo gets more rain than Seattle.

John Bishop was tired of explaining this to his out-of-town friends. Eventually, he just answered 'yep' to the weather questions and moved on.

This October morning, for instance, was unusually dry. A warm trend over the last week made the sidewalk shimmer in the early sunlight and the trees crackle with wilting leaves.

At five-thirty Bishop did what he did every morning at this time; fifty pushups, a hundred sit-ups, laced up his shoes and went for a three-mile run through the dark streets.

An hour later he showered, ate breakfast and dressed for work.

He wore beige chinos and a blue dress shirt, just like every workday. He laced up his dress Oxfords, making sure the shoes had no scuffs or dirt on them, then carefully centered the row of buttons on his shirt over the buckle on his belt and lined up with his pants zipper. It was an old habit from time in the Army, and a subtle sign to others who had also been in the military.

He got into his Jeep, waited a moment for the engine to smooth out to a steady idle, then released the clutch and drove off.

At this time of day, it was a twenty-minute drive to the University of Washington. Bishop joined the morning commuter traffic, turned off at the same exit he always turned off at, and followed Skagit Lane to a series of parking spots under a large sign that said 'Faculty Only'.

He parked between two other cars, took his briefcase off the passenger seat and went into the University building.

Three or four people nodded to him as they passed, and he nodded back. He jogged effortlessly up the stairs to the third floor and opened the heavy metal door to the hallway.

A cluster of young men and women, all in green tee shirts and black shorts, ran along the hallway toward him. They stopped as they saw him and stood up straight.

"Morning, sir." One said, firmly.

The others all muttered the same thing.

Bishop nodded. "Morning, all."

The group continued down the hallway. Bishop turned back to them and called out.

"Farrow!"

One of the young men ran back to meet him. "Sir?" He asked.

"See me in my office before class." Bishop said.

The young man's face fell. "Sir, yes, sir." He said and ran back to join the others.

Bishop continued on to the end of the hall and turned left. There was a single office door, and on the wall beside the door were three black plastic signs with white lettering, alphabetically listing the names of three instructors. Bishop's name was at the top of the list.

The office had a reception desk facing the entrance, and off to the side were three separate rooms, each with an instructor's name on them. He went into the room marked 'J. Bishop' and placed his briefcase on his desk. At five minutes to eight he pulled three manila folders out of his briefcase and placed them in the 'IN' tray beside him. He glanced at the tabs on the folders, confirming their contents. These were the case studies for today's class. Bishop taught strategic intelligence in warfare, and the case studies explained to his students why this was so vital.

He scribbled some quick notes on a pad, shorthand for the points he wanted to convey, then arranged the folders in order of delivery.

A knock at the door made him turn. The young man from the hallway, now in dress slacks and an Army green polo shirt, stood waiting in the doorway.

Bishop waved the man in. "Come in. Sit down." He said.

The young man sat sheepishly across from him.

Bishop opened the drawer in his desk and took out three stapled pages.

He placed them on the desk. "What do you call this?" He asked.

The young man glanced down, then back up. "My report on North Korea, sir."

Bishop shook his head. "Did you just Google, copy and paste, or did you talk to the tourist bureau at the North Korean embassy?"

The young man blushed a deep red. "No, sir. I researched it myself. What's wrong with it?"

Bishop sighed. "Trees died for the paper in this report, Farrow. If I had a parrot, he wouldn't crap on it. You have no arguments, no theories, no supporting evidence, no conclusion. All it says to me is 'North Korea, bad place, hungry people.'"

Farrow pursed his lips. "I thought I was making a valid point, sir."

"How exactly were you making a point?"

"I thought I expressed my thoughts on the subject quite clearly, sir." The man said.

Bishop looked out the window at the parking lot. "Do you date, Farrow?"

"Sir?"

"Girls, Farrow. Do you like girls?"

"Very much, sir." He answered, indignantly.

"Where do you meet these, alleged girls, Farrow?"

"At the U W bar, usually, sir."

"So, when you meet a girl in a bar, how do you make your move? 'Me like you, come with me now' or do you warm her up first?"

The young man's face slowly broke into a wide smile. "I think I understand, sir. May I redo the report?"

Bishop handed the pages over. "Nine AM tomorrow. My parrot thanks you."

The young man nodded and left. Bishop finished making class notes and poured himself a coffee, sat back down and looked at his watch. Eight twenty-eight.

A clip-clop sound of shoes coming down the hall got louder, then the owner of the shoes came into the reception area.

The shoes belonged to a woman in her early thirties, very thin, almost painfully so, with wheat colored hair pulled back in a short ponytail and hazel eyes over an aquiline nose. She had a clutch of manila folders in her arms, pressed against her so they didn't scatter all over the floor. She glanced over at Bishop and nodded.

"Good morning, Bish." She said cheerily.

"Hey. Morning, Kelly." He answered.

"Did you get the files you requested?" She asked casually.

"Files?" He repeated.

"Case studies for the course. You asked for them last week?"

Bishop glanced at his 'IN' tray. "Right. Got them here. Thanks, Kelly."

She nodded and went into the other offices, placed half of the folders on the second desk then the rest on the third desk. She smoothed her grey skirt and went back to Bishop's desk.

"Did you sign for that other file yet?" She asked.

"Other file? Which other file?"

She huffed and shook her head. "I got a call from some plebe at the Army library, said that he was sending over a case study. He said someone has to sign for it."

Bishop shrugged. "Doesn't ring a bell. It may have been from last semester- they get behind sometimes, after all."

"Either way, if it comes in the morning's mail I'll leave it on your desk."

She walked out of the office and down the main hall, the sound of her shoes going clip-clop getting fainter as she went.

Bishop finished his coffee, gathered his class notes and took a small green USB stick from his desk. He checked his watch. Eight fifty-three.

He walked the zigzag halls to a wide brown wooden door marked Classroom C325 and opened it. The room was laid out like a standard lecture hall. Four levels of student desks formed an arc around the lectern down below. Bishop stood at the lectern, scanned the room quickly and flipped on the microphone in the lectern and nodded.

"Good morning, class." He barked.

The thirty-five young men and women all answered back "Good morning, sir."

Bishop smiled and inserted the USB stick into a terminal inside the lectern.

He pressed some buttons and a large white projection screen appeared.

He looked around at the students, watching their faces, their curiosity and apprehension. As the projection screen lit up a movie came on.

It was a scene from a western movie, a typical small-town street that showed a cowboy coming out of a saloon. The camera followed the cowboy as he walked down the middle of a dusty street, looked around and unclipped the leather strap on his six-shooter's holster.

A series of shots rang out and the predictable happened. The cowboy fired from the hip and a figure with a rifle groaned, then fell off a roof. The cowboy swiveled around and fired down the road, then another figure leaped out from behind a post, threw its arms up and fell over. Two others were dispatched the same way, after which the cowboy holstered his gun and went back into the saloon.

Bishop turned off the video and pointed at the screen.

"Who can tell me what he did wrong?"

Many hands went up. Bishop pointed to a young woman. "Mendoza?"

She stood up. She started speaking, but it was almost a whisper. Bishop shook his head.

"I'm not good at lip-reading, Esther. Louder."

The class laughed. The woman blushed slightly, took a deep breath and spoke forcefully.

"He didn't have situational awareness, no observable intelligence on the battlefield, and I'm pretty sure that even an average shot with a rifle would have gotten him before he took a hip shot with that cheesy revolver."

The class laughed again and she sat down.

Bishop grinned. "Very good. He was outgunned and outmanned. Let's for the sake of argument say he had done his recon, got all his ducks in a row before he left the saloon. What is the very first thing he did wrong?"

Hands went up. Students gave opinions, from facing the sun to being out in the middle of the street instead of along the sidewalk, to not turning around often to see who was going to shoot him in the back. Bishop shook his head at all of them.

One student finally put her hand up. Bishop pointed to her. "Cohen?"

She stood up. "His gun was in his holster with the snap done up."

Bishop nodded. "What would you have done, Cohen?"

"Either unsnap the holster or have the gun in my hand at the ready, sir."

Bishop stretched his hands in front of him and clapped. "Finally." He said.

"Right answer, Cohen. Preparation is important. If he had the time to walk out of the safe building and into the street, he had the time to unsnap the holster."

He looked around at the class. There were nods and smiles, and a few puzzled looks. "How does this relate to the world today?"

He turned on the screen again, this time to a devastated city street, bombed out and covered in rubble. "July, twenty seventeen, the battle for Mosul. Turn to page fifty-three in your workbooks." He said.

The students opened their books to that page. Bishop waited till they all looked at him. "All right. Now, about the battle of Mosul."

At exactly twelve thirty-five Bishop walked into the restaurant where he always ate, just a few hundred feet from his classroom, ordered his usual turkey sandwich and sat by the window waiting for his food. He took out a scribble pad and doodled notes for the afternoon.

The restaurant had a captive market; most of the staff, some of the students and a number of visitors ate there. The food was good, reasonably priced and the service was quick.

While Bishop waited, people he knew came in to grab take-out or order lunch. He nodded politely and went back to his scribble pad.

Kelly, his receptionist, raced in with a slip of paper in her hand. The other two instructors in his office had an arrangement; she picked up lunch for both of them and they paid for hers in exchange.

She read the order number to the woman behind the counter, and the woman picked up two large paper bags and set them on the counter. Kelly thanked her and turned to leave. She spotted Bishop and went over to him.

"Hey, Bish, that courier file came by for you." She said.

Bishop frowned. "What file is that again?"

The paper bag in Kelly's left hand shifted and she rested it on the table to get a better grip. "Dunno. They just said it was for you. You can…"

The paper bag slipped again. "Gotta go. Ask me later."

She rushed out the door.

Bishop shook his head and went back to his scribble pad. The woman behind the counter called his name and he took the sandwich to his table. Had he called for a case file and forgotten about it? Probably. It sometimes happened.

At four forty-five, Bishop turned off the projection screen for the day and turned to the students in his class. "Any questions?"

Nobody spoke. "No? Good. Nine AM tomorrow. See you then."

He folded up his notes and pressed the button to roll the projection screen back up. Students filed past him on the way out, nodding as they went. One student stayed in his seat, frowning.

Bishop waited till the rest had gone then stood beside him. "Farrow? You have a question for me, I presume?"

The student furrowed his brow, thinking. "Sir, what would you have done back there?"

"In the saloon scenario?"

"Yes, sir."

Bishop smiled. "I wouldn't have gone out the front door."

He walked to the blackboard and picked up a piece of chalk. He drew two long horizontal lines, the street, and a number of boxes on either side of them, the buildings.

He put a circle inside one box. "The saloon. If I was here, I'd look out the windows first, for any obvious threat. Then, if I felt safe, I'd go out between these two buildings."

He drew a curved line from the saloon box, stopping between two other boxes.

"Stop between these two buildings. Look around. From here, it's hard for someone on a roof to get a good shot at you."

The young man nodded. "So you're saying what, don't be a hero?"

Bishop put the chalk down. "My drill sergeant used to say that a hero is the guy who gets killed so you don't have to. See you tomorrow, Farrow."

Bishop went back to his office, signed off attendance sheets and crossed off completed work from his students. Tomorrow there would be a snap test, so the answers they gave would give him a good feel for how the year was going.

He checked his watch. Five fifteen. Nobody came with questions, nobody was scheduled for a meeting. Time to get out and go home. He grabbed all the file folders from his desk, dumped them into his briefcase and walked out to his Jeep.

An hour later he was home, put his briefcase beside his desk, popped a frozen lasagne in the microwave and poured himself a tall glass of milk. He sipped his milk, picked up another briefcase, the one with tomorrow's lessons on it, and placed it on top of his desk. Tomorrow night, as he did every second night, he would arrange two days' worth of lessons, place the briefcase with the next day's lesson plans on the desk and the following day's briefcase beside the desk, to avoid confusion.

The lasagne was ready, the milk was gone, so he poured a second glass to drink with his meal.

He settled back in his easy chair after dinner, picked up the book he'd been struggling through and read from the bookmarked page.

It was a historical essay on the outbreak of the First World War; lessons learned from the mistakes of commanders in the field that he could bring to his class. Bishop was ten pages into the night's reading, taking notes he would verify later. The phone rang. He picked it up.

"Hello?"

A familiar voice spoke, urgent in her tone. "Bish, it's Kelly. You have to come to your office. Now."

He sat up. "Kelly? What is it?"

She sighed deeply. She only did that when she was very upset. "You got to come see this, Bish. Hurry."

Bishop jumped into his Jeep and roared down his street, quiet at this time of night, creeping through stop signs and jumping red lights before they went green.

His military ID would give him some defense if he was stopped by the police; the urgency in Kelly's voice might also allow him some leeway.

It took nineteen minutes to get to his office. He sprinted into Clark Hall, bounded up the stairs, pulling himself along the banisters, and thirty seconds later got to his office door.

Kelly was on her knees, trying to sort a snowstorm of papers scattered all over the floor. She swore softly to herself as she collected them, slamming short stacks of forms and cardboard attendance sheets onto her desk then going back to do the same with more papers.

Bishop watched this, stunned, for about a minute. "What the hell happened?" He said at last.

"Damned if I know. Security was doing rounds and called me about this shit." She snapped.

That was uncharacteristically blunt of her, Bishop thought.

He squatted down to pick up papers. "Student prank, do you think?"

Kelly shook he head. "If it is, some bastard mother is going to fail his year big time."

Bishop looked at the papers scattered on the ground. "How can I help?"

Kelly shook her head. "I have a system. You just stack the shit on my desk and get out of my way. All right?"

Bishop shrugged. "OK. Can I get you a coffee or a sandwich or anything?"

"How about giving me the balls of whoever did this?" She sneered.

"Assuming they actually have balls."

She looked up at him. "How the hell can you be so calm at a time like this?"

"I'm not calm. I'm as pissed as you are, and when I find this idiot I'm going to make him pay." He answered.

"But for now, Kelly, let's just get this mess cleared up."

She sat down, cross-legged, and shook her head. "Yeah, you're right, John. Screw it, I can get this done by myself in a couple of hours."

"Want me to grab you a burger or something? There's a place down the street that's still open."

She leaned back and wrinkled her nose. "Sure. Cheeseburger, lots of onions, lots of ketchup."

He stood up and turned for the door.

"And a medium coke." She added.

Twenty minutes later, Bishop came back with a large paper bag full of food and an icy cola. He set these in a clear spot on Kelly's desk and looked around at the floor.

Most of the papers were now in three stacks on her desk, according to the instructor they belonged to, with only a few loose sheets and a dozen manila envelopes still on the ground. The majority of the records had been digitized, of course, so only current class information was in paper form.

Kelly sat back on her swivel chair and reached out to grab the food. She took a large slurp of the soda and plunged her hand into the bag, pulling out a clump of fries. Bishop sat on the edge of the desk beside it, watching her.

"I swear, Bish, if I find out who did this…" she started.

"Yeah, I'm going to put out an 'all hands' message tomorrow morning." He echoed. "I don't expect any of them will fess up, but you never know."

Kelly sucked on the straw and put the soda down, then reached into the bag for the burger.

"Look, you can't do any more for me tonight. Security is coming around to check on me. Go home, Bish."

He stood up. "All right. Listen, if you need me for anything, or you get a strange feeling or anything at all, call me."

She nodded, her mouth stuffed with burger. "Yep. And thanks again, Bish."

Bishop got home forty minutes later. He didn't drive as quickly as he had getting to the University, and he kept glancing at his cell phone in case Kelly called him back. He rolled to a stop outside his house, locked the Jeep and went up the steps to the front door.

He checked his watch. Ten PM. Time for a quick coffee then bed. He opened the front door and stopped. Something was wrong.

There are times when that little voice in your head says something very loudly, screams for you to listen. Those are the times when you look around every corner and expect a man with a knife to come at you.

Then there are other times when the same voice whispers. You sort of hear it, but you're not sure what it's telling you. This night, the voice was speaking, barely above that whisper.

Bishop took three steps into his front hall and stood still. There was no sound of movement, no breathing from around the corner, nothing. Still, he felt *something*.

"Hello?" He called. No answer.

He went to the hallstand, where he usually dropped his keys, and pulled the M9 pistol out of the holster that he'd screwed to the underside of the stand.

He slid his feet forward, not lifting them off the floor, moving one foot forward, then the other foot just behind it, then the first foot forward again, silently.

He got to the doorway of his living room and turned quickly to scan the room, his pistol close to his chest, pointing downwards.

The little voice in his head was louder now. There was nobody there. Still, he went through every room, every closet, every cupboard in the house, looking for something, anything, out of place.

He convinced himself that he was just feeling jittery about the mess at the University, until his eyes fell on his briefcase, by the phone on his desk. It was turned around the wrong way.

Bishop was a creature of habit. It came with his time in the military. That freed up his mind to concentrate on war, not having to remember where he put his keys or what to make for lunch.

His briefcase was a standard Samsonite, dark plastic case, just like a second one he had. He always put it flat along the front of his desk, with the top half of the case facing up. The case was upside down. it was a small detail, but it was not how he had left it.

Bishop picked up the case and turned it over. With practiced caution, he pulled at the catches to unlock the case then ever so gently opened it an inch. He squatted down, looking for wires or anything explosive. Nothing.

He opened the case another inch and looked again. He did the repeatedly until the case was completely open. No sense getting killed for being in a rush.

There was nothing in the case. Nothing. His lesson plans were gone. That made no sense. Why take the lesson plans? He had an idea. He dialed a number and waited. Kelly's voice came on right away.

"Yeah?" She barked.

"Kelly, it's Bishop. Have you found anything missing from the papers yet?"

"Diddley squat. Everything's here." She said.

"It's like they took all the papers from all the drawers and just tossed them into the air. It makes no sense, Bish."

Bishop thought for a moment. "Why did you call me before? Why not Powell or Sterns?"

"Most of their papers weren't touched, just yours. That's why I figure it was the work of one of your students, maybe." She said.

"Well, I think it was actually a diversion, Kelly. Someone broke into my house and took the lessons I had ready for tomorrow."

There was a moment of silence at the other end. "No shit. Well, crap, this does paint a different picture, doesn't it? Why would anyone want to do that, Bish?"

"No idea. We'll talk in the morning. Get some rest, Kelly."

Bishop locked up the house, checked all the windows and went to bed like he always did. This night, however, he slept with the Beretta M9 under his pillow, unlike he ever did.

Chapter 2: Incident Report

He was scrunched down, gripping his rifle tight, pressed against the small recess in the rock face. The man beside him was bleeding, gasping for breath, and all Bishop could do was tell him to stay calm until help came. The 'put-put' sound of bullets striking the rocky sand were maybe two feet from Bishop's leg, and the wounded man, sheltered slightly by Bishop's body, winced every time a puff of dirt sprayed up. It seemed like hours since they'd radioed for help. Bishop considered calling again but it might let the other guys triangulate him.

Two welcome sounds came over the rise behind him; the angry wail of a Warthog, flying low over the desert, sounded like sustained thunder. It growled, the nose gun spraying the area with hundreds of rounds. The other bullets stopped coming. Seconds later, the chop-chop-chop of a Huey helicopter coming from the same direction. It hovered for a moment, then dropped to the sand as a soldier swung out the machine gun. Bishop lifted the wounded man to his feet, hurried them both to the open Huey, and watched the ground fade away as they flew to safety.

 Bishop skipped his run this morning. He did his sit-ups and push-ups, then he assembled some lessons that he'd been saving for later in the month and placed them in the empty briefcase. He would carry on with tomorrow's lessons as planned. Hopefully this mess would get resolved, either as a dumb prank or an attempt to change grades. It wasn't the first time that had been tried, after all.

He took his regular route, down Meridian Avenue, left on 130th Street to join I-5 south to 45th Street, then east on 45th and south on 15th Avenue to the university.

He was on autopilot, following the traffic, his mind running through scenarios of why anyone would steal a set of lessons. East on 45th. There was nothing special about them, nothing odd. Anyone with a computer could find the same information online. Right turn onto 15th Avenue.

He was thinking about anything unusual that he might have missed, however insignificant. He was so deep in thought he almost missed seeing the woman who cut him off. She was driving a beater, a crappy old yellow sedan. She moved in front of him then jammed on her brakes.

Bishop banged into the back end of her car. Not hard, just enough to rock it slightly. His Jeep had the rough steel bumper he'd ordered specially, and it left a waffle mark on the plastic bumper of her car.

She pulled over. Someone else behind him pulled over too, and Bishop heard a man's voice asking if everyone was okay. The woman got out and looked at her bumper.

Bishop got out of his car and glanced back at the man. "Yeah, we're fine, thanks." He said.

Bishop walked over to the woman. She was very pretty, with deep brown eyes and thick red lips. She was wearing a very short, very tight skirt and a short-sleeved sweater that seemed to have been painted on.

"Hey, miss, are you all right?" Bishop asked.

She patted the sides of her auburn hair. "I...I think so. I'm a little shaky, though."

Bishop sighed. "You cut me off. Didn't you see me in your rear-view?"

The woman smiled, a smile that made Bishop forget about his break-in for a moment.

"I'm so sorry. It was totally my fault. You're right, I should be more careful."

She paused and looked down. "Tell you what. If you like, I'll give you my number, and you can call me later to see I'm still okay. How's that?"

Bishop smiled. "Sure. Just to check you out... uh, to check on you, check to see you're all right."

She grinned. "Come to my car, I'll give you my card."

She got in her car and Bishop opened the passenger door. She glanced in her rear-view mirror; suddenly her expression changed.

"You know what, I'm fine after all. Let's forget about it." She said.

She put her car in gear and started off. Bishop had to lean back to avoid getting clipped by her door. He turned back to look at his Jeep and saw the person who had asked if he was all right driving away. The little voice spoke to him again. Bishop ran back to the Jeep. His briefcase was gone.

In the distance, he saw the woman's car race down 15th Avenue, and the person who had stopped behind him racing off down a side street, out of sight.

Bishop pursed his lips. "Son of a bitch. What now?" He muttered.

He didn't know which one to go after. He decided to catch the woman's car. She was going quite fast, weaving through traffic. She moved to the right, passing other cars in the curb lane. She was a block or so ahead of him, but he was slowly gaining on her.

She looked at him in her mirror, frowned and sped up. Bishop thought he had lost her, but he just barely saw a yellow car swing violently into a laneway to the right; Bishop slammed his brakes and backed up to chase her. By the time he turned into the lane he couldn't see her car.

He went slowly down the laneway, looking around till he saw a hint of yellow in an old parking garage. He blocked the garage entrance and went in.

The woman was there, looking for a way to get out. Bishop walked up to her.

"What the fuck is going on here, lady?" He growled.

She smiled the same coy smile. "Look, forget the damage, OK? It's not a big deal, really."

Bishop shook his head. "Wrong. Your buddy stole my briefcase. Why?"

Her smile faded. "Let it go. It will be back in your office this morning, Captain."

Bishop watched her for a few seconds. "So you know who I am, and you know what he took. You also broke into my house, then. You've got five seconds to explain then I call the cops."

Her eyes widened. She smiled the coy smile again. "You wouldn't do that. Really, would you?"

"Try me."

She sighed. "I have no idea what was in it. I was hired to stop you, that's all. I did not break into your house. All I got was your name, where to stop you, and to keep you busy for thirty seconds. Period. You still want to call the cops? Go ahead. I'll deny everything."

Bishop gritted his teeth. "What's your name?"

She shook her head slowly. "Nope."

He brushed past her to the car and opened the driver door. There was a small purse on the passenger seat and a cell phone beside it. He took them out and put the purse on the trunk of her car. He opened the purse wide.

She glared at him, mouth open. "What are you doing? That's private property." She snapped.

"No shit. How does that feel?"

He pulled out her wallet and a pair of sunglasses. He opened the wallet, found her driver's license and put it in his shirt pocket. He took her cell phone and dropped it on the ground, then lifted his polished Oxford shoe and smashed the phone's screen.

He tossed her purse back into her car, reached around the steering wheel, pulled out her car keys, then threw them over a tall fence.

He looked at her driver's license. "Olivia Young. That's a pretty name. Nice meeting you."

He put the license into his pocket.

The woman glared at him. "You're a real rat bastard, you know that?"

Bishop walked up to her, nose to nose. "Who do you think you're messing with, lady? I'm Army Intelligence. You think you can scare me? Think again. I sure as hell am not afraid of some amateur bimbo."

He turned and walked back to his Jeep.

"Hey." She called out.

He turned to look at her.

She shrugged. "Nothing personal, you know, it was just the job."

He nodded. "Anything else you want to say? No? Fine, nothing personal for me either."

Bishop drove to the university, looking behind him for any other cars the whole time.

He felt almost normal, walking up the familiar stairs, down the familiar hall, into his office.

Kelly was already there, going through memos on her computer and typing responses.

She looked up. "Hey. Morning, Bish. Got everything put away last night." She said.

"Good. Were you here very late?"

"Nah. An hour or two, maybe. The restaurant just brought your briefcase back, by the way."

Bishop frowned. "Restaurant?"

"They said you left it behind when you were there last night. Somebody on the staff knows you, they said, so they dropped it off just now."

Bishop opened his briefcase. Everything was still there. The lesson plans taken from his house were there, too. "This was stolen from my Jeep this morning." He said.

Kelly stared up at him.

"I bumped into a car- it was a setup. While I talked to the woman who hit me, the guy in the car behind me took the case." He explained.

Kelly leaned back. "Any idea who they were? Why did they do this?"

He put the woman's driver's license on Kelly's desk. "The car I bumped was hers. Olivia Young. Slinky looking hottie. She claims she was only hired to stop me so the guy could snick my case."

He sat in his chair and sighed. "Jeez, Kelly, I have no idea what's going on here. Has anything strange happened, anyone odd contacted you lately? Anyone at all?"

She thought for a moment. "Nope, nada, zip. Any red flags come to mind for you?"

"None. In the old days I'd have said that my colleagues in MI were testing me, but I've been out of there for a few years now. There'd be no reason to do it."

He rubbed his nose. "I'm going to make some calls and see."

He sat at his desk and picked up his phone. It gave short beeps instead of the usual dial tone, meaning there were voice mail messages for him.

Hadn't he checked his messages recently, he wondered. Friday, last week. He hated the phone system, and he explicitly forbade his students from leaving him voice mails.

He pressed the button to retrieve messages then pulled out the instruction sheet to remember his password. A mechanical voice came on, a woman's voice, flat and emotionless.

"You have three messages." It said.

He pressed a button. "First message." It said.

There was nothing, just a second of dead air then a click. He deleted it and pressed the button again. "Second message." It said.

There was the sound of someone breathing, then a man's voice, furtive and rushed.

"Look, it's me. Let me know it's there, all right?" Then more dead air, then click.

He pressed the button again. "Third message." The woman's voice said.

The same man again. "You have to call me! Call me! I'm putting myself in..." The voice stopped.

Bishop scratched his head. Did this have to do with the woman in the car, the break-in at his house, the office mess? How would he know? The phone number that had left the last message was still on his screen. He called it.

The phone rang three times, then he heard a click and a man's voice, rough and shaky. "Hello?"

"Hello, who's this?" Bishop asked.

There was a long pause. "This is Jerry." The man answered.

"Did you leave me messages on my phone?"

There was slight pause. "Why would I do that?"

Bishop heard traffic noise in the background. "Jerry, where are you?"

The man grunted, confused. "I'm outside of the shelter."

"Shelter? What shelter?"

The man mumbled something. "Um, the Gospel Mission on East Howell Street."

Bishop listened to the man's voice, thinking. "Listen, Jerry, you didn't call me?"

"No."

"Is this your phone?"

The man sounded indignant. "It is now. I found it in the trash. It's mine now."

"How about I buy it from you, Jerry? Fifty bucks, cash."

There was another pause. "Seventy-five."

"Deal. I'll be there in twenty minutes." Bishop said.

He turned to Kelly. "Tell my students no class this morning. I'll be back as soon as I can."

He left his briefcase under his desk and got into the Jeep. It took about ten minutes to drive to the Gospel Mission. An old man, a skinny old man in a lumberjack shirt over a worn sweater, was standing outside, leaning against a shopping buggy. Bishop pulled to a stop and got out.

"Hi, are you Jerry?" Bishop asked.

The man looked to be around fifty, with droopy eyelids and the expression of someone who no longer gives a rat's ass.

"Yeah." He croaked.

He pulled a cell phone out of his shirt pocket and held it out, then looked at it and brought it close to his chest. "You the guy with the money?" He asked.

Bishop pulled out his wallet. He peeled off four twenties and held them out. "Here. Eighty dollars. Buy yourself a hot meal."

The man took the money with one hand and held out the phone with the other. Bishop took the phone, gently, and pressed the button on the front.

It opened with no password, no pictures on the screen, nothing personal. The man with the shopping cart stuffed his money into the same shirt pocket where the phone had been, grunted something and turned to push his cart along.

Bishop said "Wait. Where did you find the phone?"

The man pointed south. "Three blocks away, in front of one of them places on Denny Way."

"Places? What do you mean, an apartment building?"

"Yeah, you know, the old ones, red brick."

"Was it just lying on the sidewalk, or what?"

He shook his head. "No, like I told you, there's a big trash bin out back, in the alley. I was looking for bottles and cans, you know."

He pointed to his shopping cart, with a collection of empty bottles to turn in for deposit.

"And the phone was just dumped in the bin?" Bishop asked.

"Yeah. like I told you."

The man leaned against the grab bar of the shopping cart and pushed it down the sidewalk.

Bishop watched him go, then drove the three blocks to Denny Way.

There was only one block that had old red brick apartment buildings, and there were only two laneways bisecting the street in that block. Bishop stopped in the road, looking both ways. He could see a single dumpster, a bright blue one wedged behind a building on the east side of the road. He turned into the lane and parked behind it.

He looked around the bin and all over the ground nearby. Apart from some fast-food wrappers, there was nothing. He pried up the lid and looked in. There were twist-tied bags of trash, a broken folding chair and other scraps, but nothing interesting. Then he spotted it. It was just a fabric sleeve, a piece of dark nylon covered by a flat slab of dirty cardboard. He reached in as far as he could and managed to grip the nylon between his two fingers. He bent his finger into a hook and pulled. The fabric lifted up and away from the cardboard, moving closer to the edge of the dumpster.

Bishop reached in further and grabbed it with his hand, pulled gently and finally got the whole piece of material out of the dumpster. It was a windbreaker, a simple, cheap windbreaker.

Bishop examined it. There was a hole in the front that could have been made by wear, but he suspected that it was likely made by a bullet.

The windbreaker also had pockets, three or four pockets, two of which were zippered shut. The nylon smelled of cat food and stale pizza, but Bishop wrinkled his nose and checked it over. There was nothing in the pockets, no name written anywhere, no indication of who it belonged to. Why zipper the pockets shut if they were empty, he wondered.

He put the windbreaker in his Jeep and turned on the phone. There were only three calls in the history, all to him. There were no stored numbers, nothing that said 'Wife' or 'Home'.

The hole in the windbreaker bothered him. If he ignored it, he might be neglecting something important. But if he didn't it might open a can of worms for him. Worms it was, he thought.

Bishop drove to the nearest police station and walked up to the front counter. A pudgy man with Sergeant's stripes sat behind the counter, writing, and glanced up as he saw Bishop.

"Hi, can I help you?" the Sergeant asked.

"Possibly. I have a mystery." Bishop started.

The Sergeant put the pen down and smiled. "Really? Did you maybe want Sherlock Holmes?"

Bishop frowned. "Maybe I should talk to a detective instead of wasting my time." He said.

The Sergeant raised one eyebrow. "Yeah? And why is that?"

Bishop held up the windbreaker and poked his finger through the hole. "I think this was made by a bullet."

The Sergeant frowned. "Wait here."

He got up and went into a back area. Three minutes later, he came back with a man wearing a dark blue suit, with a small pin on the lapel. When the man got to the counter Bishop could see that the pin showed a small Space Needle with a police badge beside it.

The man was somewhere in his late thirties, Bishop guessed, with the beginning of salt-and-pepper hair over his ears. He had a neatly trimmed goatee, which also showed some grey around the mouth. He was easily Bishop's height, and walked like he owned the building.

"Hello, I'm Detective Porezki." The man said. "And you are?"

Bishop opened his wallet and pulled out a business card. "Captain John Bishop, retired. Now I'm an instructor at U of W."

The detective read the card. "I see. How can we help you, Captain?"

"John, please. Or just Bishop. I've had a very interesting couple of days, Detective."

Porezki rubbed his upper lip. "Let's go to my desk, shall we?"

They went into the back area. Bishop was expecting a cluttered squad room, like in the movies. Instead, it was a series of glass cubicles, neat and sterile. Porezki ushered Bishop into one of them and Bishop told him the whole story- the scattered papers, the break-in, the car bump, the phone messages. He handed the phone and the windbreaker to Porezki, who made notes and nodded as he examined them.

Porezki put the cap back on his pen and placed it inside his jacket. He leaned back and looked down at the windbreaker.

"So, you have no idea who called you? No idea what they were looking for in your house?"

"No, none."

"I don't know how else to ask you, but do you take any recreational drugs? Do you buy them from unsavory people?"

"I don't even drink anymore. I quit when I got my DD214. Sorry, my discharge papers when I served my twenty years."

Porezki smirked and rubbed his nose. "Yeah, my discharge papers are on my kitchen wall."

Bishop leaned forward. "So, what does this all mean to you?"

Porezki shrugged. "Beats me. I don't think you're making this up, and I don't think you're a wacko. We get our share, you understand. I'm going to have the lab check out the windbreaker, and we'll let you know what we find. The voice mail message came from this phone, you said?"

Bishop nodded.

"Well, it's probably a burner. Same serial and type as a bunch of phones we've seen before."

"So, do you want to keep it as well?" Bishop asked.

"Not really. Forward us the voicemail messages to this number," He handed Bishop a card.

"We'll get the forensic geeks to analyze the sound. Apart from that, not much else we can do."

"What about fingerprints?" Bishop asked.

"We could check it, but I doubt we'd get much off it. How about you keep it in case you get a call?"

Bishop fingered the phone, turned it over, then put it in his pocket. "All right. You'll keep me posted?"

"Yeah. I'll let you know if there's anything more we need from you, Captain."

"Bishop, or Bish. My friends call me Bish."

"Bish it is. See you later."

Bishop went back to the University. He walked into class just after lunch, wondering what he should tell the students. Maybe he could get them to help figure out what happened?

On the other hand, the term 'bull in a china shop' came to mind. They were much more likely to cause trouble or muddy the waters if they got involved.

Still, best not to lie to them. He stood at the front of the classroom, one hand leaning on the lectern. All the students watched him, intently.

"As you may have heard, we had some excitement." Bishop started.

"However, the matter has been turned over to the police. Details will follow when they are forthcoming. Now, page seventy-three, the Battle of Loos."

The students dutifully opened their textbooks and Bishop taught the day's lesson. By five in the afternoon, most had forgotten the excitement of the morning, and they filed out quietly, clutching their workbooks with the next day's assignments written down.

Bishop didn't feel like going home. He felt that whoever had broken in wouldn't come back, but he still felt the need to stay out for a while. He drove to a coffee shop down the street, bought a meal and ate with his briefcase pressed between his legs.

He paid the bill and got into his Jeep. One last stop to make. He reached into his pocket and pulled out the driver's license of the woman who had hit him. Her picture didn't do her justice.

Her place was listed as an apartment on Mercer Street, on the other side of Highway I-5.

He drove to the address, wondering what to say when he got there. What could he ask her? Would she be angry or upset at seeing him again?

There was no parking on Mercer, but just around the corner from the building he found an empty parking spot. He hid his briefcase under the seat and walked around the corner to the apartment entrance.

It was a beige, three-storey walk-up, with four wide concrete steps leading to an ornate wood front door. The door had a row of buttons, with names beside them. 'O. Young' was listed as apartment 214. He took out the license to double-check the address before he pressed the button. A twenty-something man carrying a kick scooter came out the front door and held it open for Bishop. Bishop nodded and muttered thanks, then he went up a wide, old wood staircase to the second floor.

At the top of the landing he saw a row of doors, and near the very back of the building he saw the brass numbers '214'.

He took a deep breath, walked to the door and knocked.

There was a soft pit-pat of slippers on wood from behind the door, then a peephole opened up for a second before someone looked out through it and it went dark.

Bishop heard a sigh. The door opened, slowly. Olivia Young, in baggy shorts and a Michigan State sweatshirt, leaned in the doorway, her arms crossed.

"Yeah, what do you want?" She grunted.

He held out the license. "I wanted to give this back to you, that's all."

She took it and tossed it on the coffee table behind her. "Fine, thanks. Goodbye."

Bishop stood there, motionless. The woman sneered at him. "Waiting for a tip, or what?"

He sighed. "Who are you?"

"You saw my license, so you know damn well who I am."

"No, I mean, who paid you to distract me? And I was very distracted, by the way."

She actually smiled. "Come in. Do you want a glass of wine or something?"

"Just a coffee, if you have it, thanks."

She waved him in and he closed the door behind him.

She nodded at a worn plaid sofa against one wall. "Have a seat. It's instant, if that's all right?"

He sat down. "Instant is fine, thanks."

She plugged in a kettle and leaned against her kitchen wall.

"My turn for questions. Who are you and why do people want your briefcase?" She said.

He shook his head. "I honestly have no idea. As I told you, someone broke into my house and went through my paperwork. They also ransacked my office. In both cases, nothing was missing. Very strange, very intriguing."

She pulled a bottle of wine from her fridge and poured herself a glass. "Sure you don't want some? No? Oh well."

She took a deep slurp and placed the glass on the stove. "So, what are you, a government agent or something? Aston Martin and tuxedo kind of guy?"

Bishop chuckled. "I teach ROTC classes at U of W. And it's a Jeep. You saw it earlier."

She picked up a coffee mug and spooned in some powder. "Oh, ROTC. You're military, right?"

"I was. I got out five years ago, and now I teach, is all. Fewer people shooting at me."

She poured hot water into the mug and looked in her fridge. "Ah, how do you take it?"

"Black is fine, thanks."

She placed his coffee on a battered trunk that served as her coffee table and sat in a wicker chair across from him. "You haven't asked me about myself yet. Not interested?" She teased.

He looked around. "You are an actress, probably local theater or commercials, and you've been in town less than a year. You don't have a wealthy family, you're single, and you don't have any pets. I guess you're allergic to cats. How am I doing?"

Her mouth opened. "Who have you been talking to?"

He waved his finger around the room. "The way you first came up to me- tight skirt and big eyes. I guess that should have twigged for me that you're an actress. Your driver's license was issued seven months ago. Probably because you moved here from Michigan. Lansing?"

"Pontiac." She corrected.

He shrugged. "Pontiac. The shirt gave it away, as did the slight accent. People come to Seattle to break into theater or work for Microsoft. You don't strike me as a geek. Also, you probably came with all your worldly goods in a U Haul, so your folks didn't bankroll the move."

She smiled at that. "What about allergic to cats?" She prompted.

He pointed to a tall thin fan in one corner. "It has a filter that removes dander. I bet one of your neighbors has cats."

She laughed out loud. "All right, I'm impressed. By the way, you still owe me a phone."

Bishop reached into his pocket and pulled out the burner phone. "Here. Now, this has a bit of a mystery around it. If you plug in your own SIM card it should be clean. If you decide to use the card that's in it, though, let me know if you get any strange phone calls."

She pressed some buttons and scrolled through several menus. "Hey, this thing has over a hundred dollars of prepay on it. Shit, I'm keeping this number." She said.

Bishop finished his coffee and got up. "Thanks for the joe. Here's my card. If you do get any odd calls on that phone, please let me know?"

She placed the card on her coffee table.

"So, if I do call you, what'll it get me?"

He smirked. "How about dinner and a movie?"

She tapped the card. "I may call you even if I don't get any odd calls."

Bishop drove home. His mind went in a dozen different directions. Why did they break into his house? Why steal his briefcase? What were they looking for? Most of all, would they be back?

Could this be a case of mistaken identity? Except that Olivia, the actress, said she'd been given his name. The phone messages were worrisome, too. Somebody obviously knew him, or thought they did, and that's why they called his extension.

Too many variables. Too many balls in the air. All he could do was wait for the dust to settle.

'Apply the Nash Equilibrium', he thought. Doing nothing different is better than doing something different right now, so do nothing different.

He parked in front of his house and pulled his briefcase out from under the seat. The little voice spoke to him, softly. There was nobody outside that seemed out of place.

His neighbor, Mrs. Otagawa, was in her front yard sweeping dead leaves into a pile. Another neighbor was walking the scraggly little creature she called a dog. Lights were on in the houses where lights should be on.

All the cars that he recognized were where they usually were. Except one.

A generic black Ford was parked on the street, and one of his other neighbors was parked on the opposite side of the street from where he usually parked. Not a big thing, but even so…

Bishop walked up to Mrs. Otagawa. "Hi, Mariko. Do you mind if I walk down your side path? I just need to get to my back door?"

She nodded, puzzled. "OK. Everything all right?" She said in her soft Japanese accent.

"Yeah, I just have to use the back door, that's all." Bishop explained.

She smiled and waved him along. "Sure, OK. Go, go."

He nodded thanks and followed her driveway along his fence to the back lane. He hopped over the short wooden fence between her back yard and the lane, then opened the gate into his own yard.

His house had three doors; there was the front door that everyone used, the back door he used to put out trash, and there was one that most people never noticed, a short wooden one that led to the basement.

He went in that way, quietly closing the door behind him. The door led to a tiny tool room in the basement, and that room led to a back set of stairs.

Bishop went up those; they led to the kitchen, and he came around the top of the stairs to the kitchen right by the fridge.

He peeked around the corner; the house was dark, but even in the dark he thought he saw a shadow in the living room, sitting on the sofa. He stood perfectly still, waiting, waiting.

The shadow became clearer as his eyes grew accustomed to the dark. Another shadow, larger, was standing by the front window.

It turned to the first shadow and he heard it speak, very softly.

"His car is here. Where did he go?" It said.

It was a man's voice, not old, not juvenile, but firm and strong.

The sitting shadow answered, an older voice, tired. "Is he still talking to the neighbor?"

Bishop flipped on the bank of wall switches by his hand and the entire downstairs lit up.

The taller shadow jumped and spun around. It was a big man, a football halfback type, in a dark suit and a poorly-knotted tie.

The sitting shadow looked like everyone's old uncle, a thin man in his late sixties, with an expression which said that nothing short of being goosed by a unicorn could surprise him.

"Can I help you gentlemen?" Bishop said, calmly.

The big man moved forward, but the older one held a hand up. The big man stopped.

"Captain Bishop?" The old one said.

"We have some questions we'd like to ask you."

"Ditto." Bishop answered.

"Like, why shouldn't I shoot you both before I call the police?" He added.

The older man chuckled. "You know perfectly well why you won't do that."

Bishop sat on the edge of his kitchen table. It wasn't so much to get comfortable, as to be within reach of his chef's knives. "Enlighten me." He said.

The older man stood up, creakily and slowly. He grunted and walked haltingly to sit beside Bishop.

"You are in possession of something very important. More than that, it's something that could be vey dangerous to possess."

"I have absolutely no idea what you are talking about. Are you two the clowns that broke in last time?"

The old man nodded. "We wanted to be as unobtrusive as possible, but circumstances preclude that now, I'm afraid. We need to take a more direct course."

Bishop frowned. "Who left me the messages on my phone?"

The old man looked at the younger one, who just shrugged. The old man shook his head.

"What were the messages, exactly?"

"Mostly dead air, One said 'let me know it's there' and the other said 'I'm putting myself in' then it stopped. Who called me?"

The old man sighed and rubbed his nose. "That's not good. It means he may be gone."

"Who?" Bishop asked.

The old man stood up. "I'm sorry. Obviously, you had no idea what we are talking about. We won't bother you again."

He turned toward the front door. Bishop touched his arm. The big man seemed anxious at that.

"Wait. Who paid the girl to hit my car?" Bishop asked.

The old man sat back down. "Girl? What girl?"

Bishop explained the accident, the phone, the homeless man, everything. He felt it was better to not hold back. The old man listened and nodded quietly.

"Look, stay out of it. You're not involved and you are far better off that way. As I say, we won't be back, period." He said.

Bishop shook his head. "You still haven't told me who you are."

The old man looked up, thinking. "Acronyms are so overdone, don't you think? CIA, FBI, NSA, DHS, and a host of other alphabet soups that simply scare people. Let's just say that your goals as an Army officer align with our goals. Leave it at that."

"How would I know what it is, if I actually had what you think I had?" Bishop asked.

The old man nodded. "Valid point. If you didn't know the difference between a diamond and a piece of glass, you might not look at it twice. What we're looking for is more ephemeral, but just as valuable, in the right hands. If you come across something you don't recognize, call me."

The old man handed him a card, blank except for a phone number.

He nodded at the younger man, who stood up and opened the front door.

"Have a good evening, Captain. We most likely won't meet again. Goodbye."

Bishop watched them walk to the Ford. The younger man opened the back door and the older man got in. they drove away.

Bishop locked his door, checked that the Beretta was still in its holster under the hallstand, then got ready for bed.

Chapter 3: Alert Status

One of the things that always amused Bishop was the absurdity, the insanity, of being in a war zone. The things some people saw as vital, others dismissed as petty.

He once spent eight days on a hilltop in the Middle East, living on bags of MRE's and bottles of warm water. He was glad of being able to drink even that water for that time.

Three days later he was in the canteen, where one of his officers complained that the espresso machine was 'just not very good' at making a latte. The irony of that amused him for weeks.

He felt that same irony now, driving to work like any other day, except now he was looking around in case he was ambushed again but at the same time thinking of lesson plans to present.

He breathed a small sigh of relief as he pulled into his parking spot. He checked his watch- eight fifteen- he'd made good time this morning, better speed than average.

He placed his briefcase on his desk and made coffee. A knock at the door made him look up.

"Farrow? Can I help you?" He said.

The student came in, unhooked a courier bag from his shoulder, pulled out a stapled report, and sat across from him. "I redid my North Korea report, sir. Does this look any better?"

Bishop took the papers and read quickly through them. "Yeah, absolutely. Well done, Farrow. Much better."

The young man grinned. "Thanks, sir. I get what you meant about the structure of the report. I'll do better in the future."

Bishop smiled. "Yeah, you need to. You've just set yourself a higher bar. See you in class."

The young man didn't move.

"Something else, Farrow?"

"The library courier asked me to give something to you, sir."

Bishop was puzzled by the statement. "How's that again?"

"Miss Rogers was just leaving the office when he showed up. I signed for this delivery."

"Go on." Bishop prompted.

"Well, sir, I thought it was strange, but she left to get lunch, I guess, and the courier asked me to hold on to the package."

Bishop shook his head. "Why on earth would he do that?"

"It didn't make any sense to me either, sir. What he told me, specifically, was to hold on to the package until I could hand it to you personally, sir."

Farrow pulled an inter-office mail folder out of his bag, the kind with names of people who had previously received the folder and placed it on the desk.

Bishop looked at the folder. It was pristine, no names on the 'deliver to' line, no scribbles, nothing.

Bishop unwound the string holding the flap down and opened the folder. There was a large, sealed envelope inside it, but what most stood out were the words TOP SECRET.

Bishop slid the envelope back into the folder, wound up the string, and thought for a moment.

"Farrow, do you have any relative outside of Seattle?" He asked.

"I have an aunt in Pocatello, sir."

"Small-town Idaho, good. That will do nicely. Is she an honest person, trustworthy?"

The young man nodded. "She's a warden of her church. I would trust her with anything, sir."

Bishop went to the tall file cabinet and pulled out two large manila envelopes, slightly different in size.

He placed the inter-office folder inside the smaller envelope and sealed it. He placed that envelope inside the larger one and left it open.

He handed them to the young man, opened his wallet and took out twenty dollars.

"I have an assignment for you, Farrow. Address the inside envelope to yourself. Address the outside envelope to your aunt. Enclose a note that she should mail the inside one back to you when she gets it, but NOT to open it. Tell her it's a class project. And tell her to send it by regular mail. Stick enough stamps on both envelopes. Let me know if twenty doesn't cover it."

He handed the envelope and the money to the young man.

"Sir? I'm afraid I don't understand." Farrow said.

"Believe me, Farrow, neither do I. When you get the envelope back, keep it safe at home. Store it in your garage if you like, but just hide it until I ask you for it. And tell nobody that you've done any of this. Can I count on you to do this?"

The young man looked at his watch. "I may be a little late for class, sir."

"Not a problem. Thank you, Farrow."

The young man left.

Kelly came in a few minutes later. Bishop decided to not say anything about the package; the fewer people who were involved, the better.

He gathered his paperwork for the morning, took a last swig of coffee and headed down the hall to the classroom.

The class went quiet as he came in. Bishop picked up a piece of chalk and went to the blackboard. In bold block letters he wrote ACCIDIT STERCORE.

One of the students laughed. The rest looked at him.

Bishop looked up at the student. "Care to share with the class, Reiser?"

The man looked sheepishly around at the students who were watching him.

"Sir, in Latin it means 'shit happens'."

The class laughed. Bishop pointed at him. "You went to a Catholic high school, didn't you?"

He nodded. "Yes, sir."

Bishop looked at the class. "See? It pays to broaden your horizons. Yes, shit happens."

He powered down the projection screen and plugged a USB into the lectern.

"All right. As you may have heard, I had an issue to deal with yesterday. We're back to normal, though. Now, let's look at the details of a World War Two exercise called 'Operation Tiger'."

Bishop ate lunch at the usual restaurant, ordered his usual meal, made his usual afternoon class notes, but his mind was trying to understand what had happened.

Certainly, the mystery envelope was the reason for the break-in and the car bump, but why it was sent to him specifically was beyond him.

He thought it might be a case of mistaken identity; there was another J. Bishop who was an Army Intelligence Captain in Washington DC. He had been getting that

Bishop's mail for weeks until someone realized it was going to the wrong Washington.

There must be dozens of 'J. Bishop's' in the military. Maybe it was intended for a person in a different branch- Marines or Air Force?

Bishop shook his head. Too many variables. He would wait until the package came back to him, then he'd decide what to do.

At five PM he said good night to Kelly, drove home and parked on the street. It started to drizzle before he left the university, and by the time he got home it was a downpour. He tucked his briefcase under his jacket, waited for a lull in the rain and prepared to race to his front door.

The same black Ford was across the street. The same young man got out of it, opened an umbrella and held it out over the back door. The young man stood in the rain, oblivious, waiting for someone to get out. The older man got out, muttered something, then the young man handed him the umbrella and got back into the car.

The older man walked slowly toward Bishop. He smiled and held the umbrella high.

"Would you like some shelter?" He asked.

Bishop nodded and tucked close, then they walked to his house door. There was no reason to argue at this point, he wanted to see where this was going.

Bishop opened the door and the older man shook himself dry, folding the umbrella and placing it in the hall.

He waved at the hallstand. "I assume you won't need your pistol, Captain?"

Bishop nodded. "So, you knew about my gun but you left it there anyway?"

The older man sat at one of the kitchen chairs and leaned forward.

"Why bother upsetting you more than necessary? I believe you are an honorable man. In retrospect, I don't think you are at all aware of everything that has transpired."

Bishop walked to the kitchen and opened the fridge. "Would you like anything to drink? Milk, water, orange juice?"

"Not for me, thanks. You have yet to ask me what all this is about, I notice. Aren't you curious?"

"I assume you're going to tell me. That is why you're here, isn't it?"

The man shook his head.

"Fifteen years in Military Intelligence, three tours of Afghanistan, and an excursion into somewhere so secret even I couldn't find out. Why exactly did you leave the Army, Captain?"

Bishop poured himself a glass of milk and sat on one of the stools by his counter.

"I got my twenty-year pension and decided it was time to teach, rather than to get shot at."

The older man knit his fingers together, thinking. "And yet, somebody knows you, trusts you, and this person wanted to give you something important, something sensitive. Why is that?"

Bishop took a sip of milk. "Beats me. Frankly, if I never find out I'm just as happy."

The man looked out into the living room, thinking. "Now, I had told you we wouldn't meet again. Normally we wouldn't, except that there has been a very troubling development."

He reached into his coat and pulled out a slip of paper. "Do you recognize this person?"

He held out a photograph, a portrait of a man in a blue shirt. Bishop looked at it, curious.

"No idea. Who is he?"

The older man put the photo away. "You said 'is'. More accurately, 'was'. He worked in the research department of a...." He paused. "military-affiliated organization. He went missing some days ago, and just yesterday his body was found in a nearby lake."

"I'm guessing it wasn't suicide?" Bishop asked.

"Not unless he wrapped himself in a carpet and threw himself into the lake."

"So, who was he?" Bishop asked again.

"That's rather immaterial. We think he got your name from other case files in the system and reading them would have told him you were a reliable contact. He most likely felt you were the right person to hear what he had to divulge."

"What about the people who took my briefcase? You had nothing to do with them?"

The old man shook his head. "There are competing parties looking for the item. They are the ones who took your briefcase, no doubt. We already knew there was nothing in it, of course."

Bishop rubbed his nose. "On the off chance that I do find this whatever it is, what does it look like, and why is it so valuable?"

The old man looked hard at Bishop for a few seconds, considering something.

"You teach military history, I'm told. Do you know why operations were given their names?"

"Which operations are you referring to?" Bishop asked.

"Operation Overlord, Barbarossa, Cobra, Bodyguard. These were all given names that had nothing to do with what they did. They were given random names for the sake of secrecy."

"Right. Your point?"

The old man smiled. "Flytrap. It's just a name. But knowing that name may make it easier for you to recognize or retrieve the item we're looking for."

"A Venus flytrap is a carnivorous plant. Does it have any relation to what we're talking about?"

"None that I'm aware of, Captain. Thank you for your hospitality. You still have my card? Good."

The old man walked to the front hall, picked up his umbrella and opened the door.

He turned back and smiled. "And the rain has even stopped. Have a good evening, Captain."

He left and closed the door behind him.

Bishop looked out the front window, watched the young man open the back door of the Ford, nod slightly as the older man got in, close the door and drive away.

Bishop watched him leave, waited a few moments then got out his phone. He dialed a number and waited. A few seconds later, Olivia Young answered.

"Hello?" She said, tentative.

"Hi, it's John Bishop. Listen, have you had dinner yet?"

She laughed. "I had some ramen noodles. Why, are you hungry?"

"I'd like to buy you dinner, somewhere nice, somewhere friendly. What's your favorite food?"

"Huh. OK, let me think. There's this killer Mexican restaurant by Pike Place Market. I've been there a couple of times. Do you like Mexican food?" She asked.

Bishop chuckled. "Love it. I can be at your place in fifteen minutes. See you then."

Bishop pulled his sports jacket out of the closet and straightened it while he looked in the hall mirror. This was beginning to feel more and more like a date, he thought. He put that thought out of his mind and drove to Olivia's apartment. There was little traffic on Mercer this evening, so he stopped on the street, turned on his emergency flashers and jogged up to the front door.

Olivia was just walking down the stairs inside the building, wearing the same tight skirt and sweater, with a short raincoat over them.

He held the door for her then let her into the passenger side of the Jeep. She smiled thanks, he got behind the wheel and headed south on I-5 towards downtown.

Olivia looked out the side window as he drove. "This is an interesting choice of car." She said.

"Thanks. I guess I'm used to driving four-by-fours. Never quite got into sedans."

She smiled. "Yeah. I drove my Saturn here all the way from Michigan. I wanted to drive something nicer, but acting doesn't pay that well yet."

He turned off the highway on the Union Street off-ramp. "Have you done anything I'd recognize? I'm not that much of a theater goer though, I have to admit."

She snickered. "I was in a fast-food commercial, as a mom with a screaming toddler. And I was in a Nordstrom's ad, gasping at the great prices. You didn't see them, I suppose?"

"No, I guess I missed those, sorry."

She opened her eyes wide. "Ah. One you might know. I was in a production of Oliver! at the Fifth Avenue. I was a washerwoman in that scene."

Bishop glanced over at her. "Sorry I missed that one too. But I saw the movie on TV years ago."

He drove the cobblestoned street between buildings in the Market District, followed Olivia's directions and found a parking spot just past the restaurant she pointed out.

He opened the passenger door for her, held her hand as she got out, and felt a slight electric rush as her hand fell into his.

The restaurant was small, with tightly packed tables and a typical touristy theme to the décor. There was mariachi music playing in the ceiling, not too oppressive, and since there were only four or five other couples in the place they were seated in a large booth.

A young man handed them glossy menus and placed water in front of them then left.

Bishop looked over the menu. "You ate here before, you said?"

Olivia nodded. "Yeah. They have great enchiladas. What do you like in Mexican?"

"The enchiladas sound good. Did you want to share an order of quesadilla first?"

She folded her menu. "Yeah, and I'm going to have a beer, if that's okay by you."

The young man came back with a notepad and pen. *"Que quieres?"* He asked.

He shook his head. "Sorry, English. What can I get you?"

Bishop handed him his menu. *"Dos enchiladas, una quesadilla por nos, Dos Equis por la senorita i un agua mineral por me."*

Olivia stared at him. "You have been here before, haven't you?"

Bishop shook his head. "No. To answer the next question, I speak some Spanish. Surprised?"

She laughed. "This could get interesting."

The waiter brought Olivia's beer, lemon and a chilled glass, then mineral water for Bishop.

Olivia poured her beer into the cold glass, squeezed lemon into the beer and took a sip.

"So, what do you do when you're not buying dinner for strange women?"

He shrugged. "I teach logistics and strategy at the U of W."

"You already told me that. Pretty heady stuff. Where do you go to learn that?"

Bishop took a sip of his mineral water. "I was in the Army for twenty years."

"I remember you said you were Army. How does that gel with why I was paid to stop you?"

"I was hoping you could tell me. Look, I found out recently that something had been sent to me, something rather sensitive, by all accounts. The person who sent it, apparently, met an unfortunate end. Just what do you know about this, exactly?"

She leaned back and took a swig of beer. "This isn't just some come-on line, is it? Not just one of those 'I'm a secret agent, sleep with me' yarns?"

Bishop shook his head. "I'm afraid not. Look, I don't know much more than what I told you. I was supposedly sent something that should not have been sent out. The person who sent it, from what I can gather, now sleeps with the fishes, as the saying goes. "

He pointed at her. "You were hired to help steal my briefcase, which only had lesson plans in it, by the way. Right now, you're the only person who has any connection to what is going on."

He decided not to mention the package sent to Farrow's aunt. The old man didn't know about it, Olivia didn't know about it, so there was no point in telling anyone else.

The young man brought three plates to their table, balanced strategically on his forearms, and placed them in front of them.

Bishop cut into his enchilada and took a bite, savoring the hot cheese.

Olivia took a wedge of quesadilla and crunched it loudly. "How's your food?"

He nodded approval. "Really good. I'll be certain to come back here again."

Olivia took another bite out of her quesadilla and rested her elbows on the table. The angle made her seem even more buxom. Bishop tried not to stare.

"So, are you married, or what?" She asked.

"Why do you ask?"

She leaned back. "You haven't mentioned a Mrs. ROTC. You like musicals, and you don't drink. You only had coffee at my place and water here. So, what's your story? Don't ask, don't tell?"

Bishop patted his mouth dry and smiled. "There *was* a Mrs. Bishop, but we grew apart after my second deployment. I can't blame her for getting lonely, so we decided, mutually, to go our own ways. How about you? Still waiting for Mr. Right?"

She took the quesadilla and seductively bit a tiny corner off, her white teeth showing under her deep red lips. "How do you know it's a Mr. Right? It could be a Ms. Right." She teased.

"Sure. In that case did you both want to come over to my place?" Bishop joked.

Olivia laughed out loud. Some of the other patrons stopped talking and looked at her. Bishop waited as she took a swig of beer. The bottle was empty; she waved at the waiter for another.

She leaned her elbows on the table and crossed her arms in front of her. She looked straight at Bishop, her deep brown eyes warming him up from his knees to his elbows.

"You don't drink, right? You had water here, coffee earlier. Why don't you drink?" She asked.

"I used to drink, but it got to the point that I couldn't buy groceries without being hammered. It took a lot of meetings, and a lot of therapy, but I've been dry for more than three years now."

She leaned back slightly, surprised. "I'm sorry. I didn't expect you to say that."

"Why? Did you think I was a Mormon, or what?"

"I just never thought, that's all. So, do you live near the University?"

"No, I own a home in Northacres." He corrected.

"Where's that?" She asked.

"About seven miles straight up I-5. It's an older area, but it's nice, peaceful."

She leaned forward again. "I wouldn't mind seeing it."

"I have ice cream in the fridge. We could have dessert there." He said softly.

"What flavor?" She teased.

"Fudge ripple."

She leaned back and waved at the waiter. "Hi, could you wrap this up to go?"

Bishop opened the door to his house and dropped the keys on the hallstand. Olivia wandered through the living room, slipped her shoes off at the end of the front hall as she did, and placed the baggie with their enchiladas on the kitchen counter.

"This is really nice." She said.

"I can't take all the credit. My wife did most of the decorating. I just left it like she did it."

"So, you got to keep the house. What did she get?"

"A lawyer from Tacoma. They live in Olympia now. He's a political mover and shaker."

She sat on a bar stool at the kitchen counter. "Nobody special in your life right now?"

She swiveled back and forth, rocking slightly, a soft smile on her lips.

 "Nobody special right now. Nobody... whatsoever." He said.

He opened the freezer door and pulled out a cardboard carton of ice cream, then scooped it into two bowls.

"Would you like coffee with this?" He asked.

She nodded.

Bishop plopped a pod into the machine and pressed the button. It hissed and spat coffee into the mug below it.

He placed a spoon in the ice cream and handed the bowl to Olivia.

She smirked. "Gee, you sure know how to show a girl a good time. Mexican food and carton ice cream."

Bishop smirked. "Yeah, but I do better on a second date."

They talked for hours, Olivia describing her life in Michigan, her parents and her desire to live on the West Coast.

Bishop described his work at the ROTC, talked about interesting people he had met and the satisfaction of teaching, but was vague about what he did in Intelligence.

It was late, close to midnight, when she said she had an early audition, and would he mind driving her home.

Bishop drove through the empty streets, the Jeep's tires hissing over the occasional wet patches, talking about places as they passed them; parks where he played with friends, restaurants he'd gone to, all trivia. She nodded and asked questions, curious about the area.

He stopped outside her building, jogged around to open her door, and helped her down to the sidewalk.

She kissed his check. "I had fun tonight. Really. Can we do this again soon?" She asked.

"That would be great. Do you want me to call you?" Bishop asked.

He was waiting for the 'I'll call you' line. He'd heard it enough times that it no longer stung.

"Call me after noon. I should be free by then. We'll have dinner. Again. Six o clock?" She smiled.

She kissed him again, firmly, on the lips.

"Dinner it is. Six. At Six." He repeated, and drove home humming to himself.

He went through the next day on autopilot, running through class lessons, explaining strategies and fielding questions, but the only thing on his mind was dinner with Olivia.

At five-thirty he put on his nicest shirt, pulled his suede loafers out of the back closet and gargled with mouthwash three times, then drove briskly to Olivia's apartment. It was exactly five fifty-eight, and she came down the inside stairs just as he got out of his car.

She was wearing a knee-length dress that looked like red silk, with a pale sweater over it. She looked casual and dressy all at once.

Bishop hopped up to the front door and held her hand, making sure she didn't stumble on her way down. He bent down to kiss her hello, and she grinned, then wrapped her arms around his neck and kissed him, passionately.

He walked her to his Jeep and held the door open for her. She slid in and wriggled, getting comfortable. Watching her legs move as she did gave Bishop a rush.

He went around to the driver's side and started the engine.

"Where are we going for dinner?" Olivia asked.

"You pick. Either a steak and lobster place, or someplace ethnic. What do you feel like?"

She shrugged. "Define 'ethnic'. Italian, Thai, Russian? Anything interesting, I guess."

Bishop thought for a moment. "Does Greek sound OK? Good. Greek it is."

They parked a few spots from the door of the restaurant. Bishop escorted Olivia as though he was guarding royalty, steered her around puddles in the driveway and to the entry canopy. A young woman in black slacks, black sweater and a black apron greeted them and sat them in a corner booth that Bishop pointed to.

He took her plastic menu and let Olivia read hers over. "See anything you like?" He asked.

She scanned the page up and down. "Can't go wrong with Greek salad and souvlaki. It's hard to mess those things up." She said.

She looked up at Bishop, her brown eyes reading him. "How about you?"

His mind went blank. "Look, can I tell you something? I don't really date much."

Her eyes widened in mock surprise. "Really? A lot of guys would be at the 'come back to my place' stage by now. I kind of got your awkwardness, yeah."

He smirked. "I'm not a monk. I've had some one-nighters, but I didn't really enjoy that much."

"And now? How is this date different?" Olivia teased.

"Well, none of the other women ever tried to steal my secret papers." He joked.

Olivia laughed out loud. The waitress came back and they ordered food, plus beer for Olivia and ginger ale for Bishop.

Olivia leaned her elbows on the table and rested her head in her hands, studying Bishop.

"I repeat, how is this different? How am I different?" she asked.

Bishop smiled. "You're not a bimbo. You can carry on a conversation for more than fifteen seconds without saying 'um'. You have an unusual background, and you are interested in different things, things like me, for instance." He said.

She grinned. "I'm not sure I've ever been described in those ways before." She said.

"How are you usually described?" Bishop asked.

"Nice ass, nice tits."

Bishop nodded. "Can't argue with that, no."

Olivia smirked and leaned back. "Thank you for seeing beyond that. You're a rare individual."

The food came and they spoke between mouthfuls. Olivia asked about places Bishop had been, places that he could talk about, and he described a month spent in the Azores, swimming in the ocean, sitting on the beach and reading books. The last part intrigued Olivia.

"What did you read?"

He looked up, remembering. "Moby Dick, War and Peace, The Iliad. I forget the rest."

"Really? I would have taken you for a Patterson or Jack Reacher fan." She frowned.

"You'd think, but no. I like the classics. They have more to teach us, I think."

Olivia shook her head. "I never read any of those. I should, I guess."

"I'm happy to give you any book I have."

She smiled. "I'd like that. Thanks."

He leaned forward. "Now, how about you, miss? What's your story?"

She shrugged. "There's not that much to tell, really. I came here because there was a role for me in a couple of commercials, then I did Oliver! and some more commercials. That's all."

"Wow, you make acting sound so... not exciting. I expected major stars hitting on you and the like. None of that happens, then?"

She squirmed, uncomfortable. "More often than not. But I prefer to date within my own species."

"Does that dating include someone like me, then?" Bishop asked.

She leaned forward and placed her hand on his. "If you want, we can discuss that over coffee and ice cream."

"At your place." She added.

Chapter 4: R&R

At seven thirty in the morning, the dull sky gave way to insistent sunlight. Bishop was half-awake, lying on his side, and became gradually aware of Olivia snuggled up to his chest, her back to him. It was Saturday. He could stay in bed with her all day, he thought.

He leaned over and kissed her shoulder. "Hey, good morning." He whispered.

She rolled onto her back and threw her arm over her eyes. "Hmm. What time is it?" She asked.

"A little before eight. Do you want some breakfast?"

She put her arm down over her breasts and smiled. "That sounds lovely. What do you have?"

Bishop thought for a moment. "Ah, toast? Coffee?"

She tilted her head up slightly and squinted at him. "You don't cook, do you?"

"Nope. Never have, never needed to."

She slid out of bed and rummaged through a pile of clothes on the floor, finding her underwear.

"All right, mister, you owe me a real breakfast."

Bishop drove them to a diner overlooking Lake Washington. He'd been there a few times before, always alone. This time, it felt like he was coming in with a trophy, Olivia, on his arm.

The waitress sat them by a window, offered menus and poured coffees, then gave a knowing smirk and walked away.

Olivia leaned forward. "You think she senses that we've had sex?" She asked.

"I sure as hell hope so, otherwise I'll have to stand on the table and tell everyone."

She snickered and covered her face with the menu. "You really don't date much, do you?"

They ordered and played with their coffees as they waited for food. Olivia squirmed in her seat.

"So, what exactly is it that you had with you? Why did I get paid to stop your car?"

Bishop shook his head. "I have no idea. Supposedly someone gave me or will give me something important. What I was told was 'I'll know it when I see it'. Beyond that I have no clue. Actually, that reminds me."

He took a sip of coffee. "The person who paid you to stop me, how did they contact you? Was it someone you knew? Someone you work with?"

She shook her head. "I got a call from my agent. He said there was a quick job for me, five hundred dollars for fifteen minutes. I couldn't say no."

"Did you get to meet the person who hired you?" He asked.

"Nope. They left a note in my mail slot. I got instructions on where to go, what you drive and when to cut you off. I got home after you stopped me- it took me a half hour to find my keys- thank you very much- and there was an envelope with the cash in my mailbox. I tossed the note and the envelope, kept the cash."

Bishop opened his mouth to ask a question. Just then the waitress came with two large plates of food and refilled their coffees.

Olivia started on her food right away, and Bishop did the same.

He leaned forward. "Do you want some of my sausage?"

She smirked. "That's rather suggestive, but sure."

He moved a couple of sausages to her plate. "You haven't had any other calls on that phone, then?" He asked.

She shook her head, chewing as gracefully as she could. "No, none."

He made a decision. "If you get any strange calls, please let me know. It's probably not going to happen, but just in case. Also, please don't accept any more cryptic assignments."

She cut a sausage in half and stuck it in her mouth. "I dunno, this one turned out pretty good."

He took a sip of coffee and looked out at the lake. "Olivia. It's a beautiful name. Who chose that for you?"

"My mom- she's Lebanese. It means 'olive tree' I think."

"Are your parents still in Pontiac?"

She nodded. "Dad teaches high school math. Mom runs a gift card store. And your family?"

Bishop nodded. "My father was Air Force. He flew heavy transports for years, then he left the Air Force and flew for United until he retired. My folks moved to Florida some years back."

"So your house was their house before?" She asked.

"Yup. Advantage to being the only child. They left me their house and I kept it in the divorce."

She took a swig of coffee. "Huh. Nice." She said.

She looked at her watch. "Uh, I have to run. I have an audition this afternoon. Could you drop me home so I can get ready?"

Bishop rested his head on his hands and leaned forward. "Can I see you again? Soon?"

She smirked. "Booty call or dinner date?"

He sat up. "Look, you're very pretty, very smart, and I'd really like to get to know you better."

She grinned. "Well, that's a lot more complimentary than the usual 'nice boobs, want to come over' that I hear."

"Confidentially, I was captivated from the moment you bumped my car." He said.

"Really? It was the sweater, right?"

"It was the legs. Those fabulous legs. Come on, eat up and I'll drive you home."

He parked on the side street and walked her home, then waited patiently while she took a shower and changed into a smart business suit. She came out and checked herself in a full-length hall mirror, tugging at the jacket to smooth out any wrinkles.

She turned to look at Bishop. "How do I look?" She asked.

He shrugged and said something incomprehensible.

"I'll take that as a yes." She said.

"What are you auditioning for?" He asked.

"The local TV station is looking for a new weather girl. I figure there are ten, maybe fifteen on the short list. I want to be on it."

Bishop waved his hand in the air. "Show me your act."

Olivia smiled a plastic smile and motioned at the mirror. "We have showers over Everett, with sunny breaks this afternoon. Seattle will see a high of fifty-four, and Tacoma will see scattered cloud and a high of sixty-one. For tomorrow, clearer skies all around and a high of sixty-three in the city."

She stood up straight. "How's that?"

"Pretty great. One thing though, I wouldn't give them the Barbie doll smile. It looks fake."

She frowned. "But they all smile like that. I've watched all the weather shows."

He shrugged. "Yeah, but your smile is radiant, just as it is. Don't embellish it."

She beamed. "OK. I'll consider that. Want me to call you after the audition?"

"I'd be insulted if you didn't."

Bishop drove home. His mind bounced between thoughts of Olivia, her smooth skin rubbing against him, and who it was that had broken into his house.

He threw his keys on the hallstand, checked underneath that his gun was still there, and opened the fridge. He reached for the milk, but stopped when his phone rang. Olivia- she had forgotten something, he thought.

"Hello?" He sang.

"Captain Bishop?" A man's voice said.

"Yes?" He was all business now.

"Detective Porezki, Seattle police."

"Oh, hi, Detective. Can I help you?"

He heard paper shuffling. "We, uh, have an interesting, um, development. I wonder if you'd mind coming down to the station?"

Bishop walked up to the same desk sergeant he had spoken to before and asked to see Porezki. This time, the sergeant escorted him to a glass office and asked him to wait, explaining that the detective would be up shortly.

Two minutes later, Detective Porezki walked in with a manila folder in his hand. "Hello, thanks for coming in so promptly." He said.

He sat across from Bishop and opened the folder. "Well, this is going a lot deeper than I ever thought it would." He started.

"We got a call from a construction crew, these guys who were clearing a clogged drain. They normally didn't work in that area, but a tree lodged in a storm pipe and they were called in. They came across this."

He slid a photograph over to Bishop. On the photograph was a large carpet, spread on the ground, and a man was lying on it, obviously dead. The man in the photo was young, twenty-something, judging from his face, and it seemed that all the blood had drained from his body.

Porezki tapped the photo. "Do you recognize this person?"

Bishop shook his head. "No, not at all. Who is he?"

"His name is Roger Morrison. Army Lieutenant Roger Morrison. Ring any bells?"

"No. I knew a Major Morrison, back in the Army, but that was twenty years ago."

Porezki glanced at the folder. "Was his name Eugene Morrison? Then this was his son."

Bishop looked more closely at the photo. "Come to think of it, there is a family resemblance. I'm so sorry for him.

Did you need me to call the Major and break the news to him?"

"That might be a problem. He died of stomach cancer three years ago. Something else…"

He pulled another sheet of paper from the folder and slid it at Bishop. "The phone messages you got on that burner phone- we traced the number to a sim card bought at a mall kiosk. The kiosk owner identified Roger here as the person who bought the phone. He's obviously the one who called you."

Bishop shook his head. "Why me? I've barely spoken to the Major in the last decade. I knew he had kids, but we never really talked about family stuff, you know?"

"What department were you in?"

"Intelligence." Bishop said.

"What did you do? What connection did you and Major Morrison have?"

"I can't answer that." Bishop said, firmly.

"Can't? Or won't?"

"Unless you have a letter signed by a three star General, I can't tell you anything."

Porezki snorted. "Lieutenant Morrison worked at the 'Society for Environmental Enhancement'. Does that ring any bells? Anything that you *can* answer?"

Bishop thought for a moment. "Did you ever see any of those old movies, you know, where the guy unbuttons his tuxedo, and the shirt rolls up like a scroll?"

Porezki frowned. Then his face lit up. "Like a dickey- a fake front. Is that what you mean?"

Bishop smiled. "Yeah. That has nothing to do with this conversation, of course, it just came into my head."

Porezki nodded slowly. "Right. I see. Anything else you *can* tell me, though?"

"Not right now, but things just got a lot clearer for me. Tell you what, I'll keep you in the loop as much as I can. No promises, but I'll do my best."

"Fair enough. Do you think that you are in any danger at all, Captain Bishop?"

"Not directly. I do want to make a couple of phone calls, though. There's someone I need to talk to right now. I will let you know what I can, when I can."

Porezki leaned back. "Military Intelligence, huh? What did you do there?"

"I collected stamps."

"Stamps?"

"On my passport. As I say, I'll keep you posted. Thanks for the update, Detective." Bishop said.

Bishop drove to a park on the west side of Seattle, one with a boat launch and a view of Bainbridge Island. Logistically, it was perfect. There was no way someone could sneak up on him without Bishop seeing them. There were cars to hide behind, a few buildings that provided him cover if needed, and a lot of civilians that would make it hard to explain if they were hurt.

Bishop pulled out the old man's card and dialed the number.

It rang twice. "Captain Bishop?" The man's voice said.

"It seems we have a problem. Lieutenant Morrison is dead." Bishop said.

The man sighed. "That's very sad news. What else do you know?"

"There was a data library we used when I was active. One that didn't have your everyday books in it. I lost access to it after I retired. Was Morrison a 'librarian' there?"

"Librarian is too narrow a term, my friend. I can tell you that he was vital to certain ongoing activities, and that losing him will have repercussions far beyond your pay grade."

"So, what happens now?" Bishop asked.

"Did you get the package yet?"

"I think I did, if it is what I think it is."

"Do you have the package with you?"

"Not anymore, and I don't expect to see it anytime soon."

There was a long pause. "You've sent it on a long voyage, I'm guessing?"

"I have sent somewhere I do not have any access to. I don't know where it is, and I don't know when it will return. Does that help you?"

He chuckled. "I admire your resourcefulness, Captain. You'll let me know when circumstances change?"

"Possibly. One more thing. Why did Morrison send it to me? I'd never met him before."

"His father worked with you. By all accounts, he believed you to be a reliable ally. The younger Morrison obviously trusted that you'd find the right home for his information."

Bishop looked around. There were no cars moving toward him, nobody looking at him.

"Is there anything about the… package that you can tell me? What it contains, why it's so damn radioactive?" Bishop asked.

The man sighed. "Did you ever read any Lewis Carroll? The hunting of the Snark?"

"Not that I can recall, no."

"He talks about these men hunting the mythical Snark, but just when they think they've found it, they all disappear."

"You're saying that possession of the object is a dangerous thing, then."

"In broad terms, yes. It's best to keep your distance, Captain. There are Snarks and Boojums and all sorts of evil creatures out there. Keep far away."

Bishop drove home. He checked every room in his house for signs that someone had been there and double-checked that his pistol was still in the front hall, still loaded.

He went through classwork for Monday; the best way to get life back to normal, he thought, was just act as though everything was normal.

By six thirty, the sun had set and the streetlights came on. He nuked a frozen dinner, poured himself a soda and sat down to eat. His phone rang.

"Hello?" He said.

"Hi, it's your date calling." Olivia's voice said.

He smiled broadly. "Hi, you. How did the audition go?"

"Um, about that. Do you want to buy me a drink?" She asked.

"I'll be there in twenty minutes."

He put on a good shirt and a dressy jacket, then drove to Olivia's apartment. She was standing out front in a shimmery short dress and a trench coat, grinning broadly.

Bishop sprinted over to her, wrapped an arm around her and kissed her. "Hello, there." He said.

She grinned and wrapped her arms around him. She kissed him passionately. "Hi to you too."

They drove to a bar she suggested and found a quiet table. Olivia wanted a margarita, and Bishop ordered a virgin Mary. A skinny young woman in black brought their drinks, and Olivia took a sip of hers. She winced at the bitter taste of salt on the glass.

"So, I had the audition today, and like you suggested, I was less plastic, more myself." She said.

"Great. How did it go?"

"They decided to go with another girl- some lollipop from Bellevue."

"Lollipop?" Bishop asked.

"It means skinny girl, big head, no shoulders. She looks like an anorexic boy with large tits."

"Ah. I'm sorry to hear that."

Olivia took another sip of her drink. "But, that being said, there were some network guys there. One of them thought I would be a good fit for their Detroit station. They want me there next week, for a month-long trial. It's a great opportunity. What do you think?"

Bishop winced. "I'd really miss you, but I agree- it's a wonderful opportunity. Besides, you'll still want to come back here to do theater work, right?"

She put her hand on top of his. "I really will miss you, you know. You're a good guy. I don't meet too many good guys."

"I'll be thinking of you too. You have my phone number- call me as often as you like."

She reached into her purse. "Ah. Phone number. I did get a strange call today. Someone asking for a Roger. Do you know what that could be about?"

Bishop sat up straight. "Can I see your phone?"

He flipped through the call log. The call was from a blocked number. He gave the phone back.

"Look, get a new SIM card and toss the old one. If you get another call like that, tell them to call me. Give them my number."

Her eyes widened. "What's going on, John?"

"I'm not sure. All I know is, I'm glad that you're going to Detroit. You'll be safer there."

"Safer? What do you mean, safer? Am I in danger?" She asked.

"I honestly don't think so, but it would still be better for you to be far away from here."

She raised one eyebrow. "I'm not sure I've ever been dumped in such an inventive way."

Bishop shook his head slowly. "Look, I'd like to be around you as much as possible. I hope that when all this is over that can happen. But for now, it's a good thing you're leaving Seattle."

She drained her margarita and waived the waitress over for a refill. Bishop sipped his tomato juice, watching her face as she thought about the conversation.

Olivia leaned closer to him. "This all got started because I hit your car, right?"

He shook his head. "No, and none of this is your fault. It started well before then. I'm not going to tell you more- that would only make things worse. But if anyone asks you, tell them everything you know, tell them what you did and who paid you and where I live. Don't hold back."

The waitress swapped her drink for a fresh one. Olivia licked salt off the glass and took a sip.

"Fine. I have to be at the airport early tomorrow afternoon. Could you drive me there?"

Bishop rested his hand on hers. "It would be my pleasure. Can I buy you dinner first?"

"Yeah," She smirked. "If that also includes breakfast."

Bishop opened his eyes and realized, groggily, that he was in an unfamiliar bed. It took him a minute- Olivia's place, it was her apartment. The smells of sizzling bacon and toast roused him.

He looked over toward the small 'efficiency kitchen' that older apartments had, and saw Olivia, wearing her Michigan sweatshirt and bikini briefs, poking at a frypan with a spatula.

She turned and smiled at him. "Good morning, sunshine. Did you sleep well?" She asked.

He rubbed his hair. "Yes, thanks. Great sex always makes me sleep well. What's for breakfast?"

She laughed. "Bacon, scrambled eggs, toast. I hope you like back bacon?"

"Love all of it. Can I help you with anything over there?"

"No, just set the table and I'll be right there." She said.

He pulled on his boxers and looked around for cutlery.

"In the drawer." She said, pointing with the spatula.

He set out two knives and forks by two plates and folded paper napkins into triangles.

Olivia poured him a coffee and he sat patiently.

She slid food onto his plate. "Here you go. Butter is there, and jam is… there." She said.

He waited till she'd put her food on her plate then buttered his toast.

"I must say, this is the best second date I've ever had." He joked.

Olivia crunched a piece of bread and smiled. "Glad you liked it."

She pointed the toast at his chest, her eyes going over the diagonal scars and crosshatch stitches under his ribs.

"That looks painful. Did you get those injuries in the Army?"

He shrugged. "It's an occupational hazard, I guess. At least I still have all my extremities."

"Where were you? Where did you get hurt?"

"A faraway land with mythical people and wondrous scenery."

She frowned. "You don't want to say?"

"Some memories are better left in the past, and others are better left unspoken."

She put her feet up on the seat of her chair, hugged her knees and crunched her toast. "My grandfather was in Korea. He almost never talked about the war, but my dad says he got very quiet whenever anyone asked him about it. I guess it's the same for you, huh?"

Bishop took a sip of coffee. "I saw some things I'd rather have not seen. I can live with myself, though, with what I did there. That's a lot better than some guys I was there with."

He looked at his watch. "When's your flight?"

"One thirty. What do you want to do after breakfast?" She asked.

"How about I go home and change? You pack and I'll pick you up here around ten. We can get an early bite at the airport so you won't have to eat the pretzels and cheese on the plane."

She grinned. "I like your thinking. More coffee?"

Bishop drove home, smiling to himself. His mind went back to the nights with Olivia, the smell of her skin and the way her smooth body slid against his.

He showered, shaved and put on a pair of dress slacks. He picked a nice polo shirt and windbreaker, then checked the look in his bathroom mirror. He drove to Olivia's place, slowly but with eagerness. He wasn't sure how much of that was worry and how much was hormones.

He jumped the steps to the front door of her building two at a time, buzzed her apartment and went in.

By the time he got to her door she was in the hallway, dragging a large suitcase out and locking up behind her.

"Hi. You're all ready to go?" He asked, stupidly.

She fumbled with her keys. "Yeah. The lights are turned off, the dishwasher is empty, all set."

She looked down for a moment and back up at him. "Look, would you mind checking my mail and making sure the place is secure while I'm gone?"

"Sure. My pleasure." Bishop said.

She handed him her keys. "I will want these back, you know."

"I'm looking forward to that day." He answered.

They had a snack at one of the places in SeaTac Airport and he walked her to the airline check-in counter. She watched her suitcase slide down the belt, then through a slot, and sighed.

She looked down at her boarding pass. "You know, when I bumped your car, I never thought that this would happen. I'm glad it did, though. Are you?"

"Oh, hell, yes. You think a guy like me could ever meet a girl like you otherwise?"

She smiled broadly. "Don't sell yourself short. Keep in touch, all right? I'll call you when I get to Detroit."

She leaned up and kissed him. He wrapped his arms around her and lifted her off the ground.

"Go. Knock 'em dead, kid. Break a leg. I expect you to do great things." He whispered.

She leaned back and wiped a tear away. "Bye." She said, and went through security.

Bishop spent the afternoon getting ready for next morning's class. He bought a frozen pizza, ate it with a bag of potato chips and made notes on the similarities between Gallipoli and the invasion of Grenada. The whole time, all he could think about was Olivia's Michigan shirt and briefs, Olivia's brown eyes, Olivia's auburn hair, Olivia's back, Olivia's...

Chapter 5: Home Soil

Monday morning, five thirty AM. Back to his old routine, back to life as normal.

Bishop went for his run, did his sit-ups, did his push-ups, ate his toast and drove to work.

He made good time, parked in his usual spot, and got to his desk before eight. Nobody tried to run him off the road, nobody in a black sedan was parked down the street, nobody called him with a strange request. Olivia called after she landed in Detroit. She said her parents had driven her home and she would let him know how the job went.

For the first time in days, Bishop was back on familiar soil, mentally. He made coffee, marked Farrow's revised assignment and waited for Kelly to show up with the morning mail.

At exactly eight thirty, Kelly clip-clopped in and smiled.

"Hey, Bish. How was your weekend?" She asked.

"Pretty good. Nothing special." He lied.

She handed him a short bundle of envelopes. "Mail's here." She said.

He flipped through the dozen or so letters. Most were the standard university crap, pleas for time and money, invitations to events he wouldn't attend anyway, notices of social causes.

One letter stood out. It was squarish, like a birthday card envelope. It was addressed to him, but the return address was just a post office box and an unfamiliar zip code.

He opened his desk drawer and took out his Ka-Bar, the Bowie knife with a thick leather handle. He carefully slid the blade under the flap of the envelope and pried it open.

Inside the envelope was a greeting card. On the front of the card there was a photo of a person paddling a kayak, but the inside of the card was blank. No message, no signature, nothing.

Bishop looked inside the envelope again. There was a sheet of paper inside, folded in four.

He took the paper out and unfolded it. Printed on it was a long string of numbers, filling the page, in groups of six digits.

One of the other two instructors that shared this office came in. Mark Powell was the instructor for software, systems programming and 'all-around geeky stuff', as he described it. He had been at the university longer that Bishop, but like Bishop had done his share of 'eating dust and killing scorpions'.

Bishop walked over to him and handed him the slip of paper.

"Mark? Good morning. I got a puzzle for you." Bishop started.

Powell looked up from his desk. "Good morning. You get lucky over the weekend?"

Bishop blushed a deep red. "Excuse me? Does it show?"

"Like a flashing beacon. You don't usually beam like that on a Monday. Who is she?"

"Long story, Mark. Anyway, I got this in the mail. What do you make of these numbers?"

Powell looked at the sheet of paper. The first row of numbers started with:

880068 452246 385578 837720 927724 000000 657747 835519

Bishop shrugged. "I don't know what it means. Does this make any sense to you?"

Powell placed the paper on the desk in front of him, folded his arms and leaned in close, studying it. "This is fascinating. Did anything else come with it?"

"What do you mean?" Bishop asked.

"Did anything else come in the mail with it?"

Bishop got the greeting card and envelope. He handed them to Powell. "Just these."

Powell examined the card, flipped it over, looked for hidden items glued into the card, everything he could think of. He shook his head. "Can I take this with me?" He asked.

"Yeah, please. I'm stumped." Bishop shrugged.

Powell put everything back into the envelope. "Leave it with me."

Bishop walked into class, just like any other Monday, and taught his lesson, just like any other Monday. He presented case studies, asked questions, fielded answers and gave assignments.

He had lunch at the usual place, ate the usual meal, and made the usual notes as he ate. The whole time, all morning and all afternoon, all he could think about was Olivia.

He got home around six, put a frozen meal into the microwave and poured himself a glass of milk. He put his feet up on the coffee table and stretched out. Today had been unusually tiring.

His phone rang. "Hello?" He said, mechanically.

"Hey, hot stuff." Said the voice on the other end.

He smiled broadly. "Hi, Olivia. I've been thinking about you all day."

"Ditto. Listen, I have a dinner with the producer and his wife in ten minutes, but I wanted to say that I miss you. Anything happen since I left?"

Bishop thought about the envelope. "Nope, nothing. I'll let you know, though. What do you have planned for tomorrow?"

She sighed. "Makeup test, then a voice test, then we'll see what my 'Q' rating is on camera."

"Well, break a leg, or whatever they say in TV land. Let me know how it goes."

She giggled. "OK. Love you. Bye."

She hung up.

The words 'love you' gave Bishop a rush. He ate dinner, cleared up the few dishes, read two chapters of U.S. Grant's autobiography and went to sleep.

At five thirty in the morning, Bishop went through his usual routine. He went for a run, did sit-ups, push-ups, ate breakfast, then drove to the university. He mentally prepared his lesson for the day as he drove, while in the back of his mind he somehow hoped that a yellow sedan would cut him off, one with Olivia driving it.

He got to work at the usual time, made the usual coffee, and sat at his desk, waiting for the coffee to perk. For the first time in a long time, he felt dissatisfied.

He liked his job, he liked the people he worked with, and he liked where he lived. After spending time with Olivia, though, it seemed that all this was just no longer enough.

It didn't hit him with a bang, or a flash of realization. It simply, slowly, dawned on him. He was not happy with his life. Olivia made him happy.

Maybe it was having sex again, maybe it was being around a pretty woman, maybe it was just feeling like a whole person again. Whatever the reason, he liked how she made him feel.

Twenty minutes later, Mark Powell came in and sat across from Bishop's desk. He had a wide grin on his face, like a child who just bought the perfect toy. He pulled out the envelope Bishop had given him.

"Boy, was that ever a lot of fun!" He gushed.

Bishop shrugged. "Enlighten me."

Powell took out the greeting card and flipped it over. "Look at the brand on the back."

Bishop read the words under a simple logo. "Rosetta Stone Cards." He said.

Powell nodded. "I checked. They don't exist. This is a home-made card."

Bishop handed the card back. "Yeah. And the punch line is?"

"The Rosetta stone unlocked the code to Egyptian hieroglyphics, see? That was the clue."

Powell flipped the card over to the front. "What do you see there?"

"A man in a boat?"

Powell shook his head. "Wrong. It's not a boat. It's a man in a kayak. A kayak."

"A kayak. Not a boat. A kayak." Bishop repeated.

Powell laughed. "Kayak. Race car. Madam I'm Adam. A man, a plan, a canal, Panama."

Bishop frowned. "Those are all palindromes?"

Powell poked the card with his finger. "You see? It was right there. The numbers were palindromes. All of them."

He unfolded the sheet of paper and laid it on the desk.

Bishop looked at the numbers. "But these aren't palindromes." He said.

Powell grinned. "No, they're not. Look at the first one. 880068. What do you have to add to the end two numbers to make it a palindrome?"

Bishop thought for a second. "Twenty."

"Right. And the twentieth letter of the alphabet is T. Second series of numbers, add eight, H."

Powell shook his head, impatient. He ran his finger along the page. "I did the same thing for the entire page. Here's the first line. T. H. E. R. E. I figure all the zeros means a space. I.S. space A. space W.E.B.S.I.T.E."

Bishop frowned. "There is a website?"

Powell nodded. "It goes on. The web address the message points to starts with 141.116.168. That's the domain IP for the Pentagon. What the hell have you gotten yourself into, Bish?"

"No idea, Mark. But for your own sake, don't go down that rabbit hole. It's toxic."

Powell handed over the paper and the greeting card. "Understood. Don't ask, don't tell, don't drop the soap in the shower. Got it."

He stood up and went on to teach his class.

Bishop scooped up the envelope and papers and put them in his desk.

Bishop taught his prepared lecture, took questions, answered questions, handed out assignments and went home.

He thought of Olivia; how she looked, how she smelled, how her lips tasted. He didn't think of her quite as often as he had the day before, but maybe that was a good thing, he told himself.

He tossed his keys on the hall stand, pulled a cardboard-wrapped meal from the freezer and stuck it into the microwave.

A knock at the door made him pause. Was Olivia back already? No. Maybe the old guy? In any case, if they were knocking, chances were they weren't going to try and ambush him.

He opened the door partway, still slightly apprehensive. The woman on the front steps was older, in her late fifties, with a sad face and drooping shoulders. She looked slowly up at him.

"Captain Bishop?" She asked.

"Yes. Can I help you?"

She sniffled. "My name is Zoe Morrison. I'm Roger Morrison's mother."

Bishop opened the door wide. "Oh, Mrs. Morrison. Please come in. I'm so sorry for your loss."

She shuffled in past him. He looked out to see if anyone else was around- no, nothing out of the ordinary. He closed the door and turned to face her. "Would you care to sit down, ma'am?"

She nodded thanks, put her purse on the counter with a 'clunk' and slid onto a kitchen stool.

"Can I get you something to drink? Coffee or a soda?" He asked.

"No, nothing for me, thanks. I just wanted to come here and talk to you about Roger."

Bishop sat and put his hand on hers. "I was so sorry to hear about him. What can I tell you?"

She looked at her shoes and sighed. "He said he trusted you. He said you were a good person, and he believed in you. He indicated that he was going to give you something, something important. Do you know what he meant?"

Bishop shrugged. "I'm not sure. I think he was trying to tell me something, but I still don't know what it meant."

The woman sighed. "Could I see what it was that he gave you? Maybe it will mean something to me that it doesn't to you?"

Bishop nodded. "Of course. How is Roger's father holding up, by the way?"

She sniffled again. "He's heartbroken. Roger was our pride and joy. I don't know if he's ever going to get over it."

"Especially since he died three years ago." Bishop said coldly.

The woman's eyes widened. Her hand creeped toward her purse, slowly.

Bishop leaned forward. "You go for that purse gun and I'll break every finger on your hand. Now, who the hell are you?"

The woman leaned back and smirked. "You are a smart one, aren't you? What gave me away?"

"Major Morrison was my CO for a time. His wife passed away when Roger was a teenager. He never remarried. Now, one last time, who are you?"

The woman snorted and slid off the stool. "Not a chance. Screw you. I'm leaving." She said.

Bishop grabbed her wrist and twisted it. She arched her back against the pain and just glared at him. "Let me go. Let me go now." She hissed.

"No. Now, you're the second woman they've sent to rattle me. Here's the scoop. I don't have what you want. It's gone. I don't know what it was, and I don't want to know. So tell your people to piss off, leave me alone and go look somewhere else. Period."

She looked at him and sneered. "How did you know about my gun?"

"It clunked when you put your purse on the counter. It's a very distinctive sound." He said.

He reached into her purse and took out a tiny black 'pocket twenty-five' automatic. There was nothing else in her purse, no driver's license, no wallet, no cash, nothing but a set of car keys. He popped the magazine out of the gun, cleared a round from the chamber, put the magazine in his pocket and handed her the purse and gun. He grabbed her arm and lifted her up.

"Get out of here." He said.

He pushed her out and closed the door behind her. He could hear her shoes clunking down his front steps, then get softer as she walked away.

The smell of tomato sauce and broccoli filled the kitchen. Bishop scooped the food out of the plastic microwave dish and poured himself some milk, thinking.

Now he had some more data to analyze the situation. He went into Army mode. The people who had come after him had done so in different ways. There was the group with the old man that distracted him by trashing his office so he would leave the house. There was the group that hired Olivia to distract him so he would leave his briefcase, and now there was someone else, apparently, who went on a frontal assault by pretending to be a relative of the dead guy.

What were they after? Did he want to find out, or was he better off just destroying whatever this package contained and letting everyone know it was gone? Maybe he could do both.

Bishop went into class at the usual time. He waited for the class to settle down, plugged a USB into the lectern, and turned on the projector.

On the screen, a plump man was doing simple magic tricks, making a handkerchief disappear then reappear, turning a coin into a magic wand, and making cards float in the air. The video ran for about ten minutes. Bishop turned the screen off.

"Now, did any of you learn something from this silly video?" He asked.

Hands went up. He chose one at random. One man said: "Subterfuge and misdirection."

Bishop smiled. "Right. Your mind sees what you expect to see. That's what magician does. That's why, during the war, the British Army employed a group of magicians to do this…"

He clicked the screen on again. A movie played, old and jerky, black and white, showing a row of tanks and airplanes in a field. "Notice anything unusual?" He asked.

Nobody answered. "The tanks are made of fabric over wood frames, the artillery cannons are cardboard. The airplanes are made of cardboard and balsa wood. The Japanese also made some planes out of straw and wicker to draw Allied fire. The tricks work. Don't discount them."

He gave concrete examples of how to get information from an enemy, how to avoid answering direct questions, how to keep one step ahead of the other side.

At lunch, he waited for the students to file past him. He crooked his finger at one man.

"Farrow. Is that package still on vacation?"

The young man looked around nervously. "Yes, sir. You asked me to leave it… there until you asked for it back. Do you want it to… find its way home now?"

"Yes, please. Well done, Farrow. And as I said, please leave it sealed when you get it."

"Roger that, sir." He smiled.

Bishop went back into his office and pulled the old man's card out of his wallet. He dialed the number and waited. Three rings later, the old man came on. "Yes, Captain?" The man said.

Bishop waited for a moment. He could hear people talking in the background, voices laughing, a woman saying something. It was a restaurant or a meeting room, it seemed.

"I have a question for you." Bishop said.

"Go on."

"Did you send a woman to my door? One pretending to be Lieutenant Morrison's mother?"

There was a slight pause. "Can you describe her?"

Bishop thought about her. "Five three, fifty to sixty, Jennings twenty-five caliber pistol."

The old man moved to a new location, the voices now gone. "Did you tell her anything?"

"Only that I knew that Morrison's parents were dead, and I had nothing for her. Who is she?"

The old man sighed. "Son, you were born with horseshoes up your ass, weren't you? Let's just say that she doesn't vote Republican or Democrat and leave it at that."

"Are you telling me she's working against your interests? Is she a spy or something?"

The old man chuckled. "That's such a broad category. Some people believe in ideals that we don't believe in, that's all."

Bishop decided to reveal a detail. "I got a greeting card in the mail. It had a sheet of paper with a series of numbers with it. Do you know what it could be?"

"Was the picture on the front of the card a man paddling a boat?" The man asked.

"You've seen it?"

"It's a broadcast message for all of us in… our business. I got one too."

"What does it mean? I couldn't figure it out." Bishop lied.

"Ask Mr. Powell. He went on the website the message mentions. We know he did."

"He never told me he figured out the code. What does it say?" Bishop lied.

The old man chuckled. "A highway map will take you to from town to town. You need a detailed street map to find the right house. The card you and I got is only the first step. The other information, what we're looking for, takes you the rest of the way."

"Leading to what, exactly?" Bishop asked.

"Flytrap."

"And what exactly *is* Flytrap?" Bishop prodded.

"Some mysteries are better left unsolved, don't you think? It's healthier that way. Let it go."

The old man hung up.

Bishop waited at his desk. Mark Powell sat across from him, waited for Kelly to bring his lunch, and casually circled errors on his own students' papers.

Bishop sat across from him. "Mark. You went on the GOV website. What were you thinking?"

Powell grimaced. "Yeah, I didn't think anyone would notice, but when I landed on the site I got a big red screen. I logged off right away, but I'm sure they tagged me."

Bishop shook his head. "Drop it, Mark. I'm serious, let it go. This is deep secret government shit that you went to."

Powell leaned back, the chair springs creaking against his weight. "OK. What I can tell you, though, is the path leads outside the US, to a site that shouldn't be on a government server."

Bishop scratched his cheek. "Any idea where it leads to?"

Powell shook his head. "Dunno. It started with the Pentagon IP, then it bounced me to Portugal, then Bosnia, then I got the red screen and I shut down."

"Which computer did you do it from?" Bishop asked.

Powell pointed at the window. "The library one. I'm not a complete idiot, you know."

"Someone said they knew it was you. Let it drop, Mark." Bishop warned.

Bishop was on autopilot for the next few days. He went to work, went home, ate dinner, woke up, worked out, went to work, and went home. Life went back to normal, except that he missed Olivia more every day, and he enjoyed his work less every day.

On one ordinary day, he got to work as usual, parked in his normal spot and made coffee at eight twenty-five, then marked some papers before class.

A knock at the open door made him look up. A young man with a large envelope stood there.

"Good morning, Farrow." Bishop said.

The young man held out the envelope and placed it on Bishop's desk. "This came in the mail yesterday, sir." He said.

Bishop flipped the envelope over. It was still clearly unopened, slightly crumpled from its trip back and forth from Seattle to Idaho, but intact. He looked up at the young man.

"Thank you very much, Farrow. Please remember, this never happened."

The young man frowned. "Sir, will this affect my marks?"

"It might help them, son."

The young man left, and Bishop put the envelope in his briefcase. He would take it home tonight, but right now this was the last place anyone would think to look for it.

At five-fifteen, Bishop did what he did every evening. He drove home, put something in the microwave for dinner, and sat at the kitchen counter eating his mac and cheese. He waited for a knock, or the sound of someone opening the screen door, anything. Nothing happened.

He put a few logs in his fireplace, lit the fire and watched the flames lick the brick inside the chimney. He sat there for a few minutes, then he went to his office and opened his briefcase.

The envelope with the inter-office manila envelope was still there. He unwound the string holding the flap closed, and casually slid the contents onto his desk.

He laid them out in a row, automatically arranging them by size. There was a softcover report folder, the blue plastic see-through kind, with a dozen stapled sheets of paper inside. Through the cover sheet he could see a page with just three typed words- TOP SECRET/ FLYTRAP.

Below that was a red stamp that read 'SAP' in big letters.

That made him pause. The Special Access Program was a level above Top Secret. Most people didn't even know of its existence. SAP, SCI and EO-RAD were on documents he'd seen in the Army, but rarely even then, and never since. He looked at the next item. It was a plain DVD, a generic commercial type, like the ones Bishop bought to burn class videos. The last item was a two-gigabyte flash drive, just like an old one Bishop had.

Two gigabytes. That was very old-school, small by modern standards. A sixteen gig would cost not much more than a pack of gum.

Bishop rummaged around his desk and found a flash drive, a twin to the one he'd been sent. He dug out an old DVD like the one Morrison had sent him, and he pulled out a dozen sheets of paper with old exams on them, copied the cover page from the report that said 'TOP SECRET/ FLYTRAP', then put the real items in a folder marked '2021 taxes' and stored them in his desk.

He put the old exams in the plastic folder with the copied front page, his own flash drive and DVD on top of it and pulled out the old man's business card. He dialed the number and waited.

Two rings later, the man's voice came on. "Yes, Captain?"

"I received an interesting package today. It was in the mail." Bishop said.

The old man sighed deeply. "Have you viewed the contents?"

"No way. I just saw the cover page. I lost my SAP access when I retired. This stuff is poison."

"What do you plan to do with this information, then? Do you intend to sell it?" The man asked.

Bishop chuckled. He was going to enjoy the next statement. "No. I'm going to burn it."

The old man moved close to the phone, his voice urgent. "Listen, John, before you do anything rash, think. Think hard. The contents of that package are vital. Valuable. Do you understand?"

"The sun came up today, and the sun will rise tomorrow. With or without whatever is in this."

"Wait. Wait. Just sit and wait. I'll be there in ten minutes. Wait." The man said.

He hung up.

Bishop looked at his watch and waited seven minutes. He placed his old flash drive on a thin piece of wood, along with his old DVD, and laid them in the fireplace. He watched the plastic curl and melt as the DVD went up in smoke, and the flash drive deconstruct itself into a circuit board and smoking solder.

The sound of the front door opening didn't surprise him. He placed the plastic folder in the flame, watched as the cover shriveled while the old exam papers burned, and listened to the footsteps of the old man thunder up behind him.

The old man peered into the flame, incredulous. "What have you done?" He hissed.

"I got rid of what your people were after. It's all gone, and I'm out of this mess." Bishop said.

The old man sighed and sat on the arm of the sofa. "Well, could have been worse, I suppose."

He peered over his glasses at Bishop. "You never examined the…no? I see. That makes sense."

He walked to the front door. "Good evening, Captain. Please lose my number, if you would."

Bishop went to the front door and watched the old man stomp over to a black sedan. The young man who had been with the old man before opened the back door and the old man got in. Something about the way the younger man stood waiting by the car said 'military'. The old man's demeanour said a General's uniform, or an Admiral's, would have looked right for him.

Saturday morning, Bishop treated himself to a break. He went to the diner where he'd gone with Olivia, ordered a large breakfast and sat staring out at Lake Washington. He felt relaxed, at ease, for the first time in days.

He still missed Olivia, but less so than the days before, and the memory of her was getting foggier with time. Also, nobody was coming after him for the items that were supposedly gone.

Despite all that, he still felt uneasy. He was good at his job, he enjoyed teaching, but it was not enough anymore. He'd been good at his role in the Army too, but that was also in the past.

One of his platoon leaders left the forces and decided to motorcycle from Indiana to Alaska. Another soldier bought a boat and spent his days fishing in Tennessee. Neither of those options appealed to Bishop. He needed to do something in town, something urban, something real.

He paid for the meal and walked out to his Jeep. He reached into his pocket for his keys and realized he still had Olivia's keys in his pocket. He had an urge to see her again, to hold her, wrap her in his arms. He couldn't, of course, but he could do the next best thing.

He drove to her apartment and opened the door. The light scent of her perfume was still in the air. He breathed in deeply, enjoying her presence second-hand, as it were. He looked around to check that she hadn't left any food to go bad, then he sat on her bed, remembering the time with her. He sighed, stood up to leave, then he heard the sound.

There was the unmistakeable thump of feet on the hard linoleum outside, then the tinkle of keys coming out of a pocket, and the metallic grating of a key going into a lock. It must be the super, doing repairs or something, he thought. He would tell him why he had Olivia's keys.

The door opened, and Bishop froze. She was in her fifties, but the droopy shoulders she'd had when she came to his door as 'Mrs. Morrison' were gone. She was firm, determined.

Her head was down as she slid a suitcase ahead of her and closed the door, then she looked up and saw Bishop. She froze for moment, then kicked the case aside and turned toward the door.

Bishop got to her before she could get it open again. He planted a foot against the door and pushed her face against it with his hand.

"You have ten seconds. Talk fast." Bishop growled.

"You don't understand. I'm not trying to... It's not what you think..." the woman started.

Bishop spun her around and pressed his hand against her shoulder. "Why are you in this apartment?"

She slapped his hand away and poked her finger into his chest. "You are way out of your league, you know that? You are so far out of your depth, it's a miracle you haven't drowned."

Bishop folded his hands in front of him. "Explain."

She snorted. "You think you just got lucky, catching her car? You were meant to. We knew right away there was nothing in your briefcase. We knew after they went through your house there was nothing there. But we also knew you might confide in a pretty woman. Once she told us that you didn't know anything, her job for us was done."

Bishop looked around. "So whose apartment is this?"

"It's hers. Really. Her agent let me borrow it. I needed to be here right now."

"Why did she leave me her keys, then?" Bishop asked.

"We heard you had them, maybe to stash the item we wanted. You might have hidden it here."

Bishop sat at the dining table, thinking. "I put her on a plane to Detroit. I told her that leaving here would keep her safe. Also, why didn't you know that Major Morrison's wife was dead?"

"Of course I knew. You were *supposed* to find out that I was an impostor. We expected you to tell me that you had the goods and that you'd turn them over to the General."

"Is that who that old man is? Is he 'the General'?" Bishop asked.

"Was. He retired. He's gone private." She barked.

Bishop smiled slightly. "You do know that I received the package after all, don't you?"

She nodded. "He said that you burned it. Did you?"

"I did." Bishop lied.

"Bullshit. If you knew a tenth of what's on that DVD you'd fly to Washington and personally hand it over to your old boss. You're a boy scout. That's exactly what you'd do."

"What *is* on that DVD then?" He asked.

She laughed. "You said *is*, not *was*. All right, let's pretend that you really destroyed it."

She took off her coat and tossed it over the back of the sofa. "Would you like a glass of… no, you don't drink anymore, do you? Coffee?"

Bishop nodded. The woman pulled down a kettle and a bottle of red wine. She made the coffee and poured herself a glass of Merlot.

Bishop leaned back on the sofa and took the coffee mug from her. "What exactly is Flytrap?"

The woman sat and smoothed the wrinkles on her pant leg. She took a sip of her wine and placed the glass on the table beside her.

"We got hit hard on nine-eleven. The people who did it don't fight like conventional soldiers. They see victory and death as equals. Their followers will keep coming no matter how many of them we take out with drones. The best way to defeat them is the same way you kill ants in a colony. We send them back to their anthill with poison. It might be biological, it might be chemical, it might be electronic, but we know we need to squash them at the source."

"This much I know." Bishop said. "What's different about Flytrap?"

The woman smiled. "Sometimes we have to work with people we dislike, to get at people we both hate. 'The enemy of my enemy' and all that. And sometimes money changes hands. The American public doesn't want to know who was paid what for doing something unpleasant. They just want to be able to drive through Dairy Queen without getting blown up."

"What about Olivia? Was she just part of the act? Was she paid to lure me in?"

She threw up her hands. "Ah. Olivia. She went way above the call of duty there, Captain. She is merely an actress, just like she told you. Her job was just to get you talking, to open up to her, but she was clearly taken with you. She took to you personally on her own. Well done, you."

Bishop rubbed his eyes. "Who are you, then? Regular Army? A Langley spook? NSA? What?"

She took a sip of wine. "All I will tell you is that if we were both in uniform, you'd salute me."

He sneered. "So what now? Do we shake hands as friends and go our own way?"

The woman sipped her wine. "Why do you think Morrison was killed? He was trying to leak our dirty secret information out to the world, and those on the other side don't want to be seen dealing with America. It would be very embarrassing for them."

"Who are we talking about? Iran, North Korea, China, all of the above?"

She shrugged. "You'd think so, but there are lots of third-string countries out there hoping to make a name for themselves. Word got out that Morrison had compiled some lists, and he had records of meetings and copies of documents. It would be very embarrassing for the Bahrainis to be seen collaborating with the Israelis against the Yemenis, for instance."

Bishop rubbed his forehead. "But why send the package to me? What made me so special?"

"You think you're the only one? He sent the same information to five others. We intercepted them before they caused any damage. You're the only one left. Do you still have the information, or did you really destroy it?"

"Search my house again if you like. It's not there." Bishop said.

He hoped she wouldn't see through the bluff. She took a sip of wine. Bishop leaned forward.

"Do you have an idea of who it was that killed Morrison?"

She shrugged. "A private contractor, we think. We are never told their names, or how to contact them or who pays them. They could be your teacher, your doctor, the mailman. They don't have business cards that say 'hired assassin'."

"The Seattle PD is looking for the person who did this." Bishop said.

"Good luck. It's like catching smoke with a butterfly net."

There was a knock at the door. The woman smiled and stood up. "That will be for me."

She opened the door. Bishop couldn't see the person in the hallway from where he was.

He heard a soft 'putt, putt…putt' and the woman collapsed.

She made a gentle moaning sound, then everything went quiet.

Bishop jumped up and ran to the door. A man was vaulting down the stairs, very quickly. The woman was on her back, with a surprised expression on her face. There were two red stains on her shirt and a third red mark on her forehead. She was dead.

Bishop thought about staying where he was, in case the man shot at him too. The man was running away quickly, though, probably too quickly to get an accurate shot from that distance. He made a decision; he ran down the stairs after the man, peeking around the corner at the top of the stairs, in case the man shot at him from below. The front door closed, and Bishop sprinted down the steps, racing toward the entrance to the building. Maybe he could identify the man, if nothing else, but all he saw was a dusty van driving away, with the words 'Custom Auto Upholstery' written on the side.

Chapter 6: Activity Report

Detective Porezki pulled on a pair of nitrile gloves and tugged fabric booties over his shoes. He walked gingerly around the body of the woman in the doorway and squatted beside Bishop.

"Well, thank you for bringing the bodies to an apartment for us. It saves so much time over having to pull them out of a lake." He joked.

Bishop grunted. "I didn't have to call you, you know. I could have just walked away."

"Yeah, as I say, I appreciate you keeping us employed. So, who was this woman?"

"No idea."

"Are you saying you've never seen her before?"

"She came to my house the other day, pretending to be Roger Morrison's mother."

Porezki made notes in his little flip book as he spoke. "Why would she do that?"

"She said she wanted to know if Morrison had sent me some sensitive information."

Porezki looked up. "And had he?"

"Let's say the answer to that is no, shall we?"

Porezki looked down again. "The woman had a small caliber pistol in her purse, but no clip or bullets in it. Know anything about that?"

"Yes. I took the magazine out when she came to my house."

Porezki snickered. "Remind me not to accept any invitations to your parties."

"You don't have a name for her either?" Bishop asked.

"We've sent out her prints, but we got a nasty message back to mind or own business. Then we got a very serious call telling us to piss off and leave her here. I've been asked to watch the fort till the men in black show up. I would really like to solve this one myself, though. Anything you can tell me that helps me out?"

Bishop nodded. "Yeah, one thing. I heard the shots-highly supressed, subsonic bullets, I'd guess, and I saw a guy running down the stairs. I didn't see his face, but he had a crappy older van, with a company name on it. 'Custom Auto Upholstery'."

Porezki glared at him. "You're sure of the name?"

"Yeah, I'm sure that was it. Why?"

Porezki flipped pages on his notebook. "A witness saw someone driving away from the lake where we found Morrison's body. That's the name they saw on the van. We didn't think much of it then, since there were several vehicles reported. But now..."

Bishop stood up. "The man who killed her probably killed Morrison. Olivia Young was here the other day. If she'd answered the door, she might be dead now."

Porezki smirked. "You're dipping your pen in that inkwell, are you?"

"Does everyone know when I'm getting laid? Do I have a neon sign that lights up, or what?"

Porezki rubbed his goatee. "Your eyes glazed over when you mentioned her name."

Bishop stood up. "Well, if there's nothing else you need right now?"

"Nope. We know where to find you. If you want to send us more bodies, put them in a cab to the station, please. It saves us on gas."

Bishop drove home and opened his fridge. No meals in there. Freezer- likewise. He considered ordering a pizza, but the thought of someone coming to the door and shooting him like they had shot the woman made him rethink that idea.

He wondered if he should go back to the Mexican place he'd gone to with Olivia. The food was good, and he'd feel safer in public, at least.

His phone rang, and he hoped it would be Olivia- the Mexican restaurant put that in his mind.

"Hi." He said cheerily.

"Bishop? We need to talk." The old man's voice said.

Bishop frowned. "Do we? What about?"

"Don't be an asshole. She's dead and I know you were there. I'll be at your house in ten."

The black sedan pulled up on the wrong side of the street and the old man jumped out before it had come to a stop. He stormed up to the front door, and Bishop held the door open. The old man stomped into the living room and put his hands on his hips, huffing from the exertion of racing up the steps.

"So how do you feel now, huh? Are you happy with yourself now?" the old man snapped.

"Let's get this straight. Olivia gave me the keys to her place. I went in to check it was all ok, then that woman came in. Some stranger shoots her, but somehow this is all my fault?"

The old man let out a lungful of air in a long hiss. "She was a good soldier, son. She worked with me in places even you wouldn't want to go. Don't ever think for a moment that getting sand in your boots makes you any better than her. It doesn't."

"Who was she, General? You told me she was dangerous, but then she told me that you were, so you were both playing me off between you. Why? To see which way I'd jump?"

He growled the answer. "She was Major Morrison's CO. She was the hand inside the puppet for our Middle East operation. She made James Bond look like a pussy, all right? And for her to get dropped by some cowboy makes absolutely no sense."

Bishop sat on the edge of his sofa. "I caught a glimpse of the man who shot her as he was running away. I never saw his face, just his van, apparently the same one that was seen in the area where Lieutenant Morrison was dumped."

The old man frowned, a thoughtful frown. "Go on."

"Morrison's jacket was in a dumpster, along with his phone. A homeless guy found the phone and sold it to me. The Seattle police have no new clues, and I don't either. All I know is, I never asked to get into this mess, and I sure as hell want no part of it."

"You burned the package he sent you." The old man said. It sounded like a question.

"Yes."

"Really? You didn't keep a copy?" He sneered.

Bishop considered his answer carefully. "I promise you that I made no copies of the data."

The old man pulled at his nose, thinking. "Morrison pulled together a lot of information from a number of sources. That was his job. His real gift, his forte, was to put one and one together and come up with twelve. He sent you information that we are very interested in securing."

"Leading to long conversations in Guantanamo for someone?" Bishop asked.

The old man chuckled. "Some things can be done by the book. Others are best done in the shadows. There are places in Arizona or Ohio that make Gitmo look like Club Med."

Bishop stood up. "Would you like a coffee? Yes? Fine, I'll make us some."

He filled the machine with water and dropped in a pod. "Your lady said that five other people got what I did. She described it as our 'dirty little secret'. She also said you're retired from the service. What do you say to that?"

The old man nodded. "Sometimes you have to be seen as an outsider to do certain things. Three years ago I 'left' and worked with a contractor overseas. You wouldn't know them- you were probably never there, but it gave me access to certain parties with foreign contacts.

"The five other people Morrison contacted were all known to each other. They were each given a piece of the puzzle and told to meet up. We convinced them to hand their pieces to us. Morrison went a step beyond, though. He set it up so that even having all the pieces, they had to be together and wait for a key from the sixth person to access the information. He was a logistical genius, but he was diagnosed as schizophrenic. We think that's what got him killed."

"Why send me a paper report, a DVD, and a USB? That seems like overkill." Bishop stated.

"We have no idea. One needs all the pieces to read everything, we think. And you say you never looked at any of it?"

"I saw the SAP below the 'Top Secret' on the cover. That was enough to tell me to 'keep out'."

"Well, let's leave it at that then, shall we? You can leave this in a diary for your grandchildren to read after you're gone." The old man said.

He stood up to leave. "I'll pass on the coffee, if you don't mind. I need to deliver some bad news to a family I know."

Bishop stood. "One last thing. The man who shot her. Do we know if he was military as well?"

"If he's who I believe he is, he was one of ours, yes. He could have been a Ranger, or Airborne, or a SEAL. But now he's a gun for hire. In any case, forget this happened. Go back to your life and we'll go back to doing what we always do. Good night."

The old man left. Bishop sipped his coffee and wondered what to do next. Maybe he could call Olivia and tell her what happened, but it might just frighten her and make her avoid him.

He could just destroy the real package, but why? Everyone believed he'd burned it anyway, and it might be useful to have as a bargaining chip in the future.

He didn't believe that Morrison was killed for being crazy. If that were true, half of the officers above Major would be dead. Morrison simply wanted to pass on his findings to someone else.

Better to have an ally outside the military, he thought. Porezki could help him with that.

Detective Porezki answered the phone in one ring. "Hello?" He said.

"It's John Bishop. Do you have time to meet me?"

"I'm not sure. Do you have another body for me?" Porezki joked.

"No, but I may have some context for you."

Porezki suggested an IHOP restaurant off Federal Way. When Bishop pulled his Jeep into the lot, Porezki's unmarked cruiser was already there.

They took a booth far from other diners and a waitress handed them menus. Porezki waved his away. "Thanks, Diane, just toast and coffee for me. You want anything, John?"

Bishop ordered a light meal and waited for the waitress to leave. He leaned forward.

"The person who killed Morrison, and who probably killed the woman, is a hired killer." He said.

"That much we guessed. And probably ex-military." Porezki answered.

"I thought so too. What made you suspect him?" Bishop asked.

"Well, for one thing right after you left the apartment a bunch of guys in uniform swarmed the place, took the dead woman away and handed us a federal writ telling us to eat shit and die. We asked about the van you saw, and they told us categorically that there is no van, there never was any van, and we should forget about even trying to find this alleged van."

Bishop chuckled. "Some days you can't win for losing. That woman never told me why she was in the apartment. I told you she had come to my house looking for sensitive information. It was a couple of levels above 'top secret' so I destroyed it without viewing it. I know better than to open that can of worms."

Porezki shook his head. "Destroyed it, huh? Ok. Let's go with that story for now, shall we?"

"Why does nobody believe me when I say that? A colleague of hers came to my house and he watched me put the package in my fireplace. It's all gone up in smoke."

"Is this person someone I could talk to?" Porezki asked.

"I doubt it. He's one of those men in black. He'd probably also tell you to piss off."

Porezki munched on a piece of toast and took a gulp of coffee. "So, we have no body, no suspect, no crime for me to investigate. This is fun. Can you call in for all the murders in my precinct so I can spend more time at home?"

Bishop took a bite of his burger and patted his mouth. "What about Lieutenant Morrison? Any progress on that front?"

Porezki pulled out a small notebook. "Yeah, that I can tell you. He was shot with a silenced nine mil, probably about three days before we found him. As I say, it was one of those lucky flukes. The city works crew wasn't scheduled to be there until next year, but there was a plugged storm drain so they did some emergency work."

"How do you know it was silenced?" Bishop asked.

Porezki smirked. "There was a slight residue of rubber and oil on the bullet. That tells us he..."

"He made his own silencer. A nine-mil bullet is subsonic-quieter. It's an old trick of the trade."

"And you know this because why?" Porezki asked.

"I read it in National Geographic?" Bishop joked.

Bishop sipped his milk. "But why dump the phone with the windbreaker after he shot him?"

"We have a few theories about that. In case someone phoned, he wrapped the phone in the windbreaker to muffle the sound. Maybe he was in a hurry, who knows."

"Why not just break the phone or take out the battery?" Bishop asked.

"We wondered that too. Maybe he hung on to it for a day or so to see who called Morrison. Maybe after then he got worried about having it and just decided to ditch it?"

Bishop shrugged. "That's the only version that makes any sense so far, yeah. The place where I found the windbreaker, do we know if it has any relationship to the van?"

"None that we know of. Still, we're increasing the patrols in the area, just in case. That said, Seattle does get more than two murders a year, so we might get busy, you know." Porezki said.

Bishop leaned back. "I want to leave all this mess behind me. I don't need the grief, Detective."

"Ziggy." Porezki said.

"S'cuse me?"

"It's actually Zbigniew Porezki, but you can call me Ziggy. It's easier to remember."

Bishop waved at the waitress. "I got the check this time. Next time, if there is one, it's on you."

Bishop drove home. He scanned the street looking for a black sedan, or worse still, a van with 'Custom Auto Upholstery' on the side. Satisfied, he opened his door, but he still pulled the hallstand pistol out of its holster and walked through every room in his house, checking the closets, under the beds and behind the shower curtain.

Satisfied that he was alone, he put the pistol back and opened his freezer. Still empty. Time to hit the grocery store. He grabbed his keys. Before he got to the front door, his phone rang.

Probably Porezki with an update, he thought. "Bishop." He said curtly.

"Hi, do you miss me yet?" Olivia's voice purred.

"Oh, hell, yes, Olivia. How is Detroit?"

She sighed. "It's all right. The people at the station are super nice, and the reviews seem good. We'll see after my second week here, though, once the novelty of a new face wears off. How are you doing?"

Bishop steeled himself. "Your agent apparently lent your apartment keys to a woman."

She chuckled. "My agent has my spare keys. She needs it for interviews or something."

"You don't know the name of the woman who's coming, who she is, then?"

There was a pause. "No. Why?"

"Because somebody shot her. I was there when they did it. I was worried they were after you."

There was a long pause. "Christ, John, what have I gotten myself into? Am I in danger?"

"Damned if I know. Listen, Olivia, stay in Detroit. Wait there until I tell you it's safe to come back, all right? Stay with your folks and just keep your head low."

She sighed. "Fine. I'm not sure if I can ever feel safe there, though. Time will tell, I guess."

Bishop said goodbye and hung up. His mind was going in a dozen different directions. He took a deep breath and went into analyst mode.

Why was Morrison killed? Answer, he released important information. No brainer. That said, the branch of the military where he worked wouldn't have killed him, even for that. He might have been demoted, or possibly court martialed, but not killed.

Who killed him? Answer, someone who wanted the information he had, or wanted to stop him from making it public. It could have been either case, actually. Or both. The shooter was just the instrument, however. He was working for someone else.

Next question; who was next on the list? Answer, they killed Morrison, and the woman, what about the General, the old man? Was he next?

Something occurred to Bishop, something so blindingly obvious he'd missed it. How did the killer know that the woman would be at Olivia's apartment?

After all, she wouldn't tell anyone she was going there, except someone she trusted. The only person that Bishop thought would fit that definition was the General, the old man.

Was he in on it? Was he playing both sides all the time while pretending to be shocked? Bishop couldn't just ask him. There were so many reasons that wouldn't be a good idea.

If the old man was involved, was there a way to make him show his hand without getting killed in the process? If he wasn't involved, could telling him possibly let the bad guys know that Bishop still had the package? This would be a tricky one to figure out.

Bishop drove to the Shoreline Market and bought a meal from one of the places in the food court. He sat in a plastic booth, crunched corn chips, slurped ginger ale, but the whole time he was looking around for anyone that seemed out of place.

What to do next, he thought? From where he sat he could see the parking lot. There were people coming and going, minivans and SUVs jockeying for spots closer to the doors, cars edging their way into traffic before racing out onto the street.

One vehicle caught his attention. It was a dusty brown van with no side windows and streaks of rust arching up from the wheel wells. Bishop sat up straight, anxious. Then he noticed the name on the side, 'Mahalia's

Bakery'. In smaller letters the van said 'Caribbean sweets our specialty'.

That was where he would start looking- the van.

Bishop browsed on his phone for 'Custom Auto Upholstery'. It was listed as being in an industrial area of Utah Avenue, across from the main railroad yard by the docks. He considered calling them, but decided to see them in person instead.

He cruised slowly along the broken asphalt, looking for the right address. On one faded door a peel-and-stick lettered sign read 'CuSTom AUTo UpholSTERY' and a hand-written one below; 'no soliciting'.

Bishop knocked on the wide wooden door and waited. He could hear a buzzing noise coming from behind the door, something he couldn't place. It took a moment to recognize that he was hearing an industrial sewing machine, the kind used to stitch leather seats.

He waited for a pause in the buzzing noise then knocked again, louder. This time, he heard two voices- a man and a woman- then the clicking of shoes coming closer.

Bishop put on a smile, hoped it looked genuine, and waited.

The wide door opened about six inches and a woman peered out at him. "Yah?" She asked.

"Hi, I wonder if you could help me. Do you own an old van, grey, I think it's a Ford or a Dodge?"

The woman closed the door and spoke to the other person he'd heard. She opened the door just a crack again and shook her head. "Sorry, no have the van. We sell the van."

Bishop looked at the woman. She was small, under five feet, barrel-shaped, with hair dyed far too black and the complexion of someone that never sees sunlight. She had an accent, but from the few words Bishop couldn't place it.

She went to close the door but Bishop held it open. "Listen, I'm just trying to keep you out of trouble. There was an accident with that van. They hit my friend's car then they drove away. Can you give me the name of the person you sold it to?"

The woman scowled and looked back over her shoulder. *"Joao! Venha aqui!"* she yelled.

Bishop waited patiently and a man walked silently up behind the woman. He was the male equivalent of her, short, round but with hair dyed an almost orange color.

"Hello, I wonder if you can help me." Bishop said.

The man said something in Portuguese and the woman walked away. He turned back to look up at Bishop. "I sell the van, no more have. Do not own the van."

Bishop nodded. "Right. I understand. It's just that it had your company name on the side, so I wouldn't want the police to arrest you because they thought you hit the car and left. That's all."

At the word 'police' the man's eyes widened. He leaned back, scratched his head, then rubbed his chin. "I do not know name. He pay cash. He say going to register next week. Is all."

Bishop frowned. "Can you describe him? What did he look like?"

The man sighed, thinking. "He look like you. Anglo. He maybe work in construction, maybe."

"Why do you say that?"

"He take out seats. No want. Good seats. Nice leatherette. I bring them back here to shop."

Bishop stood up straight. "Back? Back from where?"

The man waved his arm over his head. "He call me to buy van. I go to his apartment."

The man looked down and thought for a moment. "Denny Way. He live on Denny Way."

Bishop remembered the windbreaker and the cell phone. It made a lot more sense now. "Do you have his address?"

The man shook his head. "No. Apartment building, red, is all I know. He call here and say meet me in front of apartment. He stand on street and buy van, he pay cash. That all."

"Cell phone? Did he call your cell?" Bishop asked.

The man shook his head. "Office. He call the office."

An office phone meant a land line. That would make it harder to find him. Still, now Bishop had an idea where to look for the van.

He smiled a plastic smile. "Thank you. You've been very helpful. I won't need to bother you again. Good evening."

Bishop cruised the front streets and back lanes around Denny Way, near where he had found the windbreaker. He imagined the sequence of events; the killer bought a van, killed Morrison, dumped the body then dumped the cell phone and windbreaker near his own home. It was a rookie mistake, but maybe he was in a hurry, or he didn't think anyone would connect the dots.

After twenty minutes of driving, Bishop saw something in a laneway. It was the back two feet of a van, sticking out of a stucco garage. He parked a few doors away and walked to the garage. The van was the same dirty brown and same model he saw leaving Olivia's apartment. The garage was small, but there was enough room for Bishop to walk between the van and a wall.

He looked at the side panel; in the dim light of the garage, he could see that the van had been spray painted, roughly. The paint still smelled fresh, and it had been sprayed on thickly, but he could still make out the faint outline of the words 'Custom Auto' bleeding through.

He walked around to the front of the building and buzzed the apartment marked 'super'.

A moment later, a wiry man came out, rubbing his hair as if he'd woken up from a nap. He looked Bishop up and down and rubbed his nose.

"You here about the apartment?" He asked.

"Um, no. I'm actually here about one of your tenants. I understand he does car upholstery? I tore the seats on my old Buick." Bishop lied.

The man frowned. "Car upholst... Oh, you mean Kendall. Yeah, he bought that van a while back, but I don't think he does that kind of work, no."

"Ah. My mistake. I saw the van and I figured I could get a deal, you know." Bishop shrugged.

The old man shook his head. "Yeah, actually, he's the tenant that's moving away. I thought maybe you saw the ad for his apartment. I'm the super for this building and the next one."

Bishop smiled. "Well, I do have a friend who's looking for an apartment. She's very nice, quiet. She's out of town right now, but she'll be back in December. What's his apartment like?"

The super smiled. "Nice. He keeps it clean. He's a very pleasant man, sober, never any trouble. We're sad to see him go, but he's being transferred, he said."

Bishop laughed. "Transferred? What kind of work does he do? Software developer?"

The super shook his head. "No. He's in the military, I think. He said he drives bigwigs or something. I'm not really sure."

Bishop hoped he didn't show a reaction to the statement.

"Well, I'd love to see the place, but I wouldn't want to disturb him if he's busy." Bishop teased.

"No, no. He's at work till tonight. You're welcome to see the unit for your friend." He said.

Bishop smiled. "Yeah, that would really be great, thanks."

He followed the super up to the third floor, waited as he fumbled through a thick set of keys and stood back while he opened the door marked 302.

"Super! Mr. Kendall? It's Barry!" He yelled.

No answer. They both walked into the apartment and the man described the unit to Bishop. He waved at the updated kitchen, the new wraparound fiberglass enclosure in the bathroom, and the nice view of the street from the living room. Bishop nodded at all this, pretending to be interested. As the super spoke, Bishop was mentally taking note of things he didn't say.

There was a series of zippered garment bags in the bedroom closet, the dark plastic kind that Bishop used to store his uniforms. There were four pairs of identical black oxfords on a shoe rack, immaculately polished and all pointing in exactly the same direction.

The gadgets in the kitchen drawer were spaced equally apart, and the dishes on a countertop rack were scrubbed spotless- no stains or leftover food.

The super mentioned the frost-free fridge, and Bishop said 'hmmm' as he opened the door. There was no water in the fridge, only milk, beer and orange juice.

This apartment couldn't have screamed 'military barrack' any louder if it was painted green.

His friend would be back in town in a few weeks, Bishop said, so he'd check with her when she came over. Bishop wrote down the cost of the apartment and the super's phone number on a card then thanked him for his time. They walked out onto the sidewalk and shook hands.

The super went back in. Bishop went back around to the garage. There was another entrance, a ramp that went under the apartment building. Bishop walked down that ramp and wandered between the two rows of parked cars. There were a few vacant spots, including one that was marked 'Apt. 302'. Bishop went back to his Jeep and drove away.

Late that night, Bishop came back. He walked down the back lane to the underground garage and looked at the spot reserved for apartment 302. There was a black Ford Five Hundred sedan in the spot, just like the car that had driven the General to Bishop's house.

So, Kendall owned the van: he was the General's driver and he probably killed Morrison and the woman. What to do next? Was the General involved? Was he the next target? Did Bishop care either way, as long as Olivia was not in danger?

Bishop went home. He drove around the block, looking for any unusual cars, then he opened his front door and pulled his pistol out of the hallstand.

Bishop always had a round parked in the chamber. There was no point in having a gun if you had to stop and rack the slide before you could use it. If someone was in the house, all Bishop needed to do was pull the trigger.

He went to his desk and pulled out the folder marked '2021 taxes'. The DVD, papers and USB drive were still there. He placed them on the desk and rested his elbows beside the papers, contemplating what to do next.

He had a tiger by the tail, he realized. He could really destroy everything this time, or he could put the package in the mail to someone he knew in DC, and it would get to the right person.

If he did that though, could he be sure that this would be the end of the matter? He could let Porezki know about Kendall. Kendall was not his concern, and Porezki would have a suspect.

Bishop's real concern was the dead woman in Olivia's apartment. Was the killer only there to kill that woman, or was he going to go after Olivia as well?

His phone rang. Bishop pulled it out of his pocket and pressed the button. "Hello?" He said.

A man's voice spoke. "So you went through my apartment. Did you find anything?" he said.

"Kendall? Is that you?" Bishop asked.

"Yes, Captain. What were you looking for in my apartment?"

"Same thing you guys looked for in my house. The package Morrison left." Bishop lied.

Kendall sighed. "You know damn well the package isn't there. I figured you were trying to flush me out. I suppose you want to track down whoever tapped the Colonel and her friend, Lieutenant Morrison."

"Didn't you kill them both?"

"What makes you think I did?" Kendall teased.

Bishop thought for a moment. "What are you- a Ranger? SEAL? MARSOC?"

"I'm not a jarhead. You figure it out."

"Okay, answer me this. Why did you kill these people- was it for the money?"

Kendall snorted. "If I really did what you are suggesting I did, then it wouldn't be for cash. Sometimes we do the things we do because we're under orders to do them."

"Are you telling me that the General is giving the orders? Or is he a target?" Bishop asked.

"Or neither. Maybe he has no clue about any of this. You just never know."

Bishop rubbed his face. "Look, I could tell the cops I found your van, and let them run you down. Or not. All I really care about right now is that Olivia Young is not in your crosshairs."

"Who's Olivia Young?" Kendall asked.

"You killed that woman in her apartment. I saw you running away."

There was a long pause. Bishop waited, silent, listening to dead air. Finally, Kendall spoke.

"Listen, Captain, I'm going to let you in on a little secret. The thing about secrets, though, is they're like bubble gum. You can't share them or they get sticky and messy. Do you agree?"

"Yes." Bishop said simply.

Kendall spoke slowly, deliberately. "I didn't kill either of those people."

"You're saying you haven't killed anyone?" Bishop pressed.

"That's not what I said. I only said that I never killed those two." Kendall clarified.

"Your van was seen where Morrison was dumped. It was also there when I saw you running from Olivia's apartment."

Bishop heard Kendall puff on a cigarette. There was another moment of silence. "I was ordered to dump Morrison's body. That's all I did. I just dumped him. I didn't kill him."

"Who told you to dump the body?"

"That's above both our pay grades. I receive orders. I follow orders." He snapped.

Bishop snorted. "I saw you running when the Colonel was shot. But you say you didn't do it?"

Kendall puffed on his cigarette again. "That wasn't me. For the record, I have no idea who it was, but it wasn't me. I saw him take off into the alley then right after that you came out the front door, so I got out of there. I didn't want to answer a bunch of questions just then."

"Why were you there?"

Kendall went 'pah', spat out his cigarette and sniffed. "My job was to follow her. Nothing more. That said, I went there to speak with her. She opened the door thinking it was me, I suppose."

"Was it you that called in the troops to remove her body?"

"Yeah. Dead is one thing. Questions about why, is something completely different."

"So, once again, is Olivia in any peril?" Bishop repeated.

"Not as far as I know. If she's just a civilian, she's not involved."

"Fine, then I'm backing out of this. You do what you have to do. Leave her and me out of it."

Kendall grunted. "Yeah, about that. You still have something they want back, something you should never have been given."

"I destroyed that package." Bishop lied.

He snorted. "Do you really expect everybody to believe that? The man who organizes his shirts by the day of the week? Who lines up his coffee cups with all the handles pointed in the same direction? Do you really think someone like that would destroy important data?"

Bishop was silent for a moment. "So, if I *did* still have it, why would it be so important for me to keep it, instead of destroying it?"

Kendall pulled out another cigarette. "OK, so the General told you some stuff, and so did the Colonel. Neither one lied, but neither one gave you the whole picture. If I let you see behind the curtain, you can't un-ring that bell, you know that, don't you?"

203

"Well, now that we've mixed our metaphors, what are you trying to tell me?"

Kendall lit the new cigarette. "You were told that Morrison pieced together a bunch of secret information, sensitive stuff, that was embarrassing if it got out. True. What they didn't tell you is where he got it from. We believe he was just doing his job, and someone accidentally left a file on his desk. He did what he was trained to do- he reviewed it. That's what got him killed."

Bishop rubbed his nose. "So Morrison realized this was something that smelled bad, and passed it up the chain of command?"

"He did his job. He just made the mistake of sending it to the one person who was responsible for hiding it, that's all. That's what got him killed."

"And the person in question?" Bishop asked.

"Has been dealt with. The General told you that several others got pieces of the package. They've handed their data over and agreed to forget all about it. What they had was so incomplete, individually, that they wouldn't understand it anyway. What you got, on the other hand, was the whole enchilada. Have you viewed the data?"

"I know better than that. It's toxic. Why the greeting card with the puzzle?" Bishop said.

"It was a test. If you could solve the puzzle with the numbers, you could read the package."

"My colleague solved it, but I never let him see the package." Bishop said.

Kendall was silent for a minute. Bishop could hear traffic in the background. Finally, Kendall said: "What do you know about metadata tags?"

"As much as anyone else does, I guess. What exactly are you trying to tell me?"

Kendall spoke slowly. "When you take a picture on your phone, or download a song, or visit a website, it comes with a hidden tag that tells you where it was from, who created it, all sorts of information. Most people never notice the metadata."

"This much I know already. Your point?"

Kendall puffed his cigarette. "Morrison's package was very special. Not only did the USB contain metadata tags, it also read the identity of the computer that viewed the information and reported the IP back to home base. The DVD had a hidden partition that did the same thing."

"And Morrison tripped over this metadata when he viewed the file?" Bishop asked.

"Even worse. He back-traced the USB and found a list of people who had seen the package. He was very good. The trouble is, he told this to the wrong person. That was the kiss of death. He should have just handed back the package and forgotten about it."

"So, what should I do, if we were to assume that I still have this information?" Bishop asked.

Kendall puffed more on the cigarette. "In two weeks, I'm told there will be a security conference in Oslo. The contents of the package, in all its glory, will be made public. The agreements between political parties, agreements that are top secret right now, will be on everything from Fox News to Al Jazeera. At that point you can use the DVD as a coaster, and we could care less.

Before that conference, though, letting the cat out of the bag would be catastrophic to the negotiations. The deals have already been made beforehand, of course, but it needs to appear that they were agreed to at the meeting, not before. Perception is everything."

"What does all that mean for me?" Bishop asked.

"If you still have the package, keep it under wraps. After the conference, you can send it to the New York Times, if you want- it's yesterday's news. If you destroyed it, then no harm, no foul."

Bishop considered this for a moment. "Do you know who did kill Morrison and the woman?"

"The man who killed Lieutenant Morrison and Colonel Saks? I saw him run off, but not his face."

"Saks was her name? He used a silencer with Morrison, probably the same one he used on her. It was most likely homemade. Do you know anyone that would fit that bill?" Bishop asked.

"Yes, her name was Saks. S-A-K-S. Meet me in the underground parking at my apartment, twenty minutes. I'm going to give you some names to work with, but do the work carefully. These people don't like you to poke the bear, you know." Kendall said.

"What about you? What are you going to do? Will you be looking for them too?"

Kendall puffed on the cigarette. "No way, Jose. I'm going to be back in Langley next week."

"Langley? Langley as in CIA headquarters, Langley?" Bishop asked.

"Did I say Langley?" Kendall said coyly. "I'm sure I meant to say Las Vegas."

"You're a spook? Army Intel? CIA operative? What?"

Kendall blew air out, exhaling his smoke. "I'm called a CMO. A Collection Management Officer. Look it up. You'd be good at it, Captain. I could put your name forward if you're interested."

Bishop snorted. "Thanks, I'm happy where I am for now. Your place, twenty minutes."

Bishop got to the parking garage in fifteen minutes. He stood beside the Ford sedan, looked around and waited. A middle-aged man came out of a white SUV carrying two bags of groceries and shuffled to a door marked 'Elevator'. The door clunked shut behind the man and Bishop waited some more. A thirty-something woman screeched in behind the wheel of an Audi, jumped out and strutted to the same door, all the while talking non-stop on her cell phone. The door slammed shut again.

A moment later the same door opened and another man walked out, looking carefully around. Bishop recognized the General's driver, Kendall.

Kendall nodded recognition and walked toward Bishop. "Got a pad and pencil?" He asked.

Bishop felt in his pocket for a piece of paper and found a gas station receipt. He took out his wallet, rested the receipt on it then went into his pocket for a golf pencil he always carried.

"You said you had some names?" Bishop asked.

"Yeah, but you never heard them from me." Kendall said.

Kendall rolled his eyes up, thinking. "First, there's…."

A sound like compressed thunder filled the garage. Kendall opened his eyes wide, spun around and looked behind him. Another sound like thunder filled the garage. Kendall fell to the ground. Bishop heard a far door slam shut. By the time he ran to it, there was nobody there. He walked slowly back toward Kendall. Kendall looked up at Bishop and shook his head.

"Run. Don't go home. Run, or you're next. Run away for two weeks, run." With that he died.

Chapter 7: Body Count

Porezki's cruiser rolled into the underground garage and parked in an empty spot.

He eased himself out of the seat and ambled towards Bishop, his mouth moving side to side as he chewed gum.

"So, what's so important that you needed to…" He started.

He saw the shape under a blanket on the ground and stopped. "Oh, fuck." He muttered.

Porezki placed his right hand on his hip, gripping his service pistol, and looked around.

Bishop held his hands up. "No, not me. It wasn't me. His name is Kendall. He asked me to meet him here to tell me something, but someone shot him from that doorway and took off."

Bishop lifted one side of the blanket, exposing Kendall's face and the pool of blood under him.

Porezki sniffed. "Why did you call me? Why not just call my people and let them do their job?"

Bishop shook his head. "If this man is who I think he is, the army guys will be here first and whisk him away. I need to find out if the person who shot him also killed Morrison. On a personal level, before he died he told me to run, or I would be next. I need to disappear for two weeks, but I also need to know who's after me. I need your help with that."

"Go on." Porezki said.

"Call your most trusted pathologist. Get the slugs out of the body before you call it in. This may be the only chance you'll get to compare the bullet to the one from Morrison. If I'm wrong, you have all day to do the police stuff. If I'm right though, the spooks will take him away in an hour."

Porezki pulled out his phone and dialed a number. He spoke softly, asked for someone then said something about 'a golf game we had'. He listened for a minute then said 'yup' and texted the address of the garage. He walked around the blanket, squatted down and glared at Bishop.

"So, are you shitting me about what's going on here, or are you just a moving bullet magnet that likes the attention?"

Bishop sighed. "I tracked Kendall down through the previous owner that sold him that van. He admitted he was working undercover, and he said he was the one who dumped Morrison's body, but he claims he didn't kill either Morrison or that woman. Her name was Colonel Saks, by the way. As I said, before he died he also told me to get scarce for two weeks."

"Why two weeks? Do you win a special prize after that?"

Bishop rubbed his nose. "In two weeks there's an international something or other that will reveal a secret Morrison had and make it public knowledge. After that I'm home free. Until then I do not want to be a warm target."

They waited for about twenty minutes, speaking little, looking furtively at the entrance to the garage. A beige sports car screeched in, swung around and stopped suddenly when its lights hit Porezki. A man in a sweater and chinos stepped out carrying a black leather doctor's bag.

"Hey, Ziggy. What gives?" the man asked.

He was taller than Bishop expected, lean, with pale blue eyes framed by white hair.

Porezki poked his chin at the blanket. "Hi, Arnold. We may have another one. Bishop here thinks this guy will be taken away by the feds, so I need you to pull bullets out of him first."

The man grunted and squatted down by the blanket. He opened his bag, tugged on a pair of surgical gloves and rummaged in the bag for something. He found his forceps then got Bishop and Porezki to turn the body over while he poked the forceps into a bullet hole and felt around.

He wrinkled his nose, thinking, then smiled. "Got it." He whispered.

He pulled out the forceps, a dull lead slug in the pincers. He took a small plastic pouch from his bag and dropped the slug into it. Bishop watched him do the same for the second slug.

All three men stood up. The man put the slugs in his pocket and closed up his bag. "I was never here. As far as anyone's concerned, I'm on my way to Bainbridge Island. Call me in an hour."

He got into his car, the engine roared to life and he disappeared in a squeal of tires.

Porezki waited for a minute then took out his phone. "Dispatch, Detective Porezki, badge number three-three-one-seven. Ten forty-five delta, repeat, ten forty-five delta, units respond."

He gave the address of the garage. Four minutes later the sound of police sirens got very loud, and ten seconds after that, two cruisers blocked the garage entrance.

Bishop turned to Porezki. "I need to ask a favor from you." He said.

As the uniformed officers cordoned off the area and took photographs, Porezki went to his car and called a third cruiser to assist. He told the two officers in that car to follow Bishop home, stay with him until he left, and then come back. Bishop went home, followed by the cruiser, packed some clothes and cash in a duffel bag and stuck Morrison's package inside.

He stopped at the front hall, took his pistol and put it in his duffel bag, under the clothes. He locked his front door, pocketed the keys and thanked the officers for their help.

The police drove off. Bishop waited till they were gone then got in his Jeep and picked up his phone. He called a number and waited, remembering what he needed to say in this situation.

A voice came on, older, tired and bored. "Yes?" It said.

"Dean Wilkes? It's John Bishop."

There was a slight pause. "Yes, John. What can I do for you?"

"My Aunt Muriel is ill, Dean. You remember dear Aunt Muriel?"

There was another pause. The voice came back, firm, definite. "How unfortunate. Can we be of any help?"

"No, thanks. I just have to make myself... to help her out. I hope you can understand that?"

"I understand completely. Powell will take over your classes. How badly ill is Aunt Muriel?"

"We'll know the outcome in the next two weeks. Can you tell my neighbor, Mrs. Otagawa, that her daughter should NOT clean my house until I get back?"

"I'll be sure to tell her. Did you pack your vitamins?"

Bishop reached into the duffel bag and felt his pistol. "Yes, thanks, I have my vitamins with me."

He put away the phone and drove downtown. Olivia's apartment no longer had police tape around it, there were no cruisers checking the area, or anybody paying special attention to it.

Bishop went around to the back; Olivia's ugly yellow Saturn was parked there. He reached into his pocket and pulled out her keys, confirming that her car key was among them. He parked his Jeep in its place and drove off in her car.

He pulled off the road at a gas station convenience store and dialed a number. The General answered in one ring. "Bishop? What the hell have you done, you idiot?" The man said.

"I just answered a call from your driver, that's all. Why was he killed?"

The General sighed. "Do you have any idea the shitstorm you've created? Do you know just how important he was to this operation? And now everything is down the crapper because *you spoke to him.* What are we supposed to do now, huh?"

Bishop looked around, checking that nobody was coming close. "Listen, I feel your pain. But I was in the room when Colonel Saks was shot, and I was in the garage when Kendall was shot. Why shouldn't I believe that I'm next?"

"As long as you have that data, and nobody knows where you have it, you're safe. If you give it up you're a dead man."

"At least for the next two weeks." Bishop added.

There was a pause. "He told you about the conference, didn't he? He's right. After the public announcement, all this is academic. Until then, keep your head down, don't be a target. Let me find a safe place for you, where you can come in and lay low until this is over."

Bishop thought for a moment. "How did the killer know that Colonel Saks was in Olivia's apartment?"

"What do you mean?" The General asked, cautiously.

"She must have told someone she was going there. That someone must have told the killer. Someone also told the killer that Kendall was going to be home. Who could know that?"

There was a long silence. "What exactly are you suggesting, Bishop?"

"Right now, you're the only common denominator in the whole affair. Kendall worked for you. Colonel Saks worked for you. Did Morrison work for you too, or was he just inconvenient? I don't believe I can count on you to keep me safe, General."

The General sighed. "You think you got it all figured out, huh? You think you're smart, that you figured it all out? Not even close, Captain. Not even close. Good luck, Bishop. You'll need it."

The General hung up.

One of the things that made Bishop good at his job, apart from being able to analyze data, was listening to the little voice in his head. Right now it was screaming.

He turned his phone completely off, went into the convenience store and bought a pay-as-you-go SIM card. He put fifty dollars worth of time on it and popped the old SIM card out.

He dialed a number which by now was familiar and waited. Two rings later, Porezki answered.

"Hello?" Porezki said, puzzled.

"It's me. I have a new SIM card, new number." Bishop said.

"OK, and the reason for that is?"

Bishop sighed. "I think that Kendall's employer killed him, or had him killed, for talking to me. I think I may be next on the hit list, so I need to go dark for the next while. Did you get anything from the bullets we pulled out of Kendall's body?"

Bishop heard paper shuffle as Porezki looked for something. "Good catch, that. You were right- same gun for Morrison and Kendall. And yes, the moment we called in the name we got swarmed by green men and black vans. That one's out of our hands as well."

Bishop blew air out the sides of his mouth, thinking. "OK, how about this? There's a retired General who's the key to all this. He's connected to everyone involved. I'm texting you his number. Can you find out where he is right now? I want to get ahead of the curve on this."

Porezki wrote something down. "Will I be able to reach you at this number?"

"Not always. At five PM tonight for an hour, then the phone's off. I'm not taking any chances."

"Where can I find you? Will you be home?" Porezki asked.

"No. I'm in the wind till this is over. I appreciate your help here, Ziggy. It means a lot."

Porezki chuckled. "Yeah, well, I don't want the feds carting your body away either, John."

Bishop hung up and turned the phone off.

There are some things you can teach people, and some things that certain people know without having to be taught them. Bishop's little voice was something you could never teach. He knew that the best place to hide a rock was in a pile of rocks, and the best place to hide a man where he can move around invisibly is within a bunch of other people moving around him.

Bishop drove to Belltown, a trendy, shopping-focused area of the city, found a car park and hid the Saturn in a dark corner.

He left his tote bag in the trunk, wandered down 3rd Avenue and stopped at a thrift store. He bought a shabby coat, a Mariners baseball cap, a pair of worn corduroy pants and a plaid shirt, all things he would never normally wear. He put them on, stuffed his own clothes into a scruffy three-dollar backpack and headed down to Pike Place Market.

Pike Place is the kind of destination that appeals to vagrants and tourists alike, and that one fact ensures it's always busy. The mix of cruise ship passengers, panhandlers and Canadian day-trippers make it a maelstrom of humanity.

Bishop bought a bowl of soup and a coffee from one of the inside stalls, making sure to only show a single ten-dollar bill, and sat in the corner of the food court, breaking pieces of bread into the soup and slurping noisily. This was to deter people from sitting with him.

He looked just this side of destitute, like a dock worker or lumberjack who had fallen on hard times.

He sat there for over half an hour, watching for anyone who paid too much attention to him, or overtly paid too little attention to him. Nobody he saw triggered his little voice; nobody made him reach for the pistol in the back of his belt.

He wandered through the market, bought a couple of sandwiches and snacks for later, then glanced at his watch. Four forty-five. He bought a can of club soda and wandered out onto a side street, shuffling his feet and looking down. People walked round him, giving him a wide berth and trying to avoid eye contact. That was what he wanted.

He found an empty bus bench, opened the can of soda and cradled it between his hands like a drunk would cradle a precious beer. Nobody sat beside him. At exactly one minute to five, he turned on his phone. At exactly two minutes after five, it rang. Bishop clicked the button quickly to stop the ringtone.

"Yeah?" He said.

"You doing OK, Bishop?" Porezki's voice said.

"Still breathing. Any word on our General?" Bishop answered.

"Yeah. What do you know about the WMA?"

"The Washington Military Alliance? It's a cybersecurity and military support organization. Is he part of the Alliance?" Bishop said.

"No, but he operates from an office right near there. Not sure if he is affiliated with them or just hiding in their shadow. What do you think?"

Bishop took out a pen and paper. "I think I should pay him a visit. Can I have his address?"

Porezki spoke slowly, spelled out a company name and made sure Bishop got it right. He waited for a second then sighed. "Listen, man, I know you're pissed at the guy for maybe smoking two people around you, and you don't want to be the third target. How about we put you in a safe house, find the guy that did this and lock him up, then you can go back to your life, huh?"

Bishop sniffed. "Listen, someone nuked Morrison, then they took out Saks and Kendall, and all you have to go on so far is a couple of bullets and a chalk outline. Sorry, Ziggy, I figure my odds are better if I don't use someone else's playbook."

"In other words, you're going to this guy's office and throw him over the balcony?"

Bishop snickered. "Much as that has appeal, I think he works for someone. He's not the top dog- he only works for the top dog. I need to find out who that is, and what's so important about the package I was sent. If the General ordered the killings, then he has to pay for that. If he didn't then he's in danger, just like the others were."

Porezki grunted. "Just promise me no cowboy shit, all right? I can turn a blind eye to you peeking through mail slots, but not heavy-duty Rambo crap."

Bishop tucked away the paper with the address on it. "Turning the phone off now. I'll call you around nine tomorrow morning."

"Do you have somewhere to stay tonight? Somewhere safe?"

"Got it covered, Ziggy. Tomorrow morning then."

Bishop shuffled along the side street, casually looking in store windows, checking in the reflection if anyone was following him. He got back to the Saturn and drove to the address Porezki had given him. It was a low, five-storey building with a drab brick façade and no balconies. There was a back alley with a loading dock, so he parked beside a delivery truck and went in. the Saturn looked like a crappy delivery vehicle anyway, and it blended in easily.

The office he wanted was on the fourth floor. Bishop walked past a couple of cleaners pushing big bins of scrap paper. That gave him an idea. He saw a flat bubble pack envelope, brown manila, on top of the pile of trash, and picked it up when the cleaners weren't watching. He changed out of the scruffy coat, found his way to the service elevator and got out on the fourth floor.

The corridor was narrower than he expected, flanked by grey metal doors with very little information on them.

One door had the number '414' on it in raised plastic, and the words 'Society for Environmental Enhancement' in black letters on a brass plaque. This was the address he'd been given by Porezki. There was a slim window on either side of the door, the window glass covered with stick-on frosting. Through a gap of about an inch between the edge of the frosting and the edge of the glass, Bishop could see a central desk in the middle of an open area, with a young woman sitting at the desk. Behind her was a number of wooden doors, with plastic tabs on the doors indicating who worked there.

One of the doors was slightly open. A man opened the door, came out and dropped a sheet of paper on the woman's desk. He waved his hand at the paper; she said something and nodded, and he laughed and said something back. He walked toward the front door, towards Bishop.

Bishop turned and walked away, slowly, looking at the blank envelope in his hands as if searching for an address down the hall. The man walked past him, headed for the main elevator, then turned back and smiled.

He was younger than Bishop, in his thirties, with a Marine haircut and an expression that was both disarming and piercing. "Hi? Are you lost?" He asked.

Bishop frowned. "Um. Center for Environmental…?"

The man grinned. "Society for Environmental Enhancement'. You just passed it."

He pointed; Bishop nodded thanks. The man continued down the hall and around the corner.

Bishop looked through the space in the glass again. The woman at the desk was by herself, it seemed. The office the Marine type had left still had its door partly open. The woman glanced at her phone and sighed. She wanted to go home, Bishop thought. He opened the door.

She looked up and smiled, then saw how he was dressed. "Yes?" She said sharply.

"Um, I was told to deliver this, for the General?" Bishop muttered.

"That's all you've got, just 'the General'? Nothing more specific?" She snapped.

Bishop shrugged. "Gord's car broke down, so he asked me to do the delivery for him? Gord told me you'd know what I meant? It's for the General, he said." He muttered.

The woman sighed. "General Sparwood. Fine. Do you need a signature?"

Bishop shook his head. The woman slid her seat back, grabbed the envelope and walked away from the open office door, ignoring him. Bishop waited till she'd gone into an office and went into the empty one the Marine had left, partly closing the door behind him.

He sat behind the desk in the office and waited. A minute later, he heard voices coming toward him. He grasped the gun in his belt, ready to pull it out if he needed to. A familiar voice spoke, the General's voice.

"There's nothing in here, Deb. It's just an empty envelope. What did this guy look like?"

Then the woman's voice. "About six feet, dirty blond hair, mid forties, maybe. No glasses, clean shaven. That's odd, cause he looked like a tramp otherwise."

Peeking through the crack in the door, Bishop could see the General stomp out into the hallway and come back in, rubbing his hair. "Bishop. Fucking Bishop. That bastard. Fuck."

The woman's voice went up a register. "Is something wrong, Alan?"

The General's voice again. "No. Nothing. Don't worry about it. Go home, Deb."

The woman nodded, pulled a small handbag from under the desk and shut down her computer. She went out the front door, closed it behind her and Bishop listened to her heels clicking down the hall as she went. He wondered how long he should stay there. The cleaners would probably be by sometime soon, so he wouldn't be locked in overnight. How long would the General stay, though, he wondered, and would he check the other offices before he went.

A minute later, the General came out to the front desk, cell phone to his ear. He leaned down and flipped at some paper by the young woman's computer, talking to someone on the phone.

"Uh huh. Uh huh. I agree." He said.

"Look, we underestimated him, that's all. I didn't expect him to get this far."

He sat at her desk, looking to the front entrance. Bishop quietly moved behind the open door.

The General rubbed his forehead. "He has no idea, no. Look, if we wait two weeks, the collateral damage will be minimal. I don't like it any more than you do, but we're stuck with it."

He listened to the other person for a minute. "Yeah, everyone buys the Oslo story. It seems so outlandish it must be true. Look, you need to get the funds through, and I need to keep a lid on this. As long as that package is in the wind, we're safe. I doubt he'll risk viewing it- the tag on the USB will light him up like a road flare. Even if he managed to leave it with someone in DC, we could intercept it before it blows up on us."

He fumbled in his jacket pocket for a set of keys. "I'm going home. Call me if you need anything. No, the apartment in Capital Hill. I have some papers there I need to file. Keep me posted."

He walked out, closed the door and locked the deadbolt behind him. Bishop waited for a minute, listened that there was no other sound in the office, then peeked through the other doors in the room. There was nobody there.

He went to the office where the young woman had taken the manila envelope- the General's office- and looked for anything that would help him. The office was sparse; there were no models of jeeps, no plaques on the wall, nothing that indicated who the General was, apart from the woman calling him Alan Sparwood.

A sheet of paper at the front desk was more informative. There was a phone list with a dozen names, phone numbers and addresses. Bishop took out his phone and photographed the paper. One of the names was 'A. Sparwood', beside an address in Capital Hill.

Bishop carefully unlocked the deadbolt, opened the door and went into the hall. A middle-aged lady in a smock pushed a cart full of cleaning supplies towards him. Bishop smiled.

"Are you doing four one four? Go ahead, we're all done for the night. Bye."

She thanked him and he took the freight elevator back to the Saturn.

The apartment listed for 'A. Sparwood' was in a high-rise, twenty odd floors of aluminum and glass, with wide concrete steps up to a tall glass entry foyer and an imposing intercom system. There was a desk for a concierge in the lobby, but nobody at the desk. Sparwood's apartment was listed on the intercom as number 1408. Bishop went around to the back alley; there was a door by a loading bay, but it was thick brown metal, with no sign of a door handle. There was also a ramp to the parking garage, but it had a thick metal grate that rolled down to block entry.

Bishop looked in the dumpster beside the loading bay, hoping for inspiration. He found a pizza box, empty but with the delivery slip still taped to it. He took it around to the front of the building and waited. Less than two minutes later, a young man and woman walked out of an elevator arm-in-arm, chatting and smiling. Bishop hunched his shoulders, waited till they got to the security door and spoke into the intercom. "Yeah, got your pizza here." He said.

"OK, be right up." He yelled as they opened the door.

The man held the door open for Bishop. "That's going to cost you two slices." He joked.

Bishop grinned. "Wish I could do that. Thanks, man."

The couple went down the steps to a glossy BMW. Bishop took the elevator to the 14th floor, the pizza box in front of him. If challenged, it would give him a reason to be here. The elevator opened to a carpeted, U-shaped hall, with elegant wall sconces and recessed doorways.

There were twelve apartments on this floor. Apartment 1408 was in one corner, a broad oak door with brass numbers. Bishop stood outside it, careful to not block the peep hole, and listened.

He could hear a voice, clearly the General's, but nobody else. The voice came louder then faded as the General moved around the room.

'I know we do.' Then a silence. 'He has no idea, none at all. 'I'm sure he bought the Oslo story.' Another silence. 'It's just ten more days, then the shipment clears customs. Hopefully nobody besides Morrison connected the dots.' A pause. 'We'll still get paid. Even with the delay. The only thing after that is to get rid of the gunny. He still thinks he's on a sanctioned mission, but if he puts two and two together it could sink us.' A few seconds of silence. 'No, I'll get Bishop to do it. I'm sure he will think he's just defending himself and we'll all come out of it smelling like roses.'

Bishop felt a cold chill at hearing those words. Then he felt rage. He listened, silent. The General spoke again. 'I'm going to check on the warehouse. I made sure the shipment was ready to go, but I want to see that all the customs forms are in place. There's no room for error on this, after all.' He was silent for a minute. 'Yeah, I'll keep in touch.'

Bishop heard the sound of keys jingling. He sprinted to the elevator, pressed the button and waited, anxious. A moment later the elevator door opened, and Bishop jumped in. He pressed the button for the lobby and pounded the 'close door' button. What seemed like minutes passed, but the door stayed open. From around the corner, he heard the sound of a door opening and closing. More keys jingling, then soft footsteps. The elevator door closed just as he heard the footsteps come around the corner and he rode downstairs, alone.

Bishop hopped down the lobby steps and ran around the corner to his car. It was dark by now, and the garish yellow Saturn would appear a drab beige under the alley's sodium streetlamps.

Bishop started the car and waited, the headlights off. Moments later, the metal grate to the underground parking lifted slowly up. A pale silver Malibu pulled up the ramp, paused for a moment then drove away from him. Bishop could clearly see the General's profile in the driver's seat as the car rolled down the alley.

He waited for the Malibu to go around the corner, followed it but kept at least two cars between them. He let the General get much further ahead on a long stretch of Olive Way, the busy road curving in a long downhill towards the waterfront.

The General zig-zagged his way to a drab brick building on Western Avenue, just blocks from the tourist meccas of Pier 54 and Ivar's Seafood Restaurant. He stopped on the street, got out and walked briskly up the steps to the building, punched a code at the door then went in.

Bishop parked around the corner, out of sight, and walked down the street from the General's car. There was an art gallery, displaying things Bishop didn't understand- tree branches in rainbow colors, plexiglass statues of unicorns, things of the sort. The gallery had windows on two corners, so Bishop could stand on the side street, look through both windows and see the General's car without being seen.

Twenty minutes later, a meek young man from the gallery came out to see if Bishop wanted to buy anything, and Bishop politely declined. A few minutes after that the General came out, got into his car and drove back towards Capital Hill.

Bishop watched him go. The General had spoken about a warehouse; this must be it. Bishop couldn't get in with the pizza thing he'd pulled before, but maybe he could still get in to see what the warehouse held.

He went into the art gallery, and the same meek young man looked up at him.

"Hello. Have you found something you like?" the man asked cheerily.

Bishop shook his head. "Not exactly. I can't go into a lot of detail, but I'm working with the police department on an important investigation."

The man's eyes widened. "We don't want any trouble. We sell art, that's all. Just art, OK?"

Bishop grinned. "The warehouse across the street. Do you know anyone that works there?"

The man nodded slowly. "Warren, at the front desk. He tried to sell us some awful paintings."

Bishop spoke warmly, putting him at ease. "Not a good fit for your gallery, huh?"

The man actually laughed. "It might as well have been dogs playing poker, only not as iconic."

Bishop laughed back. Mirroring an emotion, he knew, is a good way to elicit cooperation. He rested his elbows on the counter. "We need to get find out about something that's stored in the warehouse. I'm not going to take anything; I just need to report what I find inside there."

The man relaxed and slouched slightly to one side. "How can I help?"

Bishop walked across the street to the warehouse, holding a large cardboard box, given to him by the man in the gallery. He pressed the intercom button on the front door and stood back.

The intercom crackled for a second then a voice came on, with a bored drawl. "Yeah?"

Bishop glanced up at the security camera over the door. He leaned back, pretending to struggle under the weight of the box, although it was filled with Styrofoam packing from the art gallery.

"I'm supposed to ask for Warren?" He said sadly.

"Speaking." Came the indifferent reply.

"I got a delivery for…Spearward?"

There was a pause. "Sparwood. For Sparwood." The man corrected.

"Oh, right. Sparward."

"SparWOOD. WOOD. Sparwood." The man corrected again.

Bishop grunted. "Yeah. So can I just leave this here and you can install it in the locker?"

The intercom crackled. "I got a bad back. You'll have to put it away."

The door buzzed and Bishop 'struggled' to open it with one hand while balancing the box with the other. He stepped into the lobby of the building. It smelled of damp drywall and pine cleaner. The hall was lit by fluorescent tubes, but half the tubes were dead or flickering in their fixtures. A man appeared from a side door, younger than Bishop expected, heavyset with a balding head and push-broom moustache. He walked with a slight limp- Bishop was sure this was an affectation- and pulled at a large ring of keys on his hip.

"Something for Sparwood, you said?" the man asked.

Bishop smiled. "Yeah, Warren, right? They asked me to ask for you. So where does this go?"

The man rubbed his stomach. "Will this take long? I got a dinner break coming up."

Bishop seized on the opportunity. "Actually, there's some assembly to do on the components. Do you mind helping me, or did you want me to assemble it and call you when I'm done?"

The man's mouth was slightly open. "What the hell are you assembling?" He grunted.

Bishop was hoping that he was not very technical. "It's a wide-band receiver substation, with RAID server redundancies. We aren't initializing it or anything, but I need to configure the routers."

The man sighed and looked at his watch. "How long do you figure this will take?"

Bishop smiled. "Oh, forty-five minutes, an hour tops."

The man grunted. "Look, I can let you stay here and assemble this... root thing, but I gotta see that you're not taking anything after you're done."

Bishop nodded solemnly. "I understand. You're obviously very careful about security."

The man snorted and fumbled with his keys. He walked a short distance to a freight elevator and lifted the heavy wooden front gate. He waved lazily behind him. "This way." He muttered.

Bishop again feigned struggle and carried the cardboard box onto the elevator platform. The man pressed a button, slid the gate closed and the elevator creaked its way up two floors.

The man pushed the gate up to open it, stepped out and led Bishop down a hall to a thick metal door. He picked a brass key from his ring, opened the door and turned on a light inside.

"This is Mr. Sparwood's unit." He said.

He pointed to the wall beside him. "Once you're done, press the buzzer to call me and I'll lock up. If you need to use the can it's at the end of the hall. Don't leave the floor, though, the doors are alarmed. Going to eat now." He spoke walking backwards into the elevator.

Bishop peered into the storage space. It was the size of an average living room. There were no cameras, no sensors he could see. Good. There was a row of file cabinets, four military green ones, lined up against one wall. There was a desk and chair, and a lamp at one end of the desk. There was also a tall metal cabinet with a lock built in the doors, like one to hold office supplies.

Bishop opened the file cabinets. There was nothing much there, just some packing slips and a few customs forms. He took photos of these on his phone. The tall cabinet was locked, but Bishop found he could jiggle Olivia's mail key in the lock and persuade it to open.

Inside were dozens of white cardboard boxes, smaller than shoe boxes, stacked neatly on the shelves. Bishop lifted the lid off one. It had about fifty sealed vials of a yellow liquid, with markings he didn't recognize. They were not in English, or an Asian language, or Arabic, or anything he could remember seeing. He took four vials, wrapped them carefully in his handkerchief then placed them in his jacket pocket. He took that box and put it to the bottom of one stack. If anyone opened an upper box, a full box, they would assume all the boxes were full. Bishop made sure everything was back in place and locked the cabinet with the same key.

He looked around but found nothing else of interest. He had spent about forty-five minutes in the unit. He opened up the cardboard box he'd brought, spread around some of the Styrofoam packing and pressed the buzzer on the wall. Five minutes later the man called Warren came back, wiping pasta sauce from his mouth. "All done?" He asked.

Bishop pointed at the tall cabinet. "Yeah, it all fits properly, right in there." He said.

He placed the Styrofoam back into the box, allowing the man to see there was nothing else in there, and they went down the elevator together. The man turned to Bishop.

"By the way, I need you to sign in. Can I get you to sign in when we get downstairs?"

"Sure, no problem." Bishop said.

The man pulled out a faded ledger book and pointed to a blank spot on the page.

Bishop wrote something and handed the book back. The man turned it around to read it.

"Kendall Saks?" He asked.

"Call me Ken." Bishop smiled and walked away.

Chapter 8: Decoy Protocol

Bishop ditched the cardboard box in an alley and walked back to the Saturn. The little voice in his head started talking, louder every moment. The hairs on the back of his neck tingled, and he couldn't ignore the feeling. He pulled out onto the street, looking behind him as he went.

The best thing to do, he thought, was to shake the tree. The evening was cloudy, moonless, so any vehicle following him would be invisible, but its headlights would certainly be visible. Bishop turned south on Madison then east along Alaskan Way, a wide industrial road that traced the waterfront. He glanced back every so often; a handful of cars seemed to be moving in a clump, a cluster of vehicles behind him, nothing unusual. He made some pointless turns then went right on Lenora, a narrow, potholed street climbing uphill. One of the cars broke from the group and followed him. Bishop drove for another two blocks, parked on the street and got out. The car he'd spotted passed him and turned the corner. Bishop fumbled with the Saturn keys, as if looking for something, and seconds later heard the sound of footsteps from around the corner.

He went into an underground garage, pretending that he was unaware of the person following him. As soon as he was inside the garage, he ducked behind a pickup truck and crouched down.

The sound of footsteps came down the ramp into the garage. In the dim light from the outside streetlamps, Bishop saw an outline, a man around his height, step into the garage and crouch down, looking around.

Bishop felt the ground by his feet and found a pebble. He tossed it across the floor and it made the predictable small clatter. The figure walked silently toward the sound. Bishop stepped out from behind the pickup, took his gun out, crept up on the man and pointed the gun at his back.

"Easy. Now, no trouble now, easy." Bishop said softly.

The man turned to face him, scowling. "You got me." The man said.

"Why were you following me?" Bishop asked.

He shrugged. "I was following Sparwood. You were following him, and I got curious why."

Bishop shook his head. "You're the gunny, right? Gunnery Sergeant?"

The man frowned. "No, I was not a Sergeant, I'm a Lieutenant. Why do you ask?"

"Why are you following Sparwood?" Bishop hissed.

"I think he's responsible for a friend's death. I want to prove it."

Bishop lowered the gun. "We have that in common. Also, I think Sparwood hoped I'd kill you."

The man looked around nervously. "Did you lure me here to kill me?"

"If I had, you'd be dead by now. We're being played, both of us. Honest. We're being used."

Bishop put his gun back in his belt. "How about I buy you dinner?"

The man sat across the booth, waved at the waitress for more coffee and attacked his second slice of pie with a vengeance. They were in a diner, sitting on the corner of two streets in the rough part of town.

He pointed his fork at Bishop. "Just to be clear, you're buying, right?"

Bishop grinned. "So, who were you with in the service?"

The man stopped eating for a moment. "75th Rangers. You?"

Bishop nodded respectfully. "I Corps."

The man paused mid-bite. "You're an Army spook?"

"I notice you answer everything with a question. Let me ask you one. Who green-lighted you?"

The man patted his mouth with a paper napkin. "Let's be clear. I ain't giving out shit for nothing. Maybe you figure you know what I am, but I ain't telling you exactly what just yet."

Bishop leaned forward, speaking softly. "I'm not a cop. If you're the tip of the spear, someone is holding it. I need to know who and why, that's all."

The man took a swig of coffee and leaned back. "All right- let's ride this bus and see where this is going. Give and take, though, not one-sided."

Bishop nodded. "Last week I got something in the mail, something I never asked for. Papers, a DVD and a memory stick in a package labeled 'Flytrap'. Ring any bells?"

The man wrinkled his nose. "They also send you a card with a guy in a boat?"

"Yes, and a letter with a coded message in it. My colleague deciphered it."

The man tilted his head to one side. "Wow, that's impressive. I never did."

"Did Sparwood ask you to decipher it?" Bishop asked.

The man took another swig of coffee and shook his head. "He has no idea I have it."

Bishop tried another approach. "What's in the warehouse?"

The man shrugged. "You were in there for an hour. You tell me."

Bishop decided to walk the thin line between the truth and an outright lie. He didn't want to admit he had four vials of liquid in his jacket, but he wanted to find out what this man knew.

"I went in there pretending to deliver something, yeah, and I looked around, but all I found was a bunch of paperwork. There was a metal cabinet, but it was locked. No idea what's in there."

The man shook his head. "I don't know what's in there either. What I now know is that you probably didn't kill Roger Morrison."

Bishop let this sink in for a moment. "I thought *you* did. You didn't?"

The man shook his head. "You're chasing your leads. I'm just following breadcrumbs too."

"What's your stake in this fight?" Bishop prodded.

"Roger Morrison was in my unit before I got out. We kept in touch, mostly to have a beer and shoot the shit. Next thing, he sends me a USB stick, then I get the card. I've been looking for clues ever since. I still have no idea what the hell the page with numbers means, though."

Bishop smiled. "We figured that out from the clue on the back of the card. The paper was a series of incomplete palindromes. The number required to make the numbers into palindromes represented a letter of the alphabet. Very clever, actually."

The man pushed his plate away. "So, who did kill Roger?"

Bishop shrugged. "Are we on a first name basis yet?"

"Not on the first date."

Bishop took a sip of his coffee and wrinkled his nose. "I thought you killed both Morrison and Colonel Saks. That's not the case, though?"

The man scooped up a chunk of pie. "Who's Colonel Saks when he's at home?"

Bishop frowned. "She. So you didn't know her either. How did you hear about Roger's death?"

The man leaned forward and stopped smiling. "I got a call from someone very high up. They sent me a large check and told me Morrison was dead, so I made it my goal to find out who did it. As I say, he was my friend."

"Who exactly *are* you then?" Bishop asked.

"My name is Bill Knight. I'm a private investigator."

"You *were* a Lieutenant, so you're not with the Army any longer, right?" Bishop asked.

The man took a sip of coffee. "Nope, not anymore. Now I track down deadbeat husbands, expose insurance scams, find stolen cars, whatever."

Bishop snickered. "Bill Knight? No relation to the Nike guy, Phil Knight?"

"Nope, but it makes people look twice when I book restaurant tables."

He folded his arms on the table in front of him and leaned forward, closer to Bishop.

"My turn. What's your reason for chasing this rabbit?" Knight asked.

Bishop told him about the windbreaker, the phone, Kendall, Saks and Porezki. Knight mentioned that he had met Porezki once. Bishop mentioned he was driving a friend's car but omitted any specific details about Olivia. He sat back and watched Knight's reaction.

Knight rubbed his nose, digesting the information. Bishop played with a spoon and put it down.

He sighed. "What do you know about some conference in Oslo that's coming up?"

Knight shrugged. "Dunno. What's the conference about? Cheese, blondes, Nokia phones?"

Bishop reverted to his Army mode, running through facts in his mind. "Why did you decide to go after Sparwood? What pointed to him?" He asked.

Knight put his fork down. "Roger worked at the 'Society for Environmental Enhancement', a cover for a place that does stuff that the military would rather not have people *know* they do. He had access to everything from

Pentagon files to the camera up Bin Laden's ass. After Roger died I staked the place out. It's amazing what people will tell a pest control guy- or someone that says he is one- so the cute piece of fluff in the office complained that Sparwood was a dick. But she also said he was really frenzied the last little while, working on something he couldn't talk about.

Anyway, it was pretty obvious he was the top dog in that kennel, but from the few things I heard him say I figure he was just the guy whipping the horses. He's working for someone above him."

Bishop nodded. "When Kendall and Saks were killed, the men in green swooped down right away and took the bodies before we could examine them. We got some evidence from Roger's body, but not a lot. Kendall, Sparwood's driver, had the job of getting rid of Roger's body. He was shot before he could tell me something. I think he realized that Sparwood was using him."

"Why would you say that?" Knight asked.

"He was willing to move Roger, and to follow Colonel Saks around until she was shot. At that point I guess he realized he was moving up on the hit parade."

Knight slid his plate away and looked nervously around. "So, what's next on your agenda?"

Bishop waved at the waitress and made a motion like writing on the palm of his hand. She nodded understanding and pulled out her receipt book.

Bishop leaned in towards Knight. "I've got a phone, but it will only be on for a short time every day. Do you want me to call you tomorrow?"

Knight pulled a business card out of his back pocket and slid it over. "Here. Twenty-four seven, you can get me at this number."

Bishop pocketed the card. Knight tapped the table lightly. "Got a safe place to go?" He asked.

"Yup."

"Care to tell me where?" Knight asked.

"Nope." Bishop said.

Knight shrugged. "Fine. Keep me posted, please."

Bishop paid the bill in cash and left a tip, large enough that she wouldn't remember him as cheap, but not so big that she would remember him as generous, and they left the restaurant.

Knight walked to his car, grabbed the door handle and turned to face Bishop. "You're sure you can keep yourself safe for the next while?"

Bishop shrugged. "I've survived worse. I'll be fine."

Bishop drove south on International Boulevard, paralleling Highway I-5, past downtown, past the airport, past the Museum of Flight, to an area populated by strip malls and low-rise apartment buildings. It was a low-rent area but still safe enough that the Saturn would most likely be there in the morning.

He turned in at a motel with a faded metal sign that read 'Jet Stream Motor Lodge' and parked by the office. The office looked like it had seen better times, but not much better. The high Formica counter had a pair of chrome bar stools on the customer side of it, and the man behind the counter looked like he was short a few pints of blood.

Bishop placed his bag on a stool and leaned on the counter.

"Hey, you got a room available?" He asked gruffly.

He didn't want to sound educated at all. The man behind the counter grunted.

"Yep. Got any ID?"

Bishop looked genuinely insulted. "Why do I need ID?"

The man shrugged. "State law. I gotta see ID."

"I'm paying cash." Bishop protested.

She man rocked his head sideways. "Still need ID, sorry."

Bishop sighed, took out a faded wallet from his front pocket and placed a driver's license on the counter. The man looked at the license, squinted and looked at Bishop.

"Randall Scott?" The man asked.

"Call me Randy." Bishop corrected.

"All right, Randy. That'll be eighty-five dollars."

"You give discounts for unemployed guys?" Bishop asked.

The man handed the license back. "If we did we'd go broke. Eighty-five dollars."

Bishop sighed and pulled two crumpled fifties out of his pocket. The man took them and gave him change, then reached under the counter and came back with a metal key on a yellowed plastic fob.

He slid the key over the counter. "Room eleven, turn right, second from the end. No smoking, no drunks, no drugs, no hookers. Are you all right with that?"

Bishop grunted thanks, swung his bag off the stool then went out the door.

Room eleven was small, with a double bed pressed up against one wall and a battered mini- fridge beside a flimsy desk. The room smelled slightly of cigarettes and beer, somewhat more of stale socks. There was no phone, Bishop noted. Just as well. He looked at the driver's license he'd given the desk clerk; it had cost him sixty dollars from a joke website, but it looked real enough to pass, so it was worth it.

The bed was on a metal frame, and there was nothing under it except for a few balls of dust. A bad place to hide the bag overnight. The bathroom was relatively clean, except for a couple of white lines in the carpet outside it. Bishop decided these must have been from junkies shooting bleach through a needle before reusing it. There was an AM clock radio on the desk, and Bishop turned it on, mostly so that anyone passing would know the room was occupied.

He lay on the bed, kicked off his shoes and closed his eyes, thinking.

There were the vials of yellow liquid in the warehouse. They would be gone in two weeks. It had nothing to do with a conference in Oslo, so forget that line of thought. The vials were the main thing. They were what three people had been killed for, at least the three he knew about.

So, question one; what did Morrison find out that got him killed? Question two; why was Saks killed? Question three; why was Kendall killed? Question four; who killed them?

Too many questions, too many variables. In the morning, Bishop had to find somewhere to analyze the yellow liquid in his pockets. He went out of the room to a row of vending machines and bought a can of soda, a bag of pretzels and two candy bars.

The room had a small, beat-up color TV, so Bishop turned off the radio and watched some moronic game show as he drank cola and munched pretzels.

The sky was totally black by now, but light came through from the neon 'vacancy' sign by the road and a glaring streetlight beside it. Bishop could hear cars whooshing by, the sound of people walking past his door, and the clatter of soda cans dropping out of the vending machine.

He took his pistol out of his tote bag, tucked it under one bed pillow, and got undressed. The sheets on the bed were flannel- rough and pilled from too much washing and overuse, but they seemed clean. Bishop rolled onto his side, placed his right hand on the pistol and fell asleep.

Seven AM the next morning, Bishop was awake. He missed going out for a run, but he did his push-ups and sit-ups, trying to ignore the smell of the carpet in his nose. He showered, packed up his tote and stashed his pistol under the crumpled clothes. He carefully wrapped the four glass vials in a pair of thick socks and placed them at the other end of the tote, then checked that he hadn't left anything behind, checked again and dropped the key off at the front desk.

The woman who was now at the desk grunted thanks, made a note that his room was empty and watched Bishop go.

He checked his watch; eight AM. He drove back towards downtown, found a Denny's on the highway and stopped for breakfast.

He parked where he could see the Saturn from his booth, ate casually and slowly, then paid in cash again and headed in the direction of downtown. At exactly nine thirty, he pulled over at a gas station and turned on his phone. He dialed the number Knight had given him.

Three rings later, Knight picked up. "Hello!" He snapped.

"Hi, it's John Bishop. Any news?"

"Apart from the fact that some son of a bitch ransacked my office, no, not really." He snarled.

"Did they take anything?" Bishop asked.

"They broke the display case with my game-winning Mariners baseball. Other than that they just made a shitload of mess. Is this what they did to your office?"

Bishop rubbed his nose. "Yeah. Look, there's something I need to get checked out. I'll call you this afternoon. You can text this number but I'll have the phone off till later, all right?"

"When will that be?" Knight asked.

"No specific time. I don't want anyone to know when to ping me."

Knight laughed. "Still haven't lost the spook touch, I see. Call me later."

Bishop turned off his phone, pulled off the back cover and popped out the battery. It was now about as trackable as a loaf of bread.

He drove up familiar streets, past the part of the University where his classroom was, and on to a wing that he didn't visit often. The building, a black slate wall with equally black windows, had a small plaque on the wall by a smoked glass door that read 'Trinity Lab'.

Bishop parked between two large SUV's and hauled his tote bag up the short steps to the front door. He manoeuvred down a hallway, up a set of stairs and along another hallway to a flat metal door. He knocked briefly then went in.

On the other side was a man in a lab coat, sitting at a desk, scribbling something in a notepad. He glanced up when Bishop came in then did a double-take and sat back.

"Bish? What brings you all the way over here?" The man asked.

"I have a big favor to ask, Vance." Bishop said.

The man nodded. "Go on."

Bishop put the tote bag on the man's desk, pulled out the socks from one end and drew out the four vials of liquid. He handed one vial to the man.

"Can you work your magic and tell me what this is?" He asked.

The man turned the vial around between his fingers, examining the marks on the glass. He shook his head. "Where did you get this, Bish?" He asked.

"It's a long story, Vance. It's need to know. Anything about this stuff ring any bells for you?"

The man placed the vial carefully on the table in front of him. "When I worked somewhere else, at a location I'd rather not discuss, we had similar ones. The image on the glass is proprietary, like a QR code for the company that made the vials. Any idea what's in them?"

"Somewhere else? Where did you work?" Bishop repeated.

"It's my turn to say 'need to know'. Let's just say they weren't making cough syrup."

Bishop leaned forward to look at the vial more closely. "Do you have any way to tell me what this stuff is, Vance?"

The man picked the vial up and turned it upside down, watching the bubble of air at the pinched end float slowly to the wider end. "Yeah, can do. What do I do once I find out?"

"Keep it under your hat. I'll call you tomorrow about this time?"

He frowned. "I can tell Kelly what I find out. You have classes this week, right?"

Bishop shook his head. "No. Aunt Muriel is sick."

He raised his eyebrows at that. "Ah. I see. I see. You keep the other vials. I don't want to know where they are, or where you are. This means a level four isolation before I crack the glass."

He reached under the counter and retrieved a small cardboard box, lined in thick foam. He placed the vial gently into the foam and rested the lid carefully on the box.

He picked up a pen and paper. "Are you reachable? What's the number?"

"I'm prairie dogging- popping up at random times. I'll call about this time tomorrow, all right?"

"Right, better that way. Do you have somewhere to stay tonight?" The man asked.

"Yeah, I'm good, thanks. I don't think I need to tell you, Vance, but this is purely hush-hush."

"No shit. Keep your head down, Bish."

Chapter 9: Tactical Retreat

Bishop placed his tote bag on the motel's bed and rested his gun beside it. This place looked clean, and it was cheap. The irony of staying at a motel just two miles from his house didn't escape him. The 'Randall Scott' driver's license was good enough for this place, too, and since he paid in cash they didn't care much anyway.

He took a chance and paid for three nights in advance. The motel offered a free breakfast too, which made it more convenient. The parking lot was hidden from the street and that also helped him feel safer.

Bishop really wanted to clear this mess up as soon as possible; whatever was in the vial was the key to the problem, and Vance was one of the best people in his field. If anyone could figure out what that liquid was, he could.

He sat in the motel room for a few hours, watched more mindless television, then as the sun went down and the streetlight came on outside his window, he packed up the tote bag, tucked his gun into the tote and went out to buy dinner.

The little voice was speaking to him the moment he got into the Saturn. He looked around, without being too obvious about it. He stared at the reflection in the window of the car door as he got in, but couldn't see anyone unusual, just one person going to the vending machines then back to their room.

The little voice was still there. Sitting down at a restaurant would make him feel too exposed. He drove to a fast-food place and ordered from the drive-thru window.

He took the paper bag of food, parked in a corner of the restaurant lot, and started eating.

He'd been there maybe five minutes, maybe more, when he saw a police car cruise through the lot, moving slowly. His little voice was speaking more loudly now, but he just kept eating. There was a five-day-old copy of a local newspaper on the seat, so he picked it up and pretended to read it as he ate.

The police car went past him, kept going, then stopped suddenly and backed up, blocking him.

Bishop watched the cruiser; two uniformed cops in the car were talking to each other, glancing over at him as they spoke. The one behind the wheel tilted his head toward the other and said something. Bishop didn't need to read their lips- they were deciding how to approach him.

He decided to put the two cops at ease, so they would not worry about him. He rolled down his driver side window, got out and stood leaning against the car with his hands in his pockets.

Both uniforms got out, one with a hand on his pistol, looking around while the other watched Bishop. That was good training, he thought.

He nodded at the cop watching him. "Evening officers. Everything all right?" He asked.

The cop nodded. He was tall, taller than Bishop, lean but with the wide shoulders of someone who works out. His partner was slightly shorter, but his shirt bulged at the biceps. These were not lightweights. These were men who knew their stuff.

The tall one smiled cordially. "Hey there, sir. How's your night going so far?" He asked.

"So far, so good, officer. Can I help you gentlemen?" Bishop asked.

The tall one pointed at the Saturn. "That's an interesting car you're driving. Is it yours?"

"Nope. It belongs to a very lovely lady I know." Bishop answered.

"I see. And her name is?"

"Olivia Young. She's in Detroit for a month, so I'm borrowing her car." Bishop explained.

"Can you confirm that? Does she know you're using her car?" The second one asked.

Bishop thought for a moment. "Probably not, but I'm sure it's fine by her."

The first cop moved slowly to one side of Bishop, the second to the other side, bracketing him.

"Can I ask what drew your attention to me in the first place?" Bishop asked.

"The manager of an apartment building reported that this car was missing from his parking lot. He said he knew the owner was out of town." The second said.

"Right. I parked my Jeep in her spot." Bishop explained.

"How about you show us some ID so we can follow up on that?" The first one said.

Bishop nodded. "Sure. Just so you know, I have a legally registered pistol in my tote bag. I will not go for it, but I do need to reach in there for some identification."

The second cop unclipped the leather safety strap on his sidearm and wrapped his hand around the grip. The first cop looked into the car, eyeing Bishop's tote.

"What kind of gun are we talking about, pal?" He asked.

"It's an M9. A Beretta 92 nine mil." Bishop said.

The second cop raised his eyebrows. "M9? You're active forces?"

"I was- a Captain, in Army Intelligence. I'm now retired." Bishop answered.

"Where were you deployed?" He asked.

Bishop shook his head. "Next question."

The second cop chuckled. "I was there too. So, Cap'n, what brings you out this fine evening?"

"Just getting myself a burger and fries, that's all." Bishop shrugged.

The first cop pulled out a flashlight and shone it through the windows of the Saturn.

"And have you got anything else we should worry about in the tote bag or the car?"

Bishop shook his head. "Nope. No booze, no drugs, nothing. You're welcome to search."

The first cop flashed his light around the car. "How did you get this scrape on the bumper?"

"Olivia bumped into my Jeep. That's how we met."

"How romantic. I tell you what, would you mind turning around so we can cuff you, just until we're sure you're not going to do something stupid?"

Bishop sighed. "Listen, we could do this dance for the next hour, but after that you'd go away and I'd eat a cold burger. Or you could call Detective Ziggy Porezki and ask him about me."

They looked at each other. The first one spoke. "OK, convince me."

Bishop smiled. "I'm going to reach into my bag and get my phone. Slowly."

He took out his phone, turned it on and pressed a number. He waited for a few seconds.

"Hey, Ziggy? I have two of Seattle's finest here who would like to ask you about me."

He handed the phone to the first cop. The cop said "Yes?"

They spoke for a minute. The cop asked 'are you sure?' then handed the phone to Bishop.

"So I guess you're into some very scary shit, huh?" He asked.

"Deep enough that I need my gum boots." Bishop joked.

The first cop tilted his head at the second. "Take care, Cap'n. Safe travels."

They got into their squad car and left.

Bishop got back into his car and ate the burger. His fries were cold by now, but not bad, still.

He finished his meal, dumped the paper bag into the garbage and drove back to the motel.

He only had three days' worth of shirts and underwear with him, so he decided to visit a thrift store and buy some clothes. He picked out a stack of things that would last a week, paid cash and stuffed the clothes into a plastic bag.

The thrift store was just around the corner from where he'd left the Saturn. He turned the corner, the bag of clothes hanging from his hand, and fumbled for the car keys. That's when he saw them.

There were two youths, kids, really, huddled by his car. One looked around for passersby, and the second one worked at the car's door lock with a screwdriver. Bishop stiffened up.

"Guys. Leave it. Piss off." He barked.

The one with the screwdriver, a skinny teen with a shock of hair in a tight afro, sneered at him.

"This your car, bitch?" He challenged.

"Yeah, now get lost." Bishop repeated.

His friend moved behind him to one side. The teen waved the screwdriver in front of him. "Tell you what, give me your wallet and you can have the car." He sneered.

Bishop dropped the bag of clothes and looked straight at the teen. "Can you write with your left hand?" He asked.

The teen looked puzzled. "Huh?"

"Write. Can you write with your left hand? You'll have to fill out the hospital admissions form."

The other one looked at the teen with the screwdriver, unsure of what to do next. Bishop continued. "Last chance, stupid. Leave now, or I break some bones."

The teen growled and lunged at Bishop, the screwdriver poking forward. Bishop let him get close, then in one smooth motion lifted the teen's forearm, tucking it over the shoulder. He used his other hand to bend the arm further back over the shoulder. It gave a sharp cracking noise as the shoulder dislocated. The teen yelped as his screwdriver fell to the ground.

The other one didn't move, frozen. Bishop looked at him with dead eyes then turned to the first teen, now on his knees in front of him. He meticulously uncurled the teen's fingers and broke each digit, one by one.

The teen screamed in agony. Bishop picked up the screwdriver by the blade, flipped it high to catch it by the handle, and sank the blade into the teen's thigh. The teen screamed like a cat.

He pulled the blade out and the teen curled up in a ball on the ground. Bishop looked at the other one. "Next." He said calmly.

The second one ran away. Bishop picked up his bag of clothes and got into the Saturn. The other teen was still on the ground, moaning in pain. Bishop ignored him and drove off.

He parked in the back of the motel parking lot, as far as possible from the street, bought a couple of cans of soda and went into his room.

He meticulously folded the new clothes into neat piles, stacked them by type and laid them out on the small dresser. It had been a long day. He was tired. He undressed and checked for soap in the shower, but before he got in his phone rang. He'd forgotten to turn it off after dealing with the police.

He looked at the display before pressing the button.

"Hello?" He asked.

"Got you right away, huh? It's Bill." The voice said.

"Knight? Is that you?" Bishop asked.

"Yeah. I'm surprised that your phone's on."

Bishop shook his head. "My bad. I forgot to turn it off earlier. I don't want to stay on this too long. What can you tell me?"

Knight moved closer to his mouthpiece and spoke softly. "Two things. Small one first. I did some talking to your friend at the warehouse. Sparwood is vacating his locker in a week. You told me he was talking about some conference in Norway?"

"Oslo." Bishop said.

"Right. But he left some documents with the guy at the warehouse. The stuff in his locker isn't going to Norway. It's going to Cambodia."

Bishop still didn't want to admit what he'd taken from the locker. "Cambodia? What could he be sending to Cambodia?"

"Beats the shit out of me. Anyway, it cost me three hundred bucks to get a copy of the shipping documents. You interested in running this rabbit down?"

Bishop looked at his watch. "Yeah. Look, I've been on this call for thirty seconds now. I'm shutting the phone off in ten. Text me a picture and I'll get it later. What's the other thing?"

"OK. The dipshit who trashed my office didn't realize I have security cameras. I got a video of the guy doing the deed. Want to see it?"

"You bet. I'll call you in the morning and set up a meet, but stay low for now, all right?"

Knight grunted. "Roger that. Out."

Bishop turned off his phone, peeked out to see nobody was near his door, then took a shower and went to sleep, the pistol under his pillow.

At six the next morning, Bishop jumped out of bed and placed his thumb on the hammer of the pistol. A sound outside startled him, something unfamiliar. He hid beside the door, against a solid wall, his pistol pointed at the ceiling, ready to aim it or use it as a club.

The sound got more defined, a clattering and banging sound, tinkling and rattling all at once. He peeked around the edge of the thick curtain to the walkway outside his room. A large woman, huffing as she pushed a shopping cart loaded with luggage, waddled past his door. She turned and barked something to a pair of sleepy children behind her, and they skipped to keep up.

Bishop put the gun back in the tote bag. He showered and dressed, tucked his pistol into the back of his pants, covered it with the rough lumberjack shirt he'd bought from the thrift store, and made his way to the motel office.

A pretty young woman was behind the desk, making notes on a sheet. She smiled genially as Bishop came in. "Hi, good morning. Can I help you?" She asked.

Bishop smiled back. "Yeah. Hi, um, where is the breakfast area, miss?"

"Jeanie." She answered.

"Sorry?"

She smiled again and scanned Bishop quickly from head to toe. "Jeanie. My name is Jeanie."

He leaned on the counter and spoke warmly, his voice oozing. "Jeanie. So, you came out of a magic lamp, did you?"

She turned a slight shade of red. "No, my mom liked that old TV show, though." She giggled.

"Jeanie. That's a very musical name. Would you care to join me for breakfast, Jeanie?"

She glanced at the wall clock. "I have a coffee break in ten minutes. You're in room twelve?"

"Right."

"Randall? That's your name?" She asked.

"Call me Randy." He smiled.

She leaned her elbows on the counter. "Is that a nickname, or a description?"

"There's only one way to find out, I suppose." He said.

She pointed her pen at the far wall. "Out the door and turn right. There's cereal, toast, coffee, tea if you're into that stuff, and there should be some scrambled eggs ready any moment."

Bishop grinned. "Thanks. I'll save you a seat."

He followed her instructions and went into a room marked 'Dining Lounge'. The space was set out like a school cafeteria, with a long counter holding a toaster, dishes and all the usual hotel breakfast stuff.

Bishop loaded up a plate with food, poured himself a Styrofoam cup of weak coffee and sat along a back wall, giving him a view of everyone coming and going.

The large woman and her children came in, swarmed the counter and filled bowls full of sugary cereal then sat in a square table in the middle of the room. They ate noisily, slopping crumbs onto the table as they scooped up their food.

Bishop dug jam from its little plastic container and spread it onto his toast. He was halfway through the second slice of toast when the young woman from the office came in.

She was taller than she seemed behind the counter, very slender, with a wide belt around her waist, and he was sure her blouse was unbuttoned lower than when he saw her before.

She poured herself a coffee and sat across from him. She took a tentative sip, testing the heat, then leaned forward and stared at him with deep green eyes. She put the cup down.

"Randy. That's an interesting name. Are you from around here?"

Bishop recalled the details on the fake driver's license. He had a story ready if anyone asked.

"No, I'm from a little town called Palouse, Washington."

She wrinkled her nose. "Palouse? For real? Where is that?"

"Ten miles from Potlatch, Idaho. About an hour south of Spokane."

She shrugged. "Interesting. What brings you to our property of the Ritz Hotel?"

He chuckled. "I was looking for a job. A friend of mine thought he could get me a spot in the machine shop where he works." Bishop lied.

"Did you get the job?" She asked.

"Time will tell. Meanwhile, I have a couple of days to myself, to hang out and see the sights."

Jeanie moved her Styrofoam cup in a circle on the tabletop. "I get off work at four. Did you want to catch dinner and a movie or something?"

Bishop placed his hand on hers. "That sounds like a very interesting proposition. I'd love to."

She wrinkled her nose. "You don't talk like a machine shop worker."

Bishop shook his head. He had several explanations ready in case that came up and decided on the best one. "I was a salesman for industrial lubricants. The company downsized, so I figured I could work in the industry where I had sold the products."

Jeanie's eyes started to glaze over as he spoke. Good- she wouldn't ask for details.

She wrinkled her nose again. "Just to be clear, you're not married or anything?"

He shook his head. "Or anything, no."

She squinted her eyes. "And... you're not wanted by the cops, or anything like that?"

He laughed. He took a swig of his coffee and wiped his mouth with a napkin. "A few of my good friends are cops, actually. No, I'm good."

Jeanie pushed her hands against the table, stood up and smiled. Her blouse puckered slightly, and Bishop glimpsed the lace around her deep red bra as she moved. He felt that move was intentional, done solely for him.

"Four this afternoon? Perfect. I'll pick you up then." Bishop nodded.

She downed the rest of her coffee and walked back to her office. Bishop watched her go, her hips swinging as she did. He thought briefly of Olivia, but quickly dismissed the thought.

Bishop went back for another plate of eggs, swilled down some more weak coffee and went back to his room. He packed his bag, buried the pistol under his clothes, and drove off.

He drove for miles, finally parking on the road along Alki Beach, away from any dead ends and bench shelters that might hide someone watching him.

He walked a couple of hundred yards away from his car, made sure nobody was nearby, and turned on his phone.

It went 'ding' immediately to tell him there were messages. He scrolled to the menu and found two texts: one was from Vance, telling him to call. The other was from Bill Knight. There was a video attached to that message, and Bishop clicked the link to view it.

The video started off as a nearly black screen. A light came on, a flashlight, it seemed, scanning in the darkness. Then a room lit up as the person with the flashlight turned on a light switch.

The figure was a man, moving carefully but with purpose. He opened file cabinets, pulled out drawers, rifled through papers on the desk, and dropped everything on the floor once he'd done with them. His head was down most of the time, even though it seemed he was unaware of the camera recording him. After about a minute, though, he looked up to scan the room for other places he could check. Bishop got a clear view of his face. He backed the video up, froze it at that scene and zoomed in to be sure.

It was the young Marine type who had directed him down the hall at Sparwood's office. Bishop let the video play. The man finished going through things, then looked around one last time, turned out the lights and left.

Bishop called Knight. "Bill, about the man who went through your office." He started.

Knight was puzzled. "What? Who? Bishop? Hi, what do you mean?"

Bishop took a deep breath. "I think I've seen the man that went through your office. He works at the same place as Sparwood. I was there, in his office."

"No shit? All right, well that makes things interesting." Knight muttered.

"How do you want to handle it?" Bishop asked.

"I'm going to call the cops and have him picked up." Knight said.

"I'd really rather you didn't, at least not just yet. He may be the person who killed three people, including Roger Morrison. I want to find out more before we pin him to a corkboard. Once we do that to him, he clams up."

Knight was silent for a moment. "Yeah, fine, you're right. I'll give you three days- three days, that's all. You find something to hammer him with or I will have him picked up."

"Three days is fine by me. Talk to you later." Bishop said.

He hung up and turned off his phone. Time to make it hard to locate him again. He drove more miles straight north to a road high on a rise of land, overlooking Blue Ridge Park. It was a very high-priced neighborhood, with expansive houses overlooking Puget Sound and out to the San Juan Islands. He parked behind a glossy Mercedes and turned his phone on again.

Vance answered in two rings.

"Bish, what the hell have you gotten into?" He snapped.

"Hey, man, what did you find?" Bishop asked.

"No idea, Bish. It looks like some type of alkyd, but I have no idea what you'd use it for."

"What about the marks on the side of the glass? Any joy there?"

"Yes and no. It seems to have come from a government lab. When I tried to trace it I got a warning screen on my PC, so I shut it down. At a rough guess, I'd say this was something experimental, something to do with one of those three-letter agencies that don't exist."

Bishop thought for a moment, then had an idea. "Would it be easy to reproduce it? Could you make some more of it?"

Vance sighed. "In a word, no. The processes used to make this are way above my skill level. The ingredients alone are worth more than I make in a month."

"For that one vial?" Bishop asked.

"Yeah. Why?" He asked, cautiously.

"I found a bunch of them. What would they be worth?"

"Rough guess? Ten thousand dollars per vial? And that's even before I know what the hell they do. They could be go-go pills for soldiers, they could be put into a water supply to poison a city, or they might just make your pee glow in the dark. Who knows?"

Bishop rubbed his nose. "Look, just flush it and forget, OK? You never saw it, you never heard about it. It's better for everyone that way."

Vance grunted. "Agreed. See no evil, say no evil."

Bishop turned the phone off. He decided the best way to stay low for the time being was to blend in with people. He didn't want to go back to Pike Place Market- a cardinal rule in the military was to never walk the same path twice. He had a date with Jeanie at four, and it was barely ten in the morning now. He wanted to find the man who had rummaged through Knight's office. That might be the same person who killed Morison. He couldn't walk up to him in the office and ask him 'pardon, aren't you the guy that killed Roger Morrison?'

He didn't even know where the man lived. Wait- he did. Bishop had taken a picture of the sheet with employees' addresses when he was in Sparwood's office. That's how he found out where Sparwood lived. If he could get the name of the other man, he could look up his home address.

Bishop looked up the phone number for the 'Society for Environmental Enhancement' and called it. A woman answered- it was the same voice as the receptionist he'd spoken to there.

"Eight seven three-three." She said, briskly.

"Hi, um, I think one of your people may have lost a cell phone?"

Suddenly attentive, "Oh, uh, do you know whose phone it is?" She asked.

"Nah, it's locked. I think I saw one of your staff drop it, though. Young guy, six feet, blond?"

"Dwayne Carlilse? Could that be him?" She said.

"I dunno. Did he lose a phone?" Bishop muttered.

"One sec. hold on. Thank you."

She put the receiver down, and Bishop heard the tapping of shoes on the hard floor. He could barely hear distant voices, then the tapping came back. "No, he says it's not him." She said.

"No problem. I just thought… wait, they're calling me. I've got them, thanks." Bishop clicked off.

Now he had two pieces of information. The Marine was called Dwayne Carlisle, and he was in his office. Bishop checked the home address for Carlisle, shut his phone off and got into his car.

Carlisle, according to the sheet, lived in an apartment off I-5, across from Northgate Mall.

The address listed on the sheet in the office was in a long strip of three-story apartment buildings, separated from the road by a low chain link fence.

Bishop stopped at a dollar store on the way for some essentials. He picked up a clipboard, a ballpoint pen, a flashlight, an orange safety vest and a hardhat. Total, eight dollars and change.

He scrounged some sheets of computer paper from the cashier at the store, clipped them to the clipboard, and drove to Carlisle's apartment. He put on the vest and hardhat, carried the clipboard and looked in through the front door.

The building was older, but in fairly good condition. The elevator worked, the floor of the lobby was clean linoleum with grippy carpet for walking surfaces, and the lobby walls had been painted recently. This was not a bad place to live.

Bishop buzzed the caretaker's office and waited. An older woman, short and wide, waddled out from a side corridor to the front door, eyed him suspiciously and sniffed. "Yes?" She snapped.

Bishop looked down at his blank sheet of paper, holding it away from the woman's view.

"Hi. Looking for… Wayne Carsoll, apartment two sixteen? He's not answering the buzzer."

She shook her head. "There is no Wayne- wait, you mean Dwayne? Dwayne Carlisle?"

Bishop looked at the blank sheet again. "Sorry, yeah. Jerry scribbles his notes. Dwayne."

"He's not here. He's at work. You'll have to come back later."

Bishop nodded. "That's fine. We'll reschedule for next week. Hopefully the infestation won't get much worse by then."

He went to leave. She grabbed his arm and he stopped. "What infestation?" She said, worried.

Bishop shrugged. "Could be anything. Termites, roaches, rats. He didn't say when he called us."

She fumbled for a thick set of keys on her hip. "This is a clean building. We don't want no bugs or mice. I should come with you and take a look. Just to be sure, you know." She said.

Bishop rocked his head from side to side. "Yeah, I suppose, just to be sure, I get it."

The woman flipped through the roll of keys till she found a specific one, then she swept her hand behind her. "Come with me." She grunted.

Bishop hid a smile and dutifully followed her into an elevator. They went down a short hallway on the second floor, then the woman stopped at a door and knocked loudly.

"Mister Carlisle, it's Arlen. Arlen, the super." She called out.

There was no answer. She waited a moment, fumbled with her keys and opened the door.

She stood to one side and let Bishop in. "Don't you want to come check with me?" He asked.

She shook her head. "No, that's fine. I hate bugs and mice. I'll be right here, waiting."

Bishop shrugged, turned on the flashlight and crouched along a wall, shining light on the baseboard. He pretended to look for things along the floor. The woman was still at the front door, not coming in at all.

Bishop moved quickly into the living room, out of her sight. The room was neat, sparse, with a couple of hardcover books on a coffee table and a relatively small TV set on a long wooden entertainment unit. There were few things on the wall, just a couple of cheesy paintings- a painting of a bowl of fruit and a country scene- nothing else.

Bishop called out to the woman. "I'm almost done, so far so good."

She answered from the doorway. "All right, let me know if you find anything."

Bishop went into the single bedroom. The bed was made, crisply, with razor straight folds in the sheets and no wrinkles in the pillows.

On the wall was a single document, a commendation from the Marine Corps for bravery, awarded to Gunnery Sergeant Dwayne Patrick Carlisle. Could he be the General's 'gunny'?

Beside it was a photograph of Carlisle in a combat uniform, receiving a medal from a superior officer. Carlisle was the same man Bishop had seen in the hallway of Sparwood's office.

Below the picture was a tall dresser, with drawers that he opened slowly, silently. The dresser drawers contained only clothes, lined up in perfect order of size and folded identically.

Except for the bottom drawer. There was a thick white beach towel folded neatly in the drawer. On top of it was a Heckler and Koch USP nine-millimeter pistol, a box of bullets beside that and a crude contraption that looked like a stubby piece of plumbing pipe.

Bishop immediately recognised what it was. It was a silencer, a homemade suppressor, likely the one that Carlisle had built to shoot Saks and Morrison.

He slid the drawer closed, walked to the front door and smiled. "False alarm. Nothing here."

The woman sighed with relief. "Good heavens. Thanks for that. Do you want me to sign the invoice or something?" She said.

Bishop chuckled. "Naw. This one's on us. Listen, do you have a business card, though? I'm all out, but if we can be of service to your building, I'll email you and you can let me know."

She grinned and waved at him. "Sure. Come with me."

He followed her to an office beside the entry door, took her card and thanked her.

Bishop got out to his car and tossed the card into the back seat.

He turned his phone on and dialled a number. Knight answered in two rings.

"Hi? Is this Bish?" He started.

"Yeah. Listen, now I'm sure I know who went through your office." Bishop said.

"No shit? Who?"

"Not so fast. I can't risk you going after him. He's a Marine, and if he thinks you are after him he will kill you. He's that good. Trust me."

Knight hissed. "Fine. What next?"

"Leave it with me. I'll keep you posted."

Bishop turned the phone off and drove back toward the motel. There was nothing more he could do today, he thought. He stopped at a burger place for lunch, then parked in the motel lot between two big pickup trucks and went into his room.

He had a date with Jeanie in three hours. He'd take a nap first.

Chapter 10: Local Asset

At ten minutes after four, Bishop was showered, shaved and ready to go out.

He took out his best windbreaker and shirt, then he used the room's steam iron to take the wrinkles out of his slacks.

He put his tote bag in the closet, taped his pistol to the underside of the bathroom sink, and picked up a couple of cans of soda and a bucket of ice from the vending machines.

Five minutes later there was a knock at his door.

Bishop opened it, smiling. Jeanie was in the same blouse and skirt as before, but she had put on a deep red lipstick that made her green eyes that much more vivid.

She looked up at him and smiled. "Hello, there. Ready to go?"

Bishop grinned. "Absolutely. Where would you like to go?"

She pulled him out the door, took his arm and walked them down to his car. "Well, I thought we could catch a movie first, then you can splurge and take me to the Olive Garden."

He squinted. "Ooh. Fancy. I'm not sure I packed my tuxedo, but sure, that sounds good."

They got to the Saturn, and he unlocked the passenger door and held Jeanie's hand as she got in. He started up and backed carefully out onto the street.

"You said a movie. Where is there a movie showing this early in the day?" He asked.

She pointed east. "There's the Film Forum at twelfth and Pike. They're showing one of my old time favorite movies, 'The Girl in the Red Velvet Swing'." She said.

Bishop frowned. "Hmm. That title doesn't ring a bell, sorry."

She smiled. "Oh, you'll love it. Sex, murder, madness, intrigue, it's got it all."

"Sounds like my Thursdays." Bishop joked, and immediately regretted saying it.

She stared at him. "Something I should know?"

"Nah, just politics at the place I used to work. It's all behind me now, I hope."

They parked out front of the theater- a glass-front box that resembled a giant Starbucks. Bishop bought the tickets and they sat in what looked like a school auditorium, two of perhaps fifteen people in the room.

Jeanie requested popcorn and cola, so Bishop shimmied to their seats in the middle of a row, as she also requested, juggling her snack and his cup of ginger ale.

The lights went down, the movie started. The movie was not that interesting for Bishop; he watched it half-heartedly, remembering enough to make conversation afterwards, but the whole time he was thinking about the vials of yellow liquid.

They were very valuable, Vance had said. They were produced somewhere in large batches, and they were now most likely going with Sparwood to Cambodia. Why

Cambodia? Was there some organization or someone there that wanted to buy the vials from him? After all, Bishop overheard Sparwood saying that after they got paid they'd be set.

There were over a hundred boxes of vials in the storage locker. Each box, he figured, had about a dozen vials in it. That meant two thousand vials, at the minimum.

Vance had said that the ingredients alone were worth ten thousand dollars per vial. Twenty million dollars. That's what the ingredients were worth. Let alone what they were synthesised to do. So Sparwood was going to take the vials to Cambodia, and probably sell them for more than twenty million dollars. He was working with someone, the person he'd heard Sparwood talking to through the apartment door, so even if he only got some of the total, it was enough to kill for.

Bishop settled back and watched the movie. It was melodramatic, saccharine, and not what he wanted to see, but Jeanie was very attractive, so sitting through the film was a price he was willing to pay.

Eventually the lights came up and the screen went dark. Jeanie stretched and smiled at Bishop.

"So, what did you think of the movie?" She asked, expectantly.

Bishop shrugged. "You know, it's not the kind of thing I usually watch, but it was interesting."

She looked at him, studying him. "You weren't really watching it at all, were you?"

Bishop shrugged. "Like I said, it's not really what I usually watch, but yes, I did enjoy it."

She smiled broadly. "Liar. I appreciate you not complaining during the movie, though."

Bishop grinned. "Not at all. May I escort you to dinner, fair lady?"

They left arm in arm, strolling casually.

He rubbed his nose. "There's no Olive Garden near here that I can see. Do you have any idea where else you might like to eat?"

"There's an Italian pizza place two blocks west. Do you like Italian?" She offered.

"Who doesn't? Have you eaten there before?"

She nodded. "Yeah, it's very nice. Old school food, no pretense, no froo-froo, no bullshit."

"That makes a nice change from Denny's. Let's go." He said.

They walked to the restaurant, talking warmly. She told Bishop all about herself as they went.

She had lived in Seattle about two years, graduated from college with no prospect of a job and worked as a salesclerk at Nordstrom's then as a telemarketer for a duct cleaning company, she said, before getting the job at the motel. Before Seattle she had grown up in Port Angeles, on the Olympic Peninsula. She had moved to Montana for a year to be with a boyfriend but missed the area more than she imagined she would. The boyfriend was now doing time for drug smuggling, she added. For the last month and a half she had worked at the motel. She enjoyed meeting interesting people, but it wasn't what she really wanted to do.

She asked Bishop about his life story. He decided not to lie too much, but didn't want to get her involved, either.

"It's a little complicated, right now." He said.

"How so?"

"Would you believe me if I told you that I can't answer that now, but in twelve days I'll be happy to tell you whatever you want?" He said.

"That sounds very intriguing. You're a machine shop man of mystery?"

"Hmm. Machine shop, right. That's something I can also clarify, just not right away."

She stopped, leaned against a building and stared at him. "Are you in some kind of trouble? I don't need that crap in my life right now, you know. I'm getting as far as I can from the crap I had before, so I really don't need to get back into the shit pile."

Bishop nodded. "I completely understand. I can swear to you that I am not involved with anything illegal, but I can also say that I can't tell you any more for the next twelve days."

"After that what happens?" She asked.

"After that all will be revealed." He answered.

She turned to continue walking. "Just so we're clear, dinner's still on you, right?"

He chuckled. "You're the second person in two days to ask me that. The other person was a man, by the way."

The restaurant was busy, bustling with a few clusters of people jockeying for the best seats, busboys in black shuffling between tables and waiters barking orders to the row of kitchen staff behind a high counter. The restaurant

The smell of sauce and crisp bread was thick in the air. Bishop spotted an empty table for two against a brick wall and motioned to a waiter that he wanted the spot.

The waiter nodded and waved him over. Bishop took Jeanie's arm and guided her to the seat. He held a chair out for her, made sure she was seated comfortably then sat across from her.

The waiter brought a basket of breadsticks and two menus, then came back with water.

Jeanie ordered something, Bishop did as well, and the waiter asked about drinks. Jeanie suggested a bottle of wine. Bishop said he wouldn't drink, but it was ok if she wanted to.

Jeanie stared at him for a moment and changed her request to a glass of house red. Bishop asked for ginger ale. The waiter left. Jeanie folded her arms in front of her and leaned forward.

"You don't ever drink?" She asked.

Bishop shook his head. "Nope. Nothing alcoholic, no."

"You're not a Mormon or something?"

He grinned. "Nothing like that, no. I had a booze problem, but I got over it, so no wine for me."

She shrugged. "Fair enough. I've had my share of guys trying to get me drunk. This makes a nice change. If you don't drink, do you have any other vices?"

He leaned towards her, almost nose to nose. "Fabulous women with red lips and green eyes."

Their food came, and they talked as they ate. Jeanie tried to get more detailed information out of Bishop, but he kept repeating that he could tell all in just twelve days.

After the waiter took the last sliver of pizza away, Bishop suggested dessert and coffee. Jeanie read the menu, wrinkled her nose and shook her head. "Nah. None of this looks good. Tell you what, I've got some Ben and Jerry's in my fridge. Would you like to try some of my dessert?"

The innuendo was not lost on Bishop. "Do you have two spoons?" He joked.

She leaned forward and whispered. "We can share a spoon, can't we?"

He paid the bill and they sauntered back to his car. She clutched him arm tight, smiling. Bishop felt good, better than he had in days, and the thought of spending the night with Jeanie gave him a rush.

He held the door open for her as she slid in, then went around to open his door. Jeanie wrinkled her nose and sneezed. She tilted her head back and sneezed again. She groaned and rubbed her nose. "Stupid allergies. Do you have a tissue?" She asked.

Bishop looked around. "Um, not sure, let me check."

Jeanie opened the glovebox and rummaged around. She pulled out a slip of paper, read it, put it back and closed the glovebox.

"You know, I feel a headache coming on. Would you just drop me at the motel?" She said icily.

Bishop frowned. "Sorry, is something wrong?"

She glared at him. "Yeah. Who the fuck is Olivia young?"

Bishop chuckled. "She's the owner of the car we're in. Why do you ask?"

"Is she dead in a ditch somewhere? Was I going to be next on the list?" Jeanie snapped.

Bishop tried hard not to laugh. "I understand your caution. I met her some time ago, and she asked me to drive her to the airport. She's a TV weather girl in Detroit right now. But if it makes you feel any better, she should be back in Seattle next month. You can meet her then."

Jeanie looked out her window, fuming. "Listen, I don't get a creepy vibe from you, despite the mystery crap and all, but you can't always judge a book by its cover, you know."

"No, you're right. Do you want me to call you a cab, or do you trust me to drive you home?"

"I'm not so sure I should let you know where I live just yet." She answered.

Bishop nodded. "I understand. Look, if you'd rather not have me stalking you at your place, can I at least interest you in coffee at my place?"

She snickered. "OK. I can go for that. Not our motel coffee, though. It sucks."

Bishop picked up food from a cheesecake place on the way back to the motel, and Jeanie held the white cardboard box in her lap, with four large paper cups of coffee in a tray at her feet. Bishop helped her out of the car as daintily as possible, struggled to keep the coffees level and held Jeanie's hand at the same time.

She giggled at his chivalry, watched him juggle the cardboard box and the coffees as he fumbled for the keys in his pocket, then shook her head and waved her hands.

"Here. Let me get the key." She said.

She stuck her hand in his pocket and grabbed the room key. Bishop yelped involuntarily at the touch of her hand there. She laughed and turned the key to fit the door lock.

"Most guys would be pleased at me doing that." She joked.

"I wasn't complaining, just surprised." Bishop explained.

Jeanie opened the room door and turned on the light. She dragged the small desk toward the bed, slid the chair across from it and sat on the edge of the bed, resting her elbows on the desk.

"So, what did you pick up for dessert?" She grinned.

Bishop opened the box and carefully lifted out a wedge of cheesecake for Jeanie, then one for himself. He ceremoniously placed her coffee cup beside the dessert, folded a brown paper napkin into a triangle, and placed a plastic fork on the napkin, beside her slice of cake.

Jeanie frowned. "What, no candles? No violin music?" She joked.

Bishop shrugged. "I've got a radio. How about some good old AM static?"

He tuned the radio, crackling through the stations, to something smooth and jazzy. He raised his cup of coffee and toasted Jeanie. She took the hint and 'clinked' cups with him.

She took a sip and pursed her lips as she put the cup down. "Just so you know, I don't usually put out on the first date." She said.

Bishop smiled. "I'm glad to hear it. I would think far less of you if you had."

She knit the fingers of both hands together in a cradle, hooked them in front of a knee and leaned forward.

"So you're not really a machine shop kind of guy. What are you really?" She asked.

He got serious. "Would it surprise you that I teach University?"

"Not really. You speak very well. What did it- a sex scandal? You took cash from the kitty?"

He considered how to answer the question. "Did you ever discover something you weren't supposed to? Something important, but it was not meant for you?"

She shook her head. "I'm not sure I understand. Are we talking about for real spy stuff or what? Or are you still just jerking my chain?"

He put his coffee down. "I was sent something from someone I've never met. That's as specific as I can get. The thing I was sent exposes a serious situation, and I have about ten days or so to shine a light on the issue without getting killed. I'm not trying to sound dramatic, I'm just trying to stay safe. If anyone asks you anything about me, tell them everything you know. Don't hold back. That's why I'm being cagey. It's not for machismo, it's for survival."

Jeanie digested all this, sipped her coffee and nodded. "And you won't tell me your real name?"

"Believe me, I'd love to, but it would only make things messy for you right now."

"You're still not married though, right?" She asked.

"Nope. Happily divorced, six years ago."

She looked around beside her and frowned. "Shit. I think I lost them." She muttered.

"Hmm?" He asked.

"My master keys. I'm in deep shit if I did. I think I left the keys in your car. Would it be terrible to ask you to look for them?" She cringed slightly, guilty at the request.

Bishop smiled. "No problem. Be right back."

He went out into the walkway along the motel. A man was struggling with the vending machine, kicking it and glaring at the slot where cans come out.

"Not giving out your cola?" Bishop joked.

The man flapped his arms in frustration. "I told the office guy a dozen times. I've been here almost two weeks and this damned machine keeps eating my dollar."

"Want me to mention it to Jeanie?" Bishop asked.

"Who's Jeanie?"

"The lady from the front desk. She's been here for the last month, she said."

The man shook his head. "No she hasn't. She got here yesterday. Damned if I know why she told you that, though. She started yesterday."

Bishop's little voice was screaming now. He ran back to his room and threw open the door. His tote bag was on the bed, the clothes spread out and the Flytrap material in a pile beside them. The three vials of liquid were arranged in a neat row, and his gun was on the far side of the bed, by the pillows. Jeanie looked up with a start when she saw him.

"It's not what you think." She started.

She looked around and started putting things back into his tote bag.

Bishop grabbed the gun and stuck it into his belt. He checked that the Flytrap items were all there, then he turned to look at Jeanie. There was terror in her eyes, the look of a trapped animal.

"Are you working for Sparwood?" He asked.

She frowned. "What? Sparwood? I don't know what that is."

"Why are you here? Sparwood- are you working for him?" He growled.

She shook her head, puzzled, still looking at him.

"Get the fuck out of my sight." He hissed.

"I can explain. I was just supposed to…" She started.

Bishop pulled out his gun, cocked the hammer and aimed at her forehead. "Go. Now." He said.

Jeanie opened her mouth to say something, then closed it and nodded sadly. She walked to the door and turned. "I'm sorry. Really. I'm really sorry." She said.

"Fuck right off." Bishop snapped.

Bishop listened to her footsteps fade as she went down the sidewalk. He waited thirty seconds, packed everything into his tote bag and left the room key on the bed.

He got into the Saturn, backed quickly out of the parking lot and drove away.

He had two objectives right now. He had to find a place to sleep for the night, and he had to change cars. Whoever Jeanie really was, she knew his car, and whoever she worked for would now know it too. Time to take stock of his assets and objectives.

He had some cash, he had the vials of liquid, he had his gun and he had a phone. All he had to do now was to survive a handful of days and then he'd be in the clear. Getting a car was not difficult. There was a van the owner no longer needed, as long as he could hot wire it. Nobody would connect him with Kendall's van. He could even sleep in it if he needed to. The night was dark, and Bishop pulled over every few blocks to be sure he wasn't followed. So far, so good.

He put the Saturn back into Olivia's parking space, drove his Jeep out and left it on a street full of SUV's and soccer mom minivans. He was certain it would blend in, and it would take weeks before anyone noticed it.

From there Bishop walked a few blocks to a main street, took a bus to Kendall's apartment and went into the garage. There was nobody around, none of the cars was ticking to indicate they'd just gotten there, and he could hear no noise from behind the door to the elevator.

He took out his trusty Swiss army knife and put the screwdriver blade into the driver side door lock. It opened with only a little effort, and Bishop slid onto the seat and closed the door.

The van must have been stolen in the past; the steering wheel lock was broken and the wheel turned freely. He looked around under the seat and in the glove box and found a large screwdriver and a tire iron.

The screwdriver was just small enough to fit into the ignition, so Bishop banged it in deep with the tire iron and twisted the screwdriver handle as hard as he could.

The engine came to life, and Bishop backed quickly out and onto the street. If the building super knew that Kendall was dead, he'd think the police had taken the van, but he if didn't know Kendall was dead he'd assume Kendall had taken the van. Either scenario worked for Bishop.

He needed a place to stay for the night. There was a thick blanket in the back of the van, an old jacket and a couple of coveralls, probably left over from when it was owned by the upholstery place. Bishop knew the perfect place to go; the scruffy dockyard area on South Nevada Street, where the waterfront met the railway, plus the industrial buildings had dock workers coming and going at all hours. He parked between a newer pickup truck and an old Dodge sedan that made his van look elegant.

He locked all the doors then climbed into the back and lay down. He rested his head on the tote bag, tucked the gun under a fold of the blanket, and went to sleep.

At seven the next morning he woke up. There were voices outside, someone speaking in Spanish, talking to someone else in Spanish, about trading shifts so the first one could go to his daughter's school play. The second one agreed, saying that the afternoon shift premium would come in handy. They both wandered off.

The van had no side windows, and the rear windows were mostly painted over. Bishop could see out through scratches in the paint without being seen, so he checked that nobody was paying attention to the van. Good- it was helpful that it was unremarkable. Bishop started the engine and headed south on Nevada. The street looped south at the entrance to the container port, paralleled the tall fence protecting the cargo facility, then Bishop turned left onto Idaho and looked for somewhere to eat.

Idaho Street was an endless row of loading docks, warehouses and low, one-story offices.

Tucked between two warehouse buildings was a strip mall, and out front was a sandwich board with a sign reading 'Evergreen Diner. Breakfast served all day.'

Bishop parked the van in a spot right outside the diner and pulled the screwdriver out of the ignition. He tucked the screwdriver under the seat, put his gun in the tote bag, and went in. The diner was sterile, generic, and smelled of French fries, but it seemed clean. A dozen square tables were scattered across the floor, set out with four chairs. There were five or six stools at a counter as well, but Bishop didn't like the idea of having his back to the front door. There were only three or four people in the diner, so he picked a table in the corner and sat down.

A matronly woman in a green smock appeared from nowhere. She had a glass carafe of coffee in one hand, a white ceramic mug and a laminated menu in the other. She smiled a plastic smile and nodded.

"Coffee to start?" She asked.

Bishop looked up at her. "Please. Thanks."

She put down the mug and filled it. She put the menu beside the mug and turned to leave.

"Actually, I know what I'd like." He said.

She put the carafe on the table, pulled out an order pad and plucked a pencil from behind her ear. "OK, shoot, hon." She said.

"Scrambled eggs, bacon, whole wheat toast. Orange marmalade for the toast, if you have it."

She picked up the menu and grinned. "Coming right up."

Bishop looked around, trying to look casual, sipped his coffee and kept the tote bag on the floor between his feet.

The waitress came back a few minutes later with a plate of food, a smaller plate of toast and a wrapped set of cutlery. Bishop thanked her and started eating.

The restaurant got busier, in waves of three and four people; regulars who called the waitress by name, truckers who obviously had been on the road all night, the odd office person in nicer clothes who came in for coffee and toast before going to work.

Bishop watched them all, without looking like he was watching them. He ate his meal, drank more coffee, thanked the waitress and asked for his bill.

A group of men sat at a table beside him. They were disheveled, stubble-faced and weary, even this early in the morning. One man slapped a clipboard on the table and flipped through a series of forms, speaking in shorthand to the others. The man across from him flipped trough his phone and said 'yep, by noon' then put the phone away.

The first man peeled a sheet of paper off the clipboard and said 'well, won't need this then.'

He slapped the paper down on the table; it fluttered off and under Bishop's seat. The man turned around and said "Sorry, didn't mean to do that."

Bishop picked the paper up and smiled. "No harm done."

He glanced at the paper and then stopped to read it fully. It was a blank form to authorize pickup of a shipment. The addresses were all blank, the other fields were all blank, but the shipping company name and official stamp were there.

The man had his hand out for the paper. Bishop waved it at him. "Hey, mind if I hang on to this?" Bishop asked.

The man frowned. "Why?"

"I'm looking for work. I figure this lets me know where I should go ask." Bishop lied.

The others around the table laughed. The first man shrugged. "Knock yourself out. I don't think we're taking on swampers, but you never know."

Bishop folded the paper neatly and tucked it into his pocket. He paid for the meal and got back into the van.

He took a deep breath, turned on his phone and opened a browser.

The address of Sparwood's warehouse was online, as was the phone number for the office. Bishop wrote some details on the blank shipping form, indicating that he was supposed to pick up something from the warehouse, then he called the number.

Three rings later an impatient voice said "Yeah?"

"Um, is this Warren?" Bishop asked.

"No, he's off today. Can I help you?" The voice was slightly less gruff.

Bishop was relieved. "Yeah, I already spoke to Warren? I got an order to pick up a shipment from, uh, Sperwand? Sparwind, no, wait, Sparwood. Yeah, that's it, Sparwood."

There was the sound of rustling paper, then the man said "Yeah, we were expecting you later this afternoon. I guess you got free sooner then?"

Bishop's heart raced. "Right. I got a cancelled delivery, so I'll be there in about thirty minutes."

The man grunted acknowledgement and hung up.

Bishop drove slowly along the road till he found what he wanted. There was a loading bay with scattered cardboard boxes, and more being thrown off the end of a loading dock.

He pulled over and called to the man throwing the boxes out.

"Hey, buddy, mind if I scarf some of your cardboard?" He called.

The man barely looked at him. "Yeah, no prob."

Bishop took four or five of the most pristine boxes and put them in the van. "Thanks, man." He said, and drove off, towards Sparwood's warehouse.

The man at warehouse was painfully thin, with the expression of someone who's just found out his goldfish died. He reeked of old sweat and cigarettes, and the small tattoo on his hand between his thumb and index finger meant he'd spent time in jail.

Bishop picked the shipment form from his breast pocket and read it. "So, uh, this Sparwood guy wants us to transport some stuff from his locker. You know what number it's in?"

The man sauntered to a ledger on his desk, flipped over pages at a glacial speed, and finally gave Bishop the locker number.

Bishop scribbled something on the paper with a stubby pencil. "Right. So, they never gave us the key. You got a master for the door?"

The man sighed and pulled a huge clump of keys from the desk. "Yeah, I go the key."

Bishop smiled at him, nodding. "Terrific. I got the boxes we're supposed to pack it into. I don't suppose you got a dolly or a cart?"

The man snorted and adjusted his belt. "Yeah, but I gotta charge you twenty bucks to rent them. We'll add it to his bill. I'm not real sure he'll go for that."

Bishop smiled. "Tell you what. I'll give you ten dollars cash, you don't mark it down and I'll bill him the twenty bucks later myself."

Bishop needed him to collude in what seemed to be a small larceny, so the man wouldn't notice what was really going on. The man's face slowly spread into a smile, thinking that he was going to cheat Sparwood but still get money from Bishop. He agreed.

Bishop loaded three large cardboard boxes onto a dolly and wheeled it to Sparwood's locker. The man took Bishop's money, fumbled with keys till he found the one that opened the locker, then he mumbled something about a 'beer run' and left.

Bishop went right to the tall metal file cabinets. He jimmied them open with Olivia's mail key, then working as quickly as he could he took the boxes of vials and stacked them in his bigger cardboard containers. It took maybe five minutes to load them all into two of the cardboard boxes. Bishop counted as he stacked. There were a hundred and fifty white boxes in the file cabinet.

That meant that, at twelve vials per box, there were eighteen hundred vials in all.

Eighteen hundred vials times at least ten thousand dollars per vial was eighteen million dollars. The number staggered him. He collapsed the third carboard box, stuck it in a dark corner and folded over the lids on his full boxes. He rang the bell, waited and a minute later the man came back. They wandered toward the freight elevator.

"All done?" The man asked.

"Yep. Ready to ship this stuff." Bishop answered.

The man turned and asked "Got a copy of the waybill for me?"

Bishop thought quickly. "Yeah, it's in my van. I'll load this stuff up and be right back."

The man grunted agreement. Bishop rolled the dolly down the sidewalk, loaded the boxes into the van, and waited three minutes. He brought the dolly back to the man and shook his head.

"Shit, I'm sorry. I think I left your waybill at my last drop. I'll be back this afternoon, all right?"

The man shrugged. "Shit happens. I'm here till six today. Just bring it over before six."

Bishop grinned. "Hey, I appreciate it. I owe you a case of beer,"

The man smiled in anticipation and Bishop left.

Chapter 11: Frontal Assault

Sometimes, the best defense is a good offense. 'The Art of War', a must-read for military officers, talks about turning your weaknesses into strengths.

Bishop now had what Sparwood wanted. He knew its value, and he knew the name of the man who had killed Morrison, Saks and Kendall. That knowledge gave him power over Sparwood.

He found a mini storage on the other side of town, in an industrial strip mall off Roosevelt Way. He paid for a month's storage on a tiny locker, barely big enough for the two cardboard boxes, and used the Randall Scott driver's license to register it. He left his tote bag in the van, but put the three glass vials and his gun in the cardboard boxes with all the other vials.

He locked up, drove off in no particular direction, and found himself on Highway 520, the floating bridge that drove over Lake Washington. He hadn't been this way in years, but he remembered that he had once gone on a picnic with his wife to Juanita Beach Park. That was a good spot to make a phone call.

He made sure nobody was watching him and turned on his phone.

He dialed a number; a woman answered in two rings. "Eight seven three-three." She said.

Bishop spoke in an official voice. "Sergeant Carlisle, please."

She paused for a moment. "Certainly. And may I ask who you are?"

"Captain Randall Scott."

She pressed some buttons at her end. "One moment, sir."

That meant she was probably military too, or ex, at least. Bishop waited for ten seconds.

A man's voice came on. "Sergeant Carlisle, Captain. Can I help you?"

Bishop inhaled. "You have a very nice apartment, Gunny."

There was a long pause. "Yeah, I wondered if you'd call me. Did you find anything interesting?"

"I found your silencer. Did you make it yourself?"

The man sighed. "You know, it's not there anymore. If you call the cops, they'll get nothing."

Bishop grunted. "Believe it or not, I'm not trying to burn you, I'm only calling to help you out. You're doing wet work for Sparwood. He is not the good guy you think he is. He's using you."

The man covered the handset and spoke to someone. Bishop couldn't make out what he said. He came back on. "I've worked with the General for years now. Why should I believe you?"

Bishop looked around. "Don't bother trying to find me. This phone will go dead in forty seconds and I'll be in the wind again. I do want to tell you something though. I heard Sparwood say that once you're no longer useful he expects me to kill you."

That got his attention. "Go on." He said.

"You want proof? Sparwood is heading to Cambodia with something very valuable. I know."

He grunted. "I know that too. It's equipment, things to do with a matter of national policy."

"Wrong. He's selling vials of chemicals, and they're worth millions. I heard him say that once he gets paid, you're expendable and I'm supposed to get the blame for killing you."

"How do I know you're not just blowing sunshine up my ass?" He asked.

"Tell Sparwood that I went to his warehouse and cleared out his stuff. See how he reacts."

"How do I know you really did take the stuff?" He said cagily.

"Get him to check the warehouse cabinet. It's empty." Bishop answered.

"Did you take his... whatever it is, to sell it?" He said.

"No. Gotta go. Bye."

Bishop turned off the phone and pulled out the battery.

He got into the van, made sure nobody was watching him, then drove to an industrial area up Highway 405. He was now in Kirkland, across the lake from Seattle, and not in familiar territory.

He took a cloverleaf exit down to a maze of streets and off-ramps, then saw the sign for a Motel 6 and pulled into the lot. At one end of the motel was an office with a bored-looking man behind the counter, a candy vending machine and a rack of pamphlets for the local casinos.

Bishop walked up to the desk and waved his phone at the desk clerk.

"Hi, I'm sorry, but my phone crapped out. Do you have any pay phones anywhere here?"

The man raised one eyebrow and shook his head. "Not since Reagan was president, no."

Bishop laughed. "Look, I really have to make some business calls. Could I use a room phone for ten minutes? They're all local calls, nothing to Patagonia or anything like that."

The man sighed and wrinkled his nose. Bishop understood the gesture.

"Okay. Five bucks. Ten minutes, five bucks. What do you say?"

The man smiled slightly and Bishop handed him five dollars. The man slipped a room card over the counter. "Number eight. Don't use the shower or the can, please, it was just cleaned."

Bishop took the card and nodded agreement.

He opened the door to the room, made sure nobody was around then closed it behind him.

He picked up the room phone and dialed a familiar number. Porezki answered in two rings.

"Detective Porezki." He said curtly.

"It's John Bishop. I have some information for you."

Porezki rustled paper and moved closer to the phone. "Morning. What have you got, John?"

"First, the deaths all happened because Lieutenant Morrison discovered that some very valuable items were being sold to someone overseas."

"What items are they, exactly?" He asked.

"I can't tell you that right now, but I can tell you that I have these items, and they're safely hidden away." Bishop said.

"This is all sounding like real life cloak and dagger shit, you know." Porezki said.

"All right, how about some real cop shit for you? I know who killed those three people."

Porezki made a sound that indicated he was grabbing more paper. "Go on." He said.

"Sorry, same answer right now. Look, I need this guy out in the wild for just a bit longer. He won't kill anyone else, really."

Porezki sounded unconvinced. "What makes you so sure that he won't?"

"Because the person who hired him expects me to kill him next. I don't intend to, by the way. I've told the killer that he was being used. He's smart, he's not going to do anything stupid."

Porezki wrote this down. "Anything else?"

"I'll keep you posted. Do you have a cell number if I need to call you?"

"This phone number forwards to my cell. Keep me in the loop, keep safe." Porezki said.

Bishop hung up and looked up another number. He dialed it and waited. Three rings later a woman answered. "Front desk." She said mechanically.

"Hi, Jeanie. You're still there? Miss me yet?" Bishop said.

She sighed. "Look, I'm so sorry about all this. It wasn't my idea, just so you know. Is there any way I can make it up to you?"

"Yeah. Tell me who paid you to go through my stuff."
Bishop sneered.

She paused for a moment. "Listen, I work for a security
company. I get gigs where I pretend to be a desk clerk, or
cleaning lady, or a secretary, and I dig up stuff. That's all.
No hard feelings?"

"No hard feelings. Can you tell me who you were
working for? Which company?"

"It won't get back to me? You won't rat me out?" She
asked, worried.

"No, I will tell them I found out some other way." Bishop
lied.

She hissed air. "All right. It was Knight Investigations.
They hired me."

"Knight? Bill Knight? He paid you to do this?" Bishop
spat.

"You know him? Shit. The bastard said you'd never clue
in. Stupid mother..." She growled.

"Where is he now?" Bishop asked.

"Probably in the office. He has a place on Yesler, near the Smith Tower."

"What's the address?" Bishop asked.

She gave him a street address and unit number, and Bishop hung up the phone.

He thanked the desk clerk for the use of the room and went back to the van.

The Smith Tower is one of the most iconic buildings in Seattle, as well-known to locals as the Space Needle. Bishop found the address Jeanie had given him; it was a modest three-story brick building that looked like it was once a factory, converted in the eighties to offices.

Knight Investigations had an office on the third floor, accessed by either a modern steel stairwell or by taking a tiny glass elevator. Bishop chose the stairs.

At the top of the stairs was a solid metal door, beside it about twenty different company names on a board, in alphabetical order. One of them said Knight Investigations. Bishop opened the door and went in.

There was a long corridor with offices on either side, one single desk just inside the door, and a harried-looking woman behind it, answering calls on a switchboard. She transferred a caller to somewhere, sighed with relief and looked up at Bishop.

"Yeah, hon, what can I do you for?" She smiled.

Bishop smiled back. "Hey there. I was hoping to talk to Bill Knight."

She leaned her elbows on the desk and rested her head in her hands. "You didn't just come up here to talk to me then?"

Bishop leaned closer to her. "Now that I think about it, that's the only reason I'm here."

She grinned. "Yeah, he's in his office, hon."

Bishop pointed to the corridor. "Remind me which one is his?"

She waved at a door on the left, partway down the hall. "Number six."

Bishop nodded thanks and followed the hallway to the door, then opened it without knocking.

Bill Knight had his back to the door, standing behind a wide desk and putting files into a metal cabinet. "Yeah, Cindy?" He said without looking.

"Hello again." Bishop said.

Knight spun around, a look of panic on his face. "Oh, shit." He muttered.

"Oh, shit, indeed. Why was Jeanie going through my stuff?" Bishop asked.

Knight sat down in an old leather chair. He motioned to the chair on the other side of the desk and Bishop sat. "I repeat, why was she going through my stuff?" Bishop said.

Knight rubbed his nose. "I told you that I got asked to look into Morrison's death. True. I was also asked, later on, to see whether you were running a false flag on this."

"You think I just pretended to look for the killer to throw suspicion from me?" Bishop asked.

Knight shrugged. "These guys can look at spaghetti on a plate and call it a straight line. They don't see things the way we do, trust me.

"I figured if I were to snoop through your stuff you'd stop me real quick, so I called one of my operatives to step in. Jeanie is very good at what she does. She did say, by the way, that she believes you're the real deal."

Bishop thought about this for a moment. "How did you find me? I changed cars, I used a fake name, I wasn't followed, and I didn't use my phone."

Knight smiled. "I heard from the cops that stopped you the other night. It's a good thing to have friends in blue. They said your Jeep was in the parking spot where a Saturn was supposed to be. Once they called in a missing vehicle report on that car, I put two and two together. I even drove past your motel to double check that you were still there, but I think you were asleep."

Knight leaned forward. "You went back to the warehouse. You took something away with you. Care to tell me what it was?"

"Not yet. In a while I will. Right now I'm waiting for a screaming phone call telling me to give it back."

"Any hints for me?" Knight asked.

Bishop thought for a moment. "Who do you know in Cambodia?"

Knight stiffened. "Go on."

"There is something in that warehouse that was being sold to someone in Cambodia. It's very valuable, and I don't know what it does. Is that any help?"

Knight turned around and pulled a file folder from the desk behind him. He opened it out for Bishop and pointed to a page.

"Sparwood owns a company in Cambodia. It's registered as an import-export business, dealing in replacement motorcycle parts and the like. Pretty sure it's just a front, but I have no idea what he could really be doing."

Bishop glanced at the page. "Right. Pretty standard stuff. Didn't Jeanie tell you what she found in my room?"

Knight squirmed in his seat. "She said there were three vials of what looked like urine or something. She assumed you were taking steroids. What were they?"

"The stuff that dreams are made of. I have no idea, but it was supposed to go to Cambodia."

"What do you mean 'was'?" Knight asked.

"Let's just say those items are MIA for now. The less you know the better."

Knight pushed away from the desk and stood up. "Fair enough. What will you do now?"

Bishop stood up as well. "As far as I know, the delivery is time sensitive. Sparwood said 'there's no room for error' about shipping the vials. If I can delay it, maybe he'll be screwed and then I can get to the bottom of this. Look, I'm not out to save the world here, I just want to get back to my real life, that's all. I've had enough excitement for five lifetimes. I don't need any more."

Knight stuck out his hand. "You know where to find me, and you know I'm here to help if I can."

Bishop shook his hand but didn't let go. "Care to tell me who paid you to sic Jeanie on me?"

Knight grinned. "Nobody local. A person in Colorado, with intimate ties to this case, and that's all I can tell you for now."

Bishop nodded and went back down the stairs to his van. The voice in his head started talking, softly at first then louder. Bishop looked around but couldn't see anything. He opened the driver door to the van.

From nowhere someone threw a hood over his head. He felt a hard metal object press against his back, and a voice whispered in his ear.

"Easy, easy. No heroics now, Captain. He just wants to ask you some questions, that's all."

Two people, men from the feel of their hands, took his arms and guided him into a vehicle. It must have been a big SUV- the step up to get in it told him that- and they held his arms, one on either side of him, until Bishop heard a metal tinkling sound. Someone put handcuffs on him.

The SUV started to move, slowly at first then briskly down the road. Bishop tried to determine which direction they were going by listening for the sound of passing over railroad tracks or other clues- ship noises, city buses, anything that could give him a bearing.

He couldn't make out any clues from his sea- no landmark noises, nothing. They drove for about twenty minutes, then there was the sound of a heavy garage door opening and the SUV rolled to a stop.

The two people pulled him out of the SUV, led him down a set of concrete steps, from the smell in the air, then another door opened, they guided him through it and sat him on a chair.

One person took a handcuff off one wrist and wrapped his arms behind the back of the chair then put the handcuff back on him. He was now sitting down, handcuffed behind his back.

The hood came off. General Sparwood glared at him, livid. Two guys were behind him, both burly, heavy muscle types. They said nothing.

Sparwood put his hands on his knees, leaned forward and sneered at Bishop.

"You're a fucking one-man disaster crew. You do know that, don't you?" He spat.

He leaned even closer. "You have stirred up shit in so many different ways, boy, and you don't have a shovel nearly big enough to dig yourself out of this mess."

Bishop smiled. "You don't have those vials anymore, do you?"

Sparwood stood up, leaned back and ran his fingers through his hair. "Look, what do you want? Are you trying to squeeze me, is that it? Do you want money?"

Bishop had a thought. "Yeah, I tell you what. Give me ten percent and I forget everything. Ten percent and I walk away. How does that sound?"

Sparwood snorted. "You expect me to just hand over two million dollars, just like that?"

Bishop smiled. "Thanks. Now I know how much it's worth to you. I wasn't sure before, until I heard you in your apartment, talking about selling the stuff. Now I know."

Sparwood turned bright red. "You think I'm just playing with you, boy? I will cut you into little pieces and you'll be crab shit in Elliot Bay by tonight. Think about it. You have nothing, no play here, no end game, no ace card. You're simply tied to a chair and I hold all the cards."

Bishop shook his head. "Wrong. If I'm not free in six hours, my colleagues will take every vial and destroy them. You will have nothing, and I suspect the people in Cambodia won't take too kindly to that."

Sparwood stood back and nodded to the two men. They glanced at each other and left the room. For the first time, Bishop was able to look around and survey where he was. His chair was in the middle of the floor, in what looked like the maintenance room of a building. There were plumbing supplies, jugs of bleach and drain cleaner, a rack of tools, all the things you needed to fix minor building issues.

The room had no windows, just one steel door with a deadbolt lock. Sparwood waited until the men had left and pulled a second chair to face Bishop. This was interrogation class one-oh-one, Bishop thought. Here comes the good cop, the soft pitch.

Sparwood knitted his fingers together and collected his thoughts.

"Now, I know you think I'm doing everything I've done just for personal gain. That's simply not the case. I've been asked to run a covert op to flush out some people who want to hurt our country. The vials are bait for the big fish, that's all. You have to believe that." He implored.

Bishop looked down and sighed. If Sparwood could pretend that this was a legitimate, sanctioned operation, Bishop could pretend to believe him.

"Listen, I've also been sent down into some dirty holes and come up smelling of shit. I get that. But why did Morrison have to die?" Bishop asked.

Sparwood rubbed his nose. "Well, son, he only knew half the story. He thought that we were really selling secrets to the Commies. That much was our fault- everyone was supposed to think we were. The people above me, though, were in on the full story. As soon as we deliver those vials, it sets off a chain reaction that cripples the entities that use them. I was never meant to keep the money. It was just a smokescreen. It just made my role in this affair believable."

Bishop didn't believe a word of it. Still, he decided to go along with the story for the moment.

"So, what about Saks and Kendall? Why did you kill them?"

Sparwood thought for a moment. "Carlisle is a Marine, and he doesn't do half a job. He thought they were a threat to the operation, and he took it upon himself to finish the job. Losing them was unfortunate, but it did make this op more legitimate, so their deaths served a purpose."

Bishop remembered Sparwood say that he was expected to eliminate Carlisle after this was over. He said nothing about it.

"So what is in those vials, then?" Bishop asked.

Sparwood smiled. "How badly do you want to know?"

"Not badly enough to die for it. How did you find me, by the way?"

Sparwood stood up and moved the second chair away. "We've been watching Knight ever since the warehouse people said that you both showed up in the same week. Do you like Thai food? We're ordering in some lunch. If you have a favorite dish, let me know."

"Couldn't we go out for it?" Bishop joked.

Sparwood chuckled. "Sit tight. We'll be back in five minutes."

Bishop sighed and leaned back, relaxing. "Fine. Lots of brown rice, no lemongrass."

Sparwood went out the steel door and locked it behind him. Bishop looked around, scanning the room for anything that could help him. No windows, one locked door, no closets, no garbage shaft. No way out except through the door.

The two beefy guys had handcuffed him to the chair, but Bishop was able to stand and lift his arms out of the way over the chair back. That was a rookie mistake on their part.

He squatted down and slipped the handcuffs under his feet. Now his arms were in front of him. He went to a bench at one end of the room and found some tools. There was a hacksaw- he could cut off the cuffs, but it would take too long. There was a grinder bolted to the bench- faster, but too noisy. Then he found a pin-on name tag, a four-inch metal rectangle that read 'Gary- Building Services'. He bent out the pin and slid it under the ratchet of the handcuff. The handcuff popped open. He slid the cuff off his wrist and did the same for his other hand.

He put the cuffs in his pocket and looked around for more things he could use. The room was concrete, but the ceiling was covered with acoustic tile. There was a large square vent in the ceiling, a duct that went somewhere. Could he get out that way?

He slid the chair under the vent and stood on it, pried the cover up and looked in. No way. It was far too small, and in any case the duct looked like it might collapse under his weight.

Option number two; he put the chair back where it was, found a bucket and filled it halfway with drain cleaner. He waited till he heard someone coming, then quickly poured bleach onto the drain cleaner and sat back in the chair with his hands behind his back.

The chemicals mixed to make a bubbling hot liquid and produced chlorine gas, as Bishop knew they would. He closed his eyes and held his breath, waiting. A few seconds later the door opened, and one of the beefy men came in. He gasped and coughed, covered his mouth with his hand and called to someone outside. The second man rushed in and tilted back Bishop's head.

Bishop pretended to be unconscious. The two men carried him out of the room and dumped him on the ground. The first one was still hacking and coughing and staggered under the effect of the chlorine gas. He fell over.

The second one dragged him out and went back in, holding his breath, to get rid of the bucket.

They had their backs to Bishop. He ran up the same stairs they'd brought him down and out into the bright daylight. Where was he, though?

He found himself outside an industrial building somewhere in Chinatown, from the looks of the area. He figured he had maybe thirty seconds before Sparwood and his goons discovered him missing and came looking for him.

They were not very careful- they hadn't taken his phone away- but Bishop couldn't just put the battery in and call for help. He had no time. There was a noodle restaurant across the street, with a laundromat and a boarded-up property beside that, with plywood over its windows.

Bishop ran towards the plywood-covered building, went around to the side and found a door where the plywood had been pried away. Squatters had stayed here, he guessed. Hopefully they weren't here now.

He squeezed behind the plywood and into the building. It was once an office building, it seemed, with a long wide corridor and cubicles on either side. Bishop looked into the offices, found one that didn't look trashed and sat at the desk. There was a phone on the desk; he picked it up but there was no dial tone. He opened the desk drawers, looking for something to inspire him. Nothing but a few paper clips and a broken stapler.

Apparently, the squatters had ransacked the place for anything saleable. Bishop pulled out his phone, deciding who he should call, then stopped. A sound from the front door got his attention. He looked around the desk again and found a flat plastic business card case. It was chromed, and it made an almost perfect mirror.

Bishop crept to the door of the office and held the case, just poking out the door. Reflected in the chrome he saw one of Sparwood's men, the one who had fallen over, walking down the corridor, peering into offices. He was holding a gun in his hand, pointed down at the ground, with his finger wrapped around the trigger guard.

Bishop picked up the stapler from the desk and waited till the man was looking in a side office. He threw the stapler down the hall, pressed himself low inside the door and waited.

The man walked quickly past the offices, glancing briefly in as he did. When he got to the office where Bishop was waiting, Bishop stepped forward and punched the man hard in the jaw.

The big man staggered backwards, his arms flailing out. His gun fell on the ground and clattered to a stop by Bishop's feet.

The man was flat on his back, glaring angrily as Bishop calmly picked up the gun and checked the clip for bullets. He slid the clip back into the pistol and squatted down to face the man.

"Forty caliber Glock. Nice piece. I can use this." Bishop said.

The man stared at him, the angry look melting to fear. "You don't need to do this, you know."

It was the first time Bishop had heard his voice. It was raspy, almost childlike, but with an edge.

"You think I whacked those people? Is that what Sparwood told you? I didn't." Bishop said.

The man's shoulders softened slightly. "Really? Convince me."

Bishop shook his head. "Car keys, please."

The man fumbled through his pocket and pulled out a set of keys. He tossed them to Bishop.

Bishop glanced at the keys. "Toyota? What kind, and where is it?"

The man scowled. "The green Camry around the corner, on Maynard Street."

Bishop took the handcuffs out of his pocket. "One to your wrist, one to your ankle." He said.

The man seemed to know what to do next. He took his cell and slid it towards Bishop without being asked. He clipped the handcuff to his wrist and ankle, as instructed.

Bishop picked the man's phone up. "This will be at the entrance of the building. Don't leave this office till I'm gone, and then you can call for help."

"When can I get my car back?" The man asked.

"Tomorrow. And your gun will be in the trunk." Bishop answered.

The man smiled slightly. "You're being a real stand-up guy, huh? A true professional."

Bishop shrugged. "I'm not the enemy here. Whatever he told you, I think Sparwood is screwing you over. He's responsible for at least three deaths, maybe more. You decide for yourself."

The man leaned back. "Good luck, Captain."

Chapter 12: Shelter in Place

Bishop found the Camry by clicking the button on the remote until he heard a 'beep' from down the street. He drove back to the van, took his tote bag from under the seat, and checked that his gun and money were there, along with the Flytrap package.

He locked the Camry's key and the Glock in the trunk, then walked away from both vehicles.

There are ways to hide in a big city that don't attract attention. Bishop considered his options. The weather was not warm enough to camp out with the homeless in a park, and if any of the homeless people went through his bag he'd lose the gun and anything else of value.

He could book into a hotel or a motel, but he didn't have enough cash to last more than a week or so in a nice hotel, and they might check his fake ID.

He could leave town until the time ran out for the deal, but then losing this sale would probably make Sparwood homicidal, he thought.

One thing people never look for, he decided, is what is already gone. He turned on his cell phone and dialed a number. Sparwood answered in one ring.

"John, what a pleasure to hear from you." He said it cordially, but with an edge.

"Yeah, you know what, General, I've decided to flush your stuff down the crapper and leave town for a month. I just wanted you to know that." Bishop drawled.

Sparwood put the phone close to his mouth and hissed. "Listen to me, you gutless piece of shit. If you think this is over, it's not. You wanted two million, I could have given it to you. But now, now, you dumb fuckhead, now I will hunt you down and kill you slowly. Give me back my stuff, do you hear? GIVE ME BACK MY STUFF!!"

Bishop could imagine Sparwood turning beet red as he screamed. He smiled, pleased.

"Yeah, well, you're going to have to bundle up if you want to catch me. I think I'll do some salmon fishing in Alaska for the next month. A friend of mine owns a lodge near Ketchikan."

There was a pause for a moment. Sparwood sighed. "Look, John, I realise we've gotten off on the wrong foot here. You obviously know this is a valuable interaction, but you can't imagine the political importance of this sale. I'm begging you, *imploring you*, where are those vials?"

"How about if you hand Carlisle over to the cops?" Bishop asked.

"Why would I do that?"

Bishop gritted his teeth. "He killed three people. One of them was my CO's son. You want your shit back, turn him in. Otherwise bring a fishing rod and join me."

"Carlisle is a decorated Marine. Why would I just throw him to the wolves? How can I trust that you'll keep your end of the bargain?" Sparwood asked.

"I heard you say you expected me to kill him. Think of this as the next best thing. You have no proof that I'll keep my end of the bargain, no. But I will promise you this; if you don't hand him over, and you come after me, if I even so much as think I hear you, I will burn you. Do you understand?"

Sparwood sighed. "I understand. Hands off you forever. Now, when can I get my items back?"

"First, you will have Carlisle arrested. Call Detective Ziggy Porezki at the Seattle Police Department. I'll text you his number. Next, wait for my call and I'll tell you where you can pick up your stuff. I'll be in Alaska. You won't find me once I get there."

Sparwood blew air out into space. "Fine. Just so you know, if you cross me, so help me…"

"That's the pot calling the kettle black, General. I got sucked into this. I just wanted to go to work and live my life. You people made this into what it is."

Sparwood grunted. "Get back to me as soon as you hear that Dwayne is in custody. Don't go cowboy on me, Bishop."

"You keep to your end, I'll keep to mine." Bishop said.

Sparwood grunted. "Yeah, yeah, well, fuck you, Captain."

"Fuck you too, General." Bishop hung up.

Bishop dialed another familiar number. "Detective Porezki, please." He said.

A moment later Porezki came on. "Hi, John. Where are we at?"

"You should be getting a call shortly from a retired General. He's going to hand you the man who killed those three people, on his orders. The killer's name is Dwayne Carlisle."

Bishop spelled it. He could hear Porezki scribbling furiously. "So, why is this guy frying his own people, exactly?" Porezki asked.

"The General is handing Carlisle over in exchange for something I promised to give him back. Something worth twenty million dollars, that he's going to sell in Cambodia." Bishop said.

"Well, that explains it. Why didn't I think of that?" Porezki joked.

He was silent for a moment. "Are we expecting that this Carlisle person will disappear into a black van as well, or do we get to keep him?"

"I believe we're getting him as payment for the stuff the General wants. He was considered expendable, in any case. The General expected me to kill him as a matter of course."

Porezki sniffed. "Would you have?"

"Would you?" Bishop asked. "No, I didn't think so."

Porezki sighed. "So, what next?"

Bishop scratched his head, thinking. "I have no idea. I don't want to hand over this thing he wants to sell, but I have no idea who to contact that has any jurisdiction over it. So, I just have to stay alive for the next week or so."

"Need a place to stay?" Porezki offered.

"I'll find one. Nowhere I can tell you about, but thanks for the offer." Bishop said.

He turned off the phone and put it into his tote. Time to get small, lay low and wait, he thought.

The city had a very good transport system. There was the monorail, ridden mostly by tourists and drunks sleeping it off, and there were the buses. The bus was where you could sit for an hour and be anonymous, especially if, like Bishop, you looked a little worse for wear just then.

He checked the schedule on a board bolted to a bus stop pole and took the next bus that came. It took him all the way to Pier 50, by the ferry terminal. Bishop bought a ticket for the first ferry to leave, heading over to Bremerton. Once abord he found a quiet bench near the middle of the boat and slumped against a wall, his eyes closed. Tourists were more likely to talk to him if he was awake, but if it looked like he was sleeping, they were more likely to leave him alone. The trip took about an hour, and twenty minutes into the passage he decided to eat something.

He bought a burger and a coke from the onboard diner, then joined the rest of the pedestrians when the boat docked, filing off in an anonymous surge of people.

Bremerton is primarily a navy town, with the shipyards and the local hotels catering to many sailors and tourists who came over. Bishop wanted to find somewhere to stay where he could be invisible, but close enough to the ferry that he could get back to Seattle quickly.

It took him about twenty minutes, walking down a residential street, to find a house with a sign out front that said 'Rooms for Rent'.

The house was older, one of those post-war clapboard houses with a wide bay window and a set of steps up to a front porch. Bishop walked up the steps to the house's screen door, deciding on the story he'd tell the owner.

He pressed the button next to the screen door and waited. He heard the sound of thumping, of feet pounding over wooden floors, and waited some more.

A minute later, a woman opened the inner door and looked at him, leaving the screen door closed.

She was in her late sixties, it seemed, pear shaped and frowning, wearing a velour track suit jacket over a pair of faded jeans. She scanned him up and down, scowling as she did so.

"Yes?" She asked sharply.

"Hi, you have a room for rent?" Bishop asked.

"Yes." The woman answered.

Bishop waited for a painful length of time. She said nothing more.

"Can I ask about the room?" He prompted.

"What is there to ask?" She snapped.

Clearly, this is why she had vacancies, Bishop thought.

"For instance, is it private, how much is it, do you have internet?" Bishop said.

The woman sighed, impatient. "Come with me."

She waved her hand behind her as she turned, and Bishop followed her.

They walked up a flight of wooden stairs on one side of the hallway, turned around at the top of the stairs and followed a narrow hallway upstairs to a dark oak door at the end of the hall.

The woman threw open the door and gestured with her hand.

"Bed, dresser; shower and toilet are through there. We have no internet, not for the roomers, in any case. I watch television every night, and you're welcome to watch with me, but I turn it off at eight, right after the news."

Bishop nodded approval. The room was small, sparse, but clean and smelled of linen and pine cleaner. It would do fine.

"This looks good. I only need a room for a week, then I'm scheduled to ship out." He lied.

She looked at him, her hazel eyes trying to read him. "What branch are you in?" She asked.

"I'm afraid I can't tell you that, ma'am." He answered.

She looked at him for a long time then sniffed, satisfied. "A hundred fifty dollars for the week. You may use the kitchen as long as you only consume your own food, and I expect it to be clean once you're done. Is that agreeable, mister…?"

Bishop nodded. "That's fine. Scott. My name is Randall Scott."

She looked at him hard, again, then nodded. "Let's go with that one, shall we?"

"I can show you my driver's license. It proves that I'm Randall Scott." Bishop protested.

"I can show you one that says I'm Queen Mary." She countered.

Bishop smiled. "You were an English teacher, right?"

Her face softened somewhat. "How did you guess?"

"'Queen Mary'. Earlier you said I 'may' use the kitchen, not I 'can' use the kitchen."

She actually smiled. "Very shrewd, young man. I'm impressed. By the way, my name is Mrs. Tyler, but you may call me Vivian."

"Is there a mister Tyler?" Bishop asked.

"Why, are you lonely?" She joked.

Bishop laughed. "I was sure there was a warm person under that shell, and I was right."

She smiled again. "I have a suspicion we will get along quite well, young man."

She gave Bishop a key to the front door, admonished him that there was no drinking, drugs, hookers or fires allowed, then took his money and pointed out the nearest restaurants.

Bishop placed his spare clothes in a small dresser in the room, hid the Flytrap package and his gun in an obscure corner of a closet, and lay on the bed, trying to decide what to do next.

He didn't like just hiding, he realized. He was much more comfortable doing something, anything, but all he could do now was wait for Carlisle to be arrested then figure out how to snag the General.

He took a power nap to clear his head, then tried to decide when to head back to Seattle. If he went back now, Carlisle might still be free, and would probably go after him.

If he stayed where he was, he could wait out the timeline for the sale, but the General might not have turned over Carlisle until he got his vials back, despite what he promised to do.

But, the general would turn Carlisle over as soon as possible, Bishop reasoned, because then he could get his vials back faster that way. Wait till after dinner then call Porezki, Bishop thought. What to do until then, though? It was only three in the afternoon.

He went for a walk, stopping to look in store windows every so often, looking at the reflection of people behind him to see if he was being followed. So far, so good.

There was a movie theater in town, one of those multiplex things with a dozen screens, and they were showing a few new releases and some older movies, most of which Bishop didn't recognize. He decided on some romantic comedy, starring people he'd never heard of, and bought a ticket.

Bishop sat through the two hours of the movie, munched popcorn, sipped soda, then checked his watch and turned on his phone.

He dialed Porezki and waited. Three seconds later, Porezki answered "Bishop? That you?"

"Hey, Ziggy. Any news yet?" Bishop asked.

Porezki was shuffling paper, from the sound he heard. "Yeah, listen, when you make shit fly, you put it in orbit. Know what I mean?"

"I'm at a complete loss as to what you mean, Detective." Bishop said.

"Okay. First, your killer, Carlisle. We got him handed to us by that General. We picked him up at the Society for the something of something. He came without a fuss, mostly because he thinks he has a 'get out of jail' card. We have him in lockup. About two milliseconds after we booked him, I get a call from somebody in DC asking to speak to you. What is going on, Bishop?"

"Damned if I know. All I can say is that the stuff I'm holding must be very valuable for someone besides the General. Did they say who they were?"

"Better than that. They left a number for you to call them. And a name. Admiral Hubert Glass. Does that name ring a bell?"

Bishop thought hard. "No, that doesn't register at all, no. Fine, what's the number?"

Porezki read out a phone number. Bishop repeated it and said he'd get back once he knew what was happening.

Bishop wondered what to do. Was this another trap to lure him in, or would it help resolve the issue? He dialed the number and waited. Three rings later, a voice came on.

"Hello, is this Captain Bishop?" The voice said.

It sounded older, tired, but with force behind it. Bishop took a deep breath.

"Yes, this is Bishop. Who are you?"

"My name is Admiral Hubert Glass. You can call me Admiral Glass, or if you prefer, just Hugh. Thank you for returning my call, Captain." He said in a smooth voice.

Bishop was unconvinced. "My pleasure, Admiral. Can I ask what you want from me?"

The man moved in his chair, from a squeaking sound, and got comfortable. "I can understand your reluctance to speak, Captain. You've been given a number of bad headings lately."

"One could say that, yes. For instance, how do I know you really are Admiral Glass, or that there really *is* an Admiral Glass?"

The man chuckled. "They said you were careful. I see they were right. You had a CO in your last deployment, a Colonel Baruch. Do you remember him?"

"I remember him very well. He is a good officer."

"He speaks well of you as well. If you like, we can speak to him and confirm that I am who I say I am. He's in our Bethesda office right now, working with the Navy on a joint project. Would it give you confidence in what I have to say if you spoke to him first?"

"It would, if it really was him I was speaking with." Bishop said.

"I admire your caution, Captain. Please hold the line."

The phone clicked, and Bishop heard nothing. A few seconds later, he heard a familiar voice.

"Baruch." It said, simply.

That was how he always answered the phone. Bishop wanted more proof. "Colonel, it's John Bishop."

"Hey, Bish, how are you doing?" The voice said.

"Doing well, sir. I'm talking with an Admiral Glass. Do you know him?"

"Hugh Glass? Yes, good guy, deep into stuff you and I skimmed the surface on. Why?"

"Should I trust him on a very sensitive matter?"

There was a pause. "Are we talking about Flytrap, Bish?"

Bishop thought for a moment. "What can you tell me about it?"

The man at the other end sighed. "Officially, it doesn't exist. Unofficially, it doesn't exist. Further up the food chain, ask Admiral Glass."

Bishop sighed. "Don't take it the wrong way, but how do I know you're really Colonel Baruch?"

The man laughed. "I still owe you eleven dollars and fifty cents. I spilled hot chocolate on your dress jacket, and you had to have it dry cleaned before a parade. I never paid you back."

Bishop smiled. "What did I say when you spilled the hot chocolate?"

The other man laughed again. "You complained that I'd eaten all the marshmallows before I spilled it."

Bishop laughed. "Thanks, sir. You're right, nobody else could know that."

"Good speaking with you, Bish. Don't be a stranger." He hung up.

"Likewise, Colonel." Bishop said to himself.

The other voice came on. "Now, Captain, can we meet to discuss the next steps?"

"All right. Where and when do you want to meet?"

"Are you in downtown Seattle?" The man asked.

"Yes." Bishop lied.

"I'm currently at the Navy base in Bremerton." The man said.

"I see, and are you coming to meet me in Seattle?" Bishop asked.

"I rather thought you might meet me here." The man said.

"I could be there in three hours." Bishop offered.

"Or, since you're actually down the street from us, you could be here in ten minutes."

That shocked him. "You're pinging my phone? What am I getting myself into?" Bishop said.

The voice sighed. "Look, you've been jerked around, shafted, threatened and had the crap kicked out of your life for days now. How about we get this thing dealt with and let you get back to normal?"

"I'd like that very much. How do I know you're not going to stick me in a dark hole for the next week?" Bishop asked.

"That's a valid point. There's a park in the area, Evergreen Rotary Park. If you walk to the very end of Sheldon Boulevard, there's a boat ramp there, with picnic benches. I'll be on the bench in twenty minutes. I will wait for exactly ten minutes. If you aren't here in that time, I will assume you don't want our help, and we'll have to proceed without you." The voice clicked off.

Bishop thought about what to do. If they could trace his phone, they could pick him up anytime. He would not be in any greater danger, he reasoned, by meeting the Admiral.

Bishop decided to go back to his room and get his gun. If there was a confrontation it would make it more possible for him to survive. He jogged out of the house and walked towards the park. The Admiral was right, it was less than a ten-minute walk. Just outside the park was a church, and Bishop stopped in the church parking lot, looking for anyone suspicious. He waited five minutes, decided it was safe, and went through to the bench by the boat ramp. He was listening for his little voice, but it was silent.

As Bishop approached the bench, he saw a man sitting there. He looked average height, older, with salt and pepper grey hair and a casual sweater over a khaki shirt. Bishop noticed the shoes; they were polished to a mirror black, poking out from tan slacks.

The man had a manila folder on the bench, his hand on it in case the wind picked up. Bishop looked around for anyone hiding behind a tree or a billboard; nothing like that stood out.

He sat across from the man and nodded. "You're Admiral Glass?" He asked.

The man held out his hand. "Captain Bishop. I see your reputation is well earned."

Bishop frowned. "Come again?"

"Lieutenant Morrison chose you as the recipient of some very strategic information." He said.

"And now you want it back?" Bishop asked.

"Heavens, no. We don't care. It's accurate to say that if you released it today it would be embarrassing, but if you release it in ten days it's old news. Have you not reviewed the data?"

"I have not. People have died because of seeing it." Bishop said.

The man shook his head. "Very wise. You were told that Morrison lost his life because he told the wrong person about Flytrap, is that not so?"

"Yes. That's what I was told." Bishop said.

"We all expected that Morrison would leak the information, and he did what we thought he would do. Having him put it out the way he did made it believable."

Bishop was confused. "I don't get it. He told a lie, because you thought he would tell this lie, but then he was killed because of that?"

The man smiled and leaned back. "We wish our enemies to believe we have something of great value, something that they want. We had arranged for one of our retired senior staff to 'steal' this information and sell it to those who wish us harm. Unfortunately, before we could implement that plan, your friend General Sparwood had the same idea. The trouble is, he is unaware that what he's selling is of less than no value."

Bishop shook his head. "I had the contents of one of those vials tested. The material in them is very valuable. It's not worthless."

The man nodded. "In your world, twenty or thirty million dollars is substantial. The game we're playing, though, has much higher stakes. Think of it as costing the government far less than deploying a carrier group for a day."

"So you were trying to convince someone to buy something that's useless? Why? What was it supposed to do?"

The man opened the manila folder and pulled out a photograph. It was blurry, indistinct. It meant nothing to Bishop.

"In the eighties, our government bought a few gallons of special paint from the Japanese. It's what they used in a microwave oven to reflect its energy. We were testing ways to make airplanes stealthier. In any case, it took months of negotiating and eventually a resolution from the Japanese Diet, their parliament, to permit the sale. We decided to never again be in the position that we were dependent on a foreign consumer manufacturer for our security."

"So, Flytrap is something to benefit Navy pilots?" Bishop asked.

"Aviators, son, aviators. The Navy doesn't have mere pilots, we have aviators." He said sternly.

He shook his head. "Imagine that you can make an airplane, or a boat, or a submarine, invisible to radar. Right now our best effort gives our fighters the radar cross section of a pigeon. Imagine if we could get it down to the size of a golf ball. That's what Flytrap is all about."

"And we're selling this to our enemies because why?" Bishop asked.

"Because we have the ability to get around it. Imagine if a Shenyang fighter jet is painted with this stuff, and the Chinese try sneaking over the border. Our radar will light it up like a Christmas tree."

"I still don't get it. Why was I sent the Flytrap information in the first place?" Bishop asked.

The man sighed. "A number of people received parts of the package. The hope was that they would accidentally or intentionally turn their data over to the other side. That would make the sale seem even more believable. Nobody did, though. Your people decoded the letter and went on the Pentagon website that red-screened them. That's as far as that trail went, by the way. That letter was also a ruse on our part. Morrison sent the entire package to you because he was given the impression that someone was selling our country's secrets, and he wanted you to act on it. We wanted him to think that was true for the next few weeks, then we were going to tell him the truth. Unfortunately for Morrison, Sparwood found the data through back channels, and he thought it was legitimate. He decided to cash in, but for that Morrison had to die."

"What about Colonel Saks, and why shoot the General's driver, Kendall?" Bishop asked.

"Saks was one of the architects of the scheme. She was trying to arrange a final meeting with Kendall. His job, in part, was to report back to her. That's why she was in your friend's apartment. Sparwood found out where she went, and he sent someone to kill her first. Kendall, I think, must have overheard Sparwood negotiating the sale of the vials. He realised he was on the wrong side of the fence after he moved Morrison's body, so he asked us to send him home the day after Saks was shot, but unfortunately we couldn't get him out in time."

"He did say he was going to Langley the next day. I guess that was him trying to tell me he was clean. Still, why would Carlisle go along with all this? He was a good Marine." Bishop said.

"Agreed. He was initially on board with everything Sparwood was doing. He truly believed that Sparwood was trying to prevent the sale of secrets to our enemies. I believe that since he's been in custody, though, he has had a change of heart."

Bishop looked down and digested the information, mentally weeding out bullshit from reality.

"You know, this could all be a very elaborate ploy on Sparwood's part to convince me to hand over his stuff. How do I know you really are who you say you are?"

The older man leaned back and smiled. "How do you know this is not a ploy to get you to turn over the material to me, and have me pass it on to Sparwood? Call your Dean. He knows me too. By the way, 'Aunt Muriel' is an old code. Ah, and the Dean also says that Mrs. Otagawa's daughter still wants to get paid for not cleaning your house."

Bishop chuckled. "Fine, now I believe you. How should I proceed from here?"

The man closed the manila folder. "Call your police friend, Detective Porezki. He'll confirm that Sergeant Carlisle is in custody. Then tell Sparwood where the material is. We'll do the rest."

"What are you going to do?" Bishop asked.

"We'll let him sell the material, then we'll charge him with espionage and murder. We'll get him for the deaths, plus it makes the whole enchilada more believable."

Bishop thought about it for a moment. "Are you the person who hired Bill Knight?" He asked.

The man laughed and rested one elbow on the bench. "Very good. You connected the dots. Yes, he knew Lieutenant Morrison personally. We thought he might help us catch Sergeant Carlisle, but as it happens he was only able to find you. You did the grunt work on this mission, Captain."

Bishop looked out at the boat dock, watching with detachment at a man steering a small speedboat onto a trailer in the water. The trailer was hitched to a pickup truck, and the driver of the pickup, another man with a look of puzzled concern on his face, waved his hands to guide the boat into place on the trailer.

Bishop turned to look at Glass. "This whole thing is pure bullshit, isn't it?"

The Admiral smiled slowly, enjoying a private joke. "I'm not quite sure I understand, Captain."

Bishop snickered. "Yes you do. This is snake oil. This stuff doesn't work, none of it. It's all fake."

Glass looked at Bishop with an expression of amusement and admiration. "Why would you say that? Why would we go to all this bother for something that doesn't work?"

Bishop looked back at the boat on the trailer. "We used to tell the Iraqis that our drones could see through walls. The ones who believed us moved their weapons around, and it made it easier to find them that way. That made them believe the lie even more. So tell me, why would we spend time and money building something that doesn't work? Surely the Chinese and the North Koreans have good enough chemists that they can spot the scam."

Glass knit his fingers together and wrapped them around one knee. He leaned back, holding his knee in the air. "Do you ever wonder why this operation was called Flytrap?" He asked.

"I was told it was a random name, that it didn't pertain to anything." Bishop answered.

The Admiral shook his head. "Not so. We called it that because we were trying to catch all the flies at once. We are targeting the people who buy the items, the ones who are the middlemen, the brokers, the shippers, all of them. Every one of them believes that the liquid in those vials does what we told people that it does. Everyone except you. As I say, Sparwood jumped in and did what we were going to do anyway, but he killed three innocent people in the process."

Bishop smiled. "Yeah, that makes far more sense. What does the liquid do, really?"

The Admiral laughed. "I have no idea. It's corrosive, and fluorescent. Beyond that, no idea."

Bishop thought for a moment. "Tell you what. I'm happy to go along with your little scheme here, but I do have one request."

"Name it, Captain."

"I will hand over the vials to Sparwood, but I'll do it in my own way."

The Admiral leaned back and eyed him. "Explain." He said.

"He has to believe that I'm not simply rolling over. He'll smell a rat if he thinks I'm just giving him the stuff free and clear."

The Admiral smiled. "What do you have in mind?"

"Money. If I ask him for money, he'll believe it's sincere, ironically."

Glass nodded. "I see. How do you intend to proceed?"

"Leave that to me. I have your phone number, and I'll let you know when I've done the deal. What do you want me to do after I give him the vials?"

He got very serious. "Nothing. Absolutely nothing. We want Sparwood to deliver those vials to the middleman in Cambodia. That's all you need to know."

Bishop shook his head. "Cambodia does not have a very large air force. Why would they want to spend all that money on useless technology?"

"They will sell it on to other, less friendly, but more affluent countries. Those countries will then spend a considerable amount of time and resources to discover they've been duped, and everyone down the line will face harsh consequences." The Admiral explained.

Bishop chuckled. "It's like when you set out ant poison, and they bring it back to the nest."

The Admiral smiled. "Very good. Precisely that, yes. Keep me posted, Captain. Good day."

He stood up and walked toward the parking lot. A large black SUV appeared from nowhere and stopped. The Admiral got in and the SUV sped off, out of sight.

Bishop sat for a long time, watching the same two men struggle with the speedboat, trying to winch it onto its trailer, yelling at each other as the boat slid back into the water then was finally cranked up onto the trailer's rollers. The men got into the pickup truck and drove away.

Bishop walked back to the rooming house, deciding how to do what he wanted to do next.

He greeted his landlady, declined her offer of a cup of tea and went up to his room. He made some notes in a small book, took a deep breath, and dialed a number.

"Detective Porezki." The voice said.

"Hey, it's Bishop. Do you have Dwayne Carlisle in custody yet?"

Porezki took a deep breath. "Yeah, thanks for that. We went into his office and arrested him, and for some unknown reason he didn't resist or complain or anything.

He's already confessed to the killing of Morrison, that Saks woman and the driver, Kendall. He's claiming it was under orders, though. Says he's not really guilty."

"He's not wrong there. Listen, you may or may not be able to arrest the person who ordered the shooting. I'll have to let you know."

Porezki groaned. "Will we need to build an addition to the morgue?"

"Not if I can help it. Listen, keep Carlisle in the dark. You may need his unbiased testimony later. Meanwhile, I have some work to do. I'll get back to you later."

Bishop scrolled through his phone and dialed another number. He waited for a few seconds.

Two rings later he heard "Knight investigations."

"Bill, it's John Bishop. I have some news for you."

Knight sighed. "Hey, John. Is any of it good news?"

"Yeah. How would you like to earn a bunch of money?"

Knight paused for a few seconds. "Go on."

Chapter 13: Frontal Attack

Bishop dialed a number and waited. Five seconds later, Sparwood picked up the phone.

"Hello?" the General said, anxious.

"I understand you kept your end of the bargain. The police have arrested Carlisle." Bishop said.

Sparwood sounded relieved. "I have done what I agreed to do. Now, are you going to keep to your part of the agreement?"

Bishop smiled to himself. "You offered me two million dollars for those vials. I'd like it now."

Sparwood moved closer to the phone mouthpiece and whispered. "Listen, I don't have that kind of money, not right now, not anywhere close to that right now. But if you wait till I get paid I will give you the money. I swear."

Bishop laughed. "Pardon me if I don't believe that, General. Once you get what you want there's not a reason in hell to pay me. What could I do- take you to court?"

Sparwood let out a soft moan. "Look, I can raise maybe… maybe just a hundred thousand, if that. I will get you the rest once I get paid. A hundred thousand- that's nothing to sneeze at, you must agree. What do you say?"

"How long?" Bishop asked.

"Pardon?"

"How long will it take you to get that money for me?"

Sparwood sounded desperate. "Um, ah, oh. How about two hours? I can send it to your bank account in two hours. Will that do?"

Bishop almost felt bad for the General. He was clearly in over his head now. His plan to sell the vials had gone wrong, and he was certainly worried that he might not get them back in time.

Bishop huffed. "Two hours. Here's the bank account number it goes into. As soon as I have that money, I'll give you the address of the place where the vials are. After that, I will wait to hear from you after you get paid. No tricks, understand? I'll be watching for any double cross."

Sparwood spoke quickly, nervously. "No, no tricks, John, no tricks. You have my word. Call me as soon as you get the money."

Bishop sat on the edge of the bed, waiting. Ninety minutes later, his phone rang.

"Hello?" He said.

"Hey, it's Bill. I just received a hundred grand. Can I keep it?" Knight said, cheerily.

"Sure. I may want three or four thousand for expenses, though." Bishop joked.

Knight laughed. "Certainly. So, what do we do now?"

Bishop leaned forward. "I left the van I was driving by your place. It's a piece of crap with 'Custom Auto Upholstery' written somewhere under the paint. In the glove box is the key to a padlock. Take the key to the front desk of the Society for Environmental Enhancement, where you went before. Tell the girl at the desk that General Sparwood needs this, then get out fast."

Knight wrote something down. "What is the key for?" He asked.

"I'll explain that to you later. Right now, the less you know the better. Let me know when you've dropped it off."

Bishop took off his shoes and lay on the bed. He felt drained by the day. He closed his eyes and let his mind wander.

Olivia was out of town. Pity, he liked her. Jeanie was around though, and probably still at the motel. Maybe he could call her. They go out for dinner once he was back in Seattle. Maybe.

He woke up an hour later, to the sound of a buzzing phone. He sat up straight.

"Bishop." He said.

"Hey. I've left that key at the reception desk, like you asked. I'm outside the building now, sitting on a bench. What's next?"

Bishop rubbed hie eyes. "Nothing. The person who paid you to investigate Morrison's death is an Admiral. He knows what's going on. From here on, just go home. Your part in this is done."

"Do I get to keep the hundred grand?" He asked.

"As far as I'm concerned, yes. I'll keep you posted."

Bishop hung up and dialed a number. The phone rang once.

"Yes?" Sparwood said, quickly.

"I just left a key with your receptionist. It's for the locker where I put your stuff."

Sparwood let out a sigh of relief. "Where is it?" He asked.

Bishop told him the address of the storage unit, had Sparwood repeat it, and confirmed it.

"Just so you know, General, I don't really think I'll get any more money from you." Bishop said.

"No?" the General asked, amused.

"I expect that if I tried, you'd just kill me. Let's just say that the money I got was my finder's fee and leave it at that, shall we?"

Sparwood laughed. "Agreed. If you leave me alone, I have no reason to wish you further harm."

"Happy to hear that. Goodbye, General." Bishop hung up.

Bishop stretched out on the bed again. It was not uncomfortable, but it was not as comfortable as his own mattress, in his own bed, and he missed the routine of his own life. He would stay here overnight, he thought, and go home in the morning. By then Sparwood would have other things on his mind, and Bishop could go back to his routine, back to his normal routine.

One of the things he learned in the army was how to get some rest when he needed to. Going into battle half asleep or fatigued was a good way to ensure that you'd make mistakes. He closed his eyes and took a nap.

At six in the evening, Bishop told Mrs. Tyler that he would be leaving in the morning, but she could keep the week's rent. That both pleased and intrigued her.

Bishop walked along the street, looking for a restaurant, somewhere he could eat quietly and think. He just wanted this week to be over.

He dialed a number and waited for three rings. Sparwood answered. "Yes, Captain?" He said.

"Did you get what you needed?" Bishop asked.

"I did. Thank you. I trust you will remove my number from your phone?"

"Right away. I can promise you I will not contact you again." Bishop said.

He turned off his phone. There was a sign up ahead, one that said 'diner' with a blinking neon arrow, and Bishop headed toward it.

Out of the corner of his eye he saw a blur, a vehicle slowing beside him. The black SUV stopped just in front of him, and the rear door opened.

Glass leaned out of the open door and smiled. "Hello. Do you need a ride?" Glass asked.

"No thanks, just walking to grab a meal." Bishop answered, still walking forward.

"Mind if we eat together? My treat." Glass offered.

Bishop looked at the front seat of the SUV. There was a very stocky young man in a windbreaker behind the wheel, and another, both wearing dark sunglasses, beside him.

They watched Bishop but seemed to ignore Glass.

Bishop took a step back. "Sure. Let's walk, it's just down here." He nodded.

Glass got out of the SUV. One of the other men went to open the front door, and Glass shook his head, almost imperceptibly. The man stayed in the vehicle.

Glass let Bishop to lead the way. He looked around and waved casually, and the SUV drove off.

"You know, I'm impressed by what you've managed to do in just a short week." Glass said.

"Thanks, but I really miss being in class, at home, all the normal activities." Bishop answered.

Glass nodded. "Have you considered coming back to the service? You have very good intuitive skills, and we could use someone with your natural abilities."

Bishop smiled. "I wondered how long it would take you to ask. I'm flattered, really I am, but no thanks. I'm out, and out for good."

Glass stopped at a store window as they walked, glancing in the reflection for anyone nearby.

"You were in Nicaragua, up to your knees in mud and cow shit for a week to rescue one of your men. Are you saying that a stint in Annapolis wouldn't be like a vacation for you?"

Bishop chuckled. "It was actually Guatemala, and no, it was not fun. But I was a decade younger then. Been there, done that, got the tee shirt."

Glass scratched his head. "Yes, I suppose. Still, would it be possible for me to request your services if required?

All above board, of course. As I say, you have a desirable set of abilities."

They reached the restaurant, one of the small storefront places that every town has, and Bishop politely held the door open for Glass.

Bishop chose a booth away from the windows, with a view of the entire room. Bishop had chosen the booth intentionally, and Glass smiled, amused by the detail, as they sat.

"See, Captain? Even now you've taken a table with site view of the terrain, and I bet you can spot all three exits without turning your head."

"Four exits. The front door, kitchen, bathroom and the side delivery door." Bishop corrected.

Glass chuckled. "You're making my point for me. Tell you what, I'll let it drop for now, but keep me in mind if you do consider my offer."

A thin man in black pants and a patterned shirt took their orders and returned minutes later with their food. Bishop poked at his salad, sipped water and glanced out the window. A familiar black SUV was parked across the street, its darkened windows shielding the occupants.

Glass sawed at his steak, gnawing on chunks of beef and talking between bites. He pointed his fork at Bishop and grunted.

"You know, Captain, I can do better than my original offer. We can bump you up, commission you as a Navy Captain and put your skills to work for your country again. What do you say?"

Bishop shook his head. "Thanks, but I'm Army. By the way, what happens when Sparwood discovers that he's selling swamp water?"

Glass smiled. "Leave that to us. We'll wait for him to get desperate, and then we'll offer him a deal, and then he'll give up the people above him."

Bishop grimaced. "Do you know the two words that will fail a mission fastest? 'And then'. It guarantees that you need something to happen before something else happens. Murphy's law states that anything that can go wrong, will go wrong. There's too much space between 'right now' and 'and then'."

Glass spoke little after that. He ordered dessert, talked about his family in Maryland, how he was flying back to see them in a week, and again offered Bishop a position working with him.

Glass waved over the waiter, paid the bill and the two men left the restaurant. By now the sky was dark, clouds hiding most of the stars and the quarter moon trying valiantly to poke through the spaces between the clouds.

Glass handed Bishop a card. It looked a lot like Sparwood's card, with only a name on the top, 'Hugh Glass', and a telephone number.

"Keep it. You never know when we could help each other." Glass said.

He walked casually across the street, the black SUV appeared from nowhere and he was gone.

Bishop stood there, watching the taillights of the SUV disappear into the distance, then walked back to his room.

He woke up late the next morning. It was almost eight thirty, and he felt as though he'd been asleep for a week. He showered, put on fresh clothes and put the rest of his belongings into his tote.

Bishop's gun was buried under the Flytrap papers, with dirty socks and a thrift store shirt piled over that. He bounded down the stairs, feeling lighter than he had in days. Mrs. Tyler was in the kitchen, to one side of the stairs, and he felt he should say goodbye before leaving.

He poked his head around the corner. "Hi. Just wanted to say thanks for the room and I'm headed back to Seattle." Bishop said.

The woman turned to him and smiled. "Good morning. I'm sorry to see you go. Would you like some breakfast before you leave?"

Bishop looked over her shoulder at the stove. "Um yeah, if it's no too much trouble, thanks."

"Of course. I'm happy to have the company. Sit down."

Bishop slid his tote under a chair and sat. Mrs. Tyler pulled some eggs and bread out of her fridge and proceeded to prepare more food.

"How do you like your eggs?" She asked.

"I'm not fussy. Whatever's easiest for you." Bishop answered.

"That's very polite of you. Over easy it is. Jam with your toast?"

He nodded. "Yes, please."

She poured a coffee and placed the mug in front of him. Moments later, he was eating toast and scooping egg onto his fork.

Mrs. Tyler sat across from him and sipped coffee. "Can I ask you a very personal question?"

Bishop looked up. "Sure."

"So what *is* your name?"

Bishop patted his mouth with a paper napkin. "My name is Retired Captain John Bishop."

"You were in the sub fleet or what?" Tyler asked.

He shook his head. "Sorry, wrong branch. I'm an Army Captain."

She shook her head. "Why the phony name? Did you think I wouldn't rent to army?"

Bishop chuckled. "Not that at all, ma'am. I was doing something that needed to be completed with a minimum of exposure, that's all."

She stared at him. "Are you telling me that what you were doing here wasn't legal?"

"It was perfectly legal. In fact, if you watch the news in a week or so, they will probably talk about what I was doing. I'm afraid I can't tell you more than that right now, though."

She shrugged and sipped her coffee.

Bishop finished his breakfast, thanked her again and took the ferry back to Seattle.

After spending days hiding out, laying low, moving around, it felt strange driving his own Jeep again, opening the door to his own house again, sitting on his own sofa again.

He went to his local store, bought some frozen meals and a bag of groceries, taking quiet comfort in being able to put them into his own fridge.

At some point he should take a cooking lesson, he thought. Good place to meet women, too.

That gave him an idea. He dialed the number of the last motel he'd stayed. A man answered.

"Hi, is Jeanie working today?" Bishop asked.

"Jeanie? Nah, Jeanie quit the other day." The man said.

"Ah, I see. I don't suppose you have a number for her?" Bishop said hopefully.

"I don't have dick for her. She didn't even pick up her last paycheck." The man grunted.

"Right. Thanks anyway." Bishop said sadly.

He made himself a coffee and sat on the sofa, relaxing. He replayed the conversation he'd had with Jeanie. She seemed to like him, and it would be good to see her again, even if only to spend time with her and talk. That would help him unwind from the week. But where was she? She had been hired by Bill Knight, maybe he knew where to find her.

He drove back to Knight Investigations, jogged up the stairs to the third floor and breezed past the empty reception desk. He opened the door to Bill Knight's office without knocking.

Jeanie was in a chair opposite Knight, going over some stapled sheets of paper and reading off numbers on similar papers Bill was holding.

Knight looked up at Bishop and smiled. "Oh, hi. I believe you two know each other?"

Jeanie smiled sheepishly and nodded. "Hi, Randall." She muttered.

"Bishop. John Bishop. But then, you did know that." Bishop smiled.

She covered her face with her hands, embarrassed. "Right. I did know that, yes."

Knight placed his stack of paper on the desk. "What brings you to our humble abode?"

Bishop leaned against the door frame. "I was rather hoping for a second date, actually."

Jeanie glanced at Knight, smiled and leaned forward. "That sounds like fun. Yeah, sure."

Bishop turned back to look at Knight. "So you're keeping the money, right?"

Knight nodded seriously. "Damn straight. It's not every day that it rains cash, you know."

Jeanie sat up straight. "What do you mean?"

Bishop poked his chin at Knight. "We convinced a bad guy to give your boss a hundred thousand dollars. I'd like some of it back for expenses, by the way. Three thousand dollars."

Jeanie glared at Knight. "And why didn't you share some of that with me, Bill? Huh?"

Knight sneered at her. "I do, Jean. It's called alimony."

Bishop leaned back. "You guys were married?"

Knight shook his head. "Jean was my sister-in-law. Her sister's my ex that's bleeding me dry. That, plus my current wife can't spell 'credit limit'. That money will save my life, I tell you."

Jeanie smirked, pleased with herself. "How about you pick me up at six? We'll go somewhere nice. Somewhere that has linen tablecloths, not like the places Bill likes to eat, you know."

Jeanie took a sticky note from Knight's desk and wrote down her address. She handed it to Bishop. "Six PM sharp. Don't make a lady wait."

Knight snickered. "Lady. Huh."

Bishop glared at him. "*Five* thousand dollars. You now owe me *five* thousand dollars."

"For what?" Knight said, indignant.

"Being rude. Plus, then I won't tell the IRS how you got the money." Bishop joked.

Knight shrugged. "Fine. Thanks for the rest of it, though, appreciate it."

Bishop smiled at Jeanie. "See you at six." He said.

Bishop went home, pulled out a dressy sweater and shirt to go with his good slacks, reminding himself that his wife had chosen that look for him almost a decade ago.

He showered, enjoying the luxury of a long hot soak, shaved and brushed his teeth extra clean. You just never know when you're going to get to kiss a woman, after all.

It was five thirty, and the address Jeanie had given him was about fifteen minutes away. He had time for a quick coffee first.

He walked into his kitchen, buttoning his shirt sleeve, when he saw her.

She was the woman he'd seen at Sparwood's office, the receptionist at the front desk. She was standing in the doorway between his living room and kitchen, her legs slightly apart, with a determined look in her eyes.

She was also holding a familiar gun, a Heckler and Koch USP pistol, pointed at Bishop's chest.

Bishop didn't panic. He assessed the situation for a brief second, then smiled.

"Serves me right for not locking my door." He said.

"You help me now or I will shoot you where you stand." The woman growled.

"By the way, we met before, but I don't think I introduced myself. I'm John Bishop." He said.

The woman shuffled her feet slightly. "I know. You're the bastard that got Dwayne arrested."

Bishop casually leaned one hand on the kitchen counter. If needed, he could grab a cleaver from the knife block and throw it at her. She didn't notice the danger.

She took a deep breath. "You put Dwayne in jail. You need to let him out." She barked.

Bishop shrugged. "It's not quite that easy, you see. I'm not a police officer."

The woman put her hands over her ears, the pistol pointing at the ceiling as she did. She took another deep breath and pointed the gun at Bishop again.

"I don't give a shit how you do it. Just get him out of jail. He shouldn't be in jail. Get him out of jail. Get him out now." She hissed.

Bishop sighed. "Fine. Tell me why he shouldn't be in jail. He killed three people, after all."

The woman shook her head. "It was all Alan's fault. Alan talked him into doing those things. Blame Alan, not Dwayne."

Bishop nodded. "Look, let me see what I can do for him. I'm supposed to be on a date right now, though. If I don't show, they might come here looking for me, given everything that's happened to me so far. Do you mind if I cancel my date first?"

She lowered the pistol slightly, thinking, then raised it again. "No tricks, OK? Just make sure you don't try anything stupid."

Bishop picked up his phone and dialed. Bill Knight answered in two rings. "Yeah? What?"

"Hi, Jeanie? Sorry to do this on such short notice, but I have to cancel dinner. Something very important came up." Bishop said cheerily.

Knight was silent for a moment. "Are you in trouble, Cap?"

Bishop laughed. "Yes, that's right. I owe you a dinner at Porezki's restaurant. Sorry, I'll make it up to you as soon as I can."

"Are you home?" Knight asked.

"That's right." Bishop smiled.

"Are they armed?" Knight asked.

"Yeah, you too, sweetheart. Bye." Bishop said.

He turned to the woman. "It's Deb, right? From the Society for the whatsis of whosis?"

She adjusted her grip on the pistol. "Porezki's? I've never heard of it. What were you really talking about?"

"It's a Polish restaurant near the Space Needle. Jeanie loves their perogies. I'd be happy to take you there sometime?" He smiled again.

She shook her head. "Dwayne needs to go free. Now, are you going to get him out of jail, or do I have to shoot you?"

Bishop examined her face, looking for a sign of hesitation, any hint of uncertainty. He saw none.

"Let me ask you a question, Deb. Why do you think I can get him out of jail?"

She huffed. "You're the one who called the police about him. You're the one who ransacked his apartment, and you're the one who framed him for selling stuff to the Chinese."

Bishop pulled out a stool and sat on it. "All right, now you've got my attention. I have absolutely no idea what you're talking about."

She hissed, squatted down a bit and glared at him. Stop LYING to me. I know you were there. He said you even told him so. Stop lying, you're LYING."

Bishop folded his arms in front of him. "Look, yes, I was in his apartment. That's where I found that gun you're holding. I also found a silencer. Nothing else that makes him guilty. Nothing. As for selling secrets, your boss Sparwood is the one who's selling the secrets. He's the one that ordered Carlisle to kill three people, that's all. If you have a gripe, take it up with General Sparwood."

She looked around, trying to collect her thoughts. "What about the money? Sparwood says you took money from him. I heard him talking in his office, and he said you were blackmailing him. Huh? What about that?"

Bishop nodded. "That's partly true. I asked for money to make him believe that I was crooked. He sent it to a bank account, but it was not mine. It went to a friend of Lieutenant Morrison, Dwayne's first victim."

She lowered the pistol slightly. Bishop could probably distract her, make the eight-foot distance to grab it away from her, but he wanted to get more information out of her first.

He sighed, mostly for effect. "All right. Here's what I can do. If you tell me where Sparwood is right now, I can probably get him to admit that he pushed Dwayne to do the things he did. I can't promise anything, but if I tell the authorities he was just a pawn of Sparwood's, we may be able to get him off easy."

She looked around the room, hoping for inspiration from the furniture. "What do you want to know?" She asked.

Bishop knew then that he had won her over. "Do you know where Sparwood is now?"

"Yeah, he's getting ready to fly to Istanbul. He'll be there on vacation for a while." She said softly.

"Then from Istanbul he files to Phnom Penh? That makes no sense." Bishop said, puzzled.

She shook her head. "Why on earth would he go to Phnom Penh?"

Bishop frowned. "He is selling the items we were talking about in Cambodia. I figured he'd go to Phnom Penh, not Istanbul."

"No, I booked the flights. From Istanbul he flies to a place called Van Ferit." She said.

She lowered the gun to her side. "What exactly is it you're trying to tell me, Captain?"

Bishop did some quick calculations. "Well, that makes much more sense. I need to make a phone call."

The woman studied him for a moment then nodded quickly. Bishop pulled a card out of his wallet and dialed a number.

Admiral Glass answered in two rings. "Hello, John. Can I help you?"

"Actually, I think I can help you, sir. Sparwood isn't going to Cambodia. He's going to Turkey, to a town called Van Ferit."

The Admiral was silent for a moment. "Why does that name sound familiar?"

"Sir, it's an hour's drive from there to the border with Iran. He lied about the vials going to Cambodia. They're going to Iran. Either that, or the Cambodians are middlemen in this deal. Either way, I thought you should know."

Glass chuckled. "Are you absolutely sure you won't reconsider my offer? You know, I think you would look right at home in Marine blue."

"Sorry, sir, but it clashes with the color of my eyes. I'll stick with green."

Glass sighed. "Fair enough. Can I repay you in some way for this assistance?"

Bishop looked over at the woman. "Not me, but this lady has a favor she'd like to ask you."

He handed the phone to Deb. She held it to her ear. "Hello? Who is this?" She asked.

Chapter 14: Mission Critical

Porezki sat in his unmarked cruiser, Admiral Glass sitting beside him, with Bishop and Deb- Carlisle's girlfriend- in the back seat. Bishop watched planes taking off behind them.

Carlisle was outside the car, pacing, clearly more nervous than Bishop had ever seen him. Porezki stuck his arm out the window and tried to calm him down.

"Relax, Sergeant. Go with the plan as discussed. Get your General to say that he is going to visit Iran and admit that he ordered you to kill three people. Once we get that on tape, walk away."

Carlisle looked unconvinced. "That's it? Nothing else?"

Glass leaned over Porezki to speak. "I have promised this young lady that we will treat you with leniency. It's as much as I can promise, but I will certainly honor that promise."

Porezki stuck his head out the window and spoke softly. "Look, if you run into problems, or if you feel you're in danger, just say the word 'Arizona'. Make it sound natural, like 'maybe next time I can take you to this place I know in Arizona', or something like that. Just don't blurt it out. He's not stupid, he'll suspect we're on to him. Anyway, we have a dozen officers scattered throughout the terminal, so you're perfectly safe."

Carlisle looked out at the low terminal building past the parking lot. "Why did he come all the way out to the Auburn airport, though? Why didn't he fly out of SeaTac?"

Deb leaned over and spoke. "I can answer that. He booked a private charter out of here to take him to Portland. He has a flight from Portland to Istanbul booked for later today."

Bishop looked over at her. "But Dwayne is right. Why drive all the way down here instead of taking the flight from Seattle?"

Deb shrugged. "Maybe he figured we would be looking for him in Seattle, but not in Portland?"

Porezki nodded. "Yeah, that makes sense. If he gets away from us we'll alert the Portland PD."

Deb sat up straight and tapped Porezki on the shoulder. "Here he is, getting out of the cab."

Porezki looked at Carlisle. "Go. Be casual, remember the script. We're recording everything."

Sparwood was across the parking lot, a hundred yards away, with dozens of people between him and Bishop. Carlisle walked slowly towards the General. Deb looked around, opened her door and ran to Carlisle. She grabbed his arm, waited till he turned around and hugged him tight. He gave her a quick kiss and smiled, then turned back towards Sparwood.

Deb slid back into the car and watched Carlisle go. Porezki turned a volume knob on a receiver beside him and everyone listened.

Carlisle walked quickly, caught up with Sparwood and touched his arm. "General, sir?" He said.

Sparwood spun around, surprised. "Sergeant? Why are you here? Why aren't you in jail?"

"I got out on bail, sir. I heard you were leaving to complete the mission. I just wanted to know if I could come along with you."

Even from where he was sitting, Bishop could see that Sparwood was annoyed. "Son, you have to have faith in my actions. I will be back shortly and sort this mess out for you. I did that for the things you had to do before, and I will sort this out for you as soon as I get back. Trust me."

Bishop snickered at those words. Porezki frowned and they listened quietly again.

Carlisle kept to the agreed script. "Sir, where are you going? Is it somewhere I can get a hold of you in case I need to?"

Sparwood moved his suitcase from his right hand to his left one. "Now, Dwayne, this trip is strictly need-to-know, son. Why would you go and ask me something like that?"

Carlisle ran his fingers through his hair. This was not going as planned. He turned bright red. "Listen, General,

I just want to know why I've been doing all this work for you, that's all. I am probably going to go to jail, and I need to know it was worth it. Can you at least give me that?"

Sparwood placed his suitcase carefully on the ground. He put his hands on his hips and stared at Carlisle. "Son, what the hell is going on? Do you expect me to believe they let you out on bail, or are you here so you could coon-dog me out here in the middle of nowhere?"

Carlisle shook his head. "I'm just asking, General. Where are you going, that's all."

Sparwood shook his head slowly. "I'm taking a short flight to see some friends, that's all. You want more answers, ask your friends in that car over there."

He poked his chin at Porezki's cruiser. He turned to leave, and Carlisle grabbed his arm.

"You will answer my questions, sir. Where are you going?" Carlisle said firmly.

"I'm going up shit creek. Let me go, Dwayne, or so help me you will regret it."

The General struggled to pull his arm free. Carlisle held tight, gripping harder, and pulled Sparwood close to him. Sparwood gritted his teeth. "I have to go. Let me go- NOW."

Carlisle yanked him closer. Sparwood growled and reached into his jacket. His arm swung out and Bishop saw a glint of silver metal. Bishop scrambled out of the car, running towards the two men, but he was too late. Sparwood planted his knife into Carlisle's ribs, just under the left armpit. Carlisle staggered back, pulled the knife out and stared at it, incredulous. He roared like an animal and stuck the knife into Sparwood's chest.

Sparwood glared at him, angry. Carlisle stood still for a moment then his knees folded and he sat on the ground cross-legged. Deb screamed and ran toward him, following Bishop.

Sparwood fell flat on his back, his arms folded up on top of him in a 'boxer' position, as blood poured out from his shirt onto the ground around him. He opened and closed his mouth gasping like a fish for a few seconds then went limp.

Carlisle rested one hand on the ground beside him to steady himself. By the time Deb had gotten to the two men, Carlisle's arm trembled and he fell forward onto his face.

Deb rushed to him, lifted him into her arms and hugged him, crying pitifully. Porezki had already called for an ambulance, but he knew there was no point. He sauntered over to the bodies of the two men and squatted down beside them.

"Y'know, Bishop, when you decide to save court time, you don't screw around." He said.

Bishop shook his head. "This is all wrong. This should not have gone this way. It's wrong, just wrong, that's all."

Deb was still cradling Carlisle, still weeping. She sniffed. "He didn't have to do what he did, he could have let him just go. He didn't have to leave me."

Bishop put a hand on her shoulder. "I'm so sorry for your loss. You shouldn't stay here. Come on, let us take you back home."

She shook her head. "No, I want to stay here with Dwayne. I want to stay. I want to be with him. I don't want to let him go."

She hugged him tight and cried quietly. Bishop stood with his back to the dead men and watched for anyone that might get too close, an old habit. Porezki radioed the other officers scattered throughout the airport terminal to stand down and wait for the ambulance to arrive.

It was an awkward silence; the two men standing by doing nothing, Deb sitting on the ground, crying. Glass stayed in the passenger seat of the car, making frantic phone calls.

An ambulance came and took the two dead men away. Protocol, Bishop learned, was that nobody ever died in an ambulance. The medics would always try to perform CPR on the men until they got to hospital, and only then the doctors in the ER would pronounce them dead.

The forensic team spent a half hour collecting blood samples from the concrete- all standard procedure, all unnecessary- then they left as well, and by that time the sun was setting.

Porezki drove Glass back to an address near the ferry terminal, and two large men in a black SUV whisked him away.

Deb was calmer now, still dejected but no longer weeping. She asked to be driven home. Porezki parked and Bishop walked her up the steps of her apartment building and held open the door.

He returned and sat in the front seat. Porezki turned slightly and said "Where to, mac?"

Bishop chuckled at the old taxi reference. "Home please, Jeeves." He joked.

Porezki drove Bishop home. When they got there he stayed still, gripping the wheel. Porezki tilted his head and wrinkled his nose.

"Listen, Cap, can you tell me what's wrong with this picture?" Porezki asked.

Bishop shrugged. "I'm not sure I understand. We have two dead guys. That's pretty fucked-up, any way you slice it."

Porezki shook his head. "Why did that Deb woman run out to kiss Carlisle? She must have known she could kiss him when he came back?"

Bishop grunted. "You cops, you always look for the details, huh? I don't know, I don't care, I just want to go home and get back to my life." Bishop said.

Porezki sighed. "Yeah, I'm overthinking it, as usual. Go home, Cap. Don't call me, I'll call you."

"Yup, I'm going to go home and get some sleep." Bishop said.

The man in the village guided them to the house of the village elder. Bishop and his men sat cross-legged on the carpeted floor, nodding at the other three Afghans and smiling politely as one of the elder's sons poured tea into melamine teacups. Bishop said 'manana', thanking the man for his hospitality.

Etiquette dictated that as guests they would not be harmed in any way, so to show respect two of the men with Bishop took off their helmets and placed them over their M 16's.

The elder said something, then the interpreter told Bishop that the elder wanted to assure peace between their peoples. Bishop agreed and asked what the elder meant by peace.

The interpreter repeated this in Pashtun, and the elder looked nervously at the three other Afghan men in the room. The interpreter quickly excused himself for a moment. As soon as he was out of the room, the elder reached behind him and brandished a sword. He jumped to his feet, swinging it high over his head. Bishop leaned back, away from the blade. One of Bishop's men was even faster, putting a bullet into the elder's forehead. He turned to the other three Afghans in the room and shot each of them one by one. Bishop and his men stood up to leave. The elder's son came into the room, struggling to rack the bolt on an old Mosin-Nagant rifle.

Bishop's man grabbed the rifle out of the boy's hands and hit him in the forehead with the butt. The man grunted 'stupid fuckers'. He broke the rifle in half over his knee. They left.

Bishop woke up from his nap. He was hungry, he felt secure for the first time in over a week, and he was hoping to actually get that second date with Jeanie. If nothing else, spending a few hours with a pretty girl would help water down the memory of the last few days.

He couldn't see anything in the fridge that he wanted to heat up; he drove to the local store and bought a chicken dinner and fries, brought them home and enjoyed having the meal on his own plates and in his own kitchen.

He still couldn't shake the feeling he had missed something, that he had overlooked something, had seen something that didn't make sense. He replayed the afternoon's events in his mind, from when they picked up Deb and Carlisle to when they saw Sparwood arrive at the airport.

Deb. Everyone just called her Deb. Why just Deb? What was her full name?

Bishop took out his phone and scrolled through his photos. He found the one he'd taken at the General's office, with Carlisle's home address on it. Three lines up was an entry for Deb. It said her full name was Deborah Bijani. Bishop closed the photo and dialed a number.

Porezki answered in three rings. "Bishop? You better not have more corpses for me." He said.

"Ziggy, I have a puzzle. Our weepy girl, Deborah. Her last name is Persian, Iranian." Bishop said.

Porezki sighed. "Why do I not like the direction this is going?"

Bishop organized his thoughts. "Sparwood said he was going to Cambodia. The customs forms I found in his storage unit said they were going to Cambodia. Deborah says he was actually going to Iran, but nothing I overheard Sparwood say supports that. We only have her word for it that he was going to the Middle East. She has an Iranian name, and he was supposedly going to Iran. Maybe she was going there instead. What are the odds I'm wrong?"

Porezki was silent for a moment, then he sighed. "Give me fifteen minutes. I have some contacts with the TSA. I sure as shit hope this is a wild goose chase though, Cap."

Bishop went to the small desk in his home office and pulled the manila envelope from his desk. He felt he could now look at the Flytrap files, since most of the people involved were dead.

The string holding the flap down was wound counter-clockwise, as a left-handed person might do. Inside, the cover page still had 'Top Secret' and 'SAP' stamped in red, but Bishop ignored them and flipped to the first printed page.

He read the dozen or so pages quickly. It was pretty basic stuff; it described selling a substance known only by an inventory code to foreign buyers and how to use the list of contacts that the sale of the item provided to find the end buyer, an organization that could hurt the USA.

Pretty standard security stuff, so far. There was nothing here that should have caused anyone to get reprimanded, let alone killed. Something else was at play, and Bishop was not sure exactly what that was.

He decided not to play the DVD or plug in the memory stick, in case they were dangerous to his computer. Twenty minutes later his phone rang.

"Bishop." He said mechanically.

"I'll be there in ten minutes." Porezki said.

He hung up.

Bishop left his gun at home- Porezki had one, after all- so Bishop waited on the front steps.

Porezki screeched up in his unmarked cruiser and flung the passenger door open.

"Get in!" He yelled.

Bishop ran down the steps and got into the car. Porezki squealed the tires and turned around sharply. He looked behind him for traffic and accelerated.

"Something clicked for you, did it?" Bishop asked.

"You can really make the sky rain shit in a hurry, huh?" Porezki said.

Bishop grabbed his seat belt and held tight. "I give up. What is all this about?"

"Your girl there, Miss Bijani. She booked a ticket out of Seattle to fly to Cairo later this evening. I called in a favor; she was booked to fly from Cairo to Tehran a couple of days after that. You called it right, Bishop. She's the one in the middle of all this. You called it right."

"What about Sparwood? Wasn't he in on this with her, then?" Bishop asked.

Porezki shook his head. "He was never going to Iran. She lied about that. He had a flight from Portland to Bangkok, then another to Phnom Penh. He was going to Cambodia the whole time. She lied, Bishop, she lied like a dog."

He slammed the car around corners and got on the radio briefly, checking traffic conditions. Bishop watched his expression, firm, resolved.

"Don't you want to call for backup?" Bishop asked.

"Shit no. This bitch is mine." Porezki snapped.

He got to the apartment building where they had let Deb out. Porezki got out of his car and looked around for anyone suspicious. "Stay behind me." He snapped.

"Like hell I will." Bishop answered.

Porezki grunted and unclipped the leather strap on his hip holster. He kept his hand on his gun as he walked up the apartment steps.

The door opened and Deb came out, pulling a large suitcase behind her. She didn't see the men till she looked up.

"Going somewhere?" Porezki asked.

She jumped. "Oh. I, uh. Yes, I just want to get away for a while." She said, unconvincingly.

"Are you going back to visit family in Iran?" Bishop asked.

She frowned. "Why would you think that?"

"Well, for one thing, you bought a ticket to Tehran?" Porezki said.

She shook her head slowly. "I haven't done anything wrong. You have no reason to hold me."

Porezki took out his handcuffs. "Conspiracy to commit murder for a start. More charges later."

She laughed. "I never killed anyone. General Sparwood and Dwayne killed each other, I didn't do anything to hurt either of them."

Porezki tilted his head. "What did you say to Carlisle? What did you tell him when you ran out and hugged him? We saw you talking to him. I think you told him that Sparwood was the reason he was going to jail, and you two could be together, but only if Sparwood was dead."

She snorted. "That's the most ridiculous thing I've ever heard. Besides, there's no way for you to know what I said to him."

Porezki smiled. "He had a wire on him. We recorded everything he said, and it picked up every word that you said. Even if you only whispered it in his ear, our techs will be able to isolate the sounds. That counts as conspiracy in my books, sweetheart."

She shook her head. "Good luck making anything stick. Dwanye was a nice guy, but he was a little doe-eyed when it came to women. He was gullible. I could have said anything to him. Prove that me talking to him got him killed."

Bishop stepped forward. "Why did you divert the General's shipment from Cambodia to Iran?"

"Who says I did?" She sneered.

"You didn't say 'no I didn't' so you just admitted it. All right, off to the big house with you." Porezki said.

He grabbed her arm and swung the handcuff onto her wrist. She leaned back, squirmed and wriggled back and forth, resisting as he tried to lock the cuff on her.

"No! NO! You Can't! NO!" She screamed, pulling back as far as she could.

Bishop watched, amused at her trying to get away. Porezki gritted his teeth and shook his head.

"Calm down, missy. Calm down or I will smack you into submission." He said in a low voice.

From behind him, Bishop heard the sound of squealing tires. He looked back to see the reason, then watched as a black SUV raced around the corner, screeching to a stop outside the apartment building. The two large men he had seen with Admiral Glass jumped out and sprinted up the steps towards Deb.

Admiral Glass got out of the SUV, walked casually up behind them and nodded at Bishop.

"You figured it out, did you?" He smiled.

Bishop shook his head. "When did you realize what she had planned, Admiral?"

Glass nodded towards Deb. "We had our suspicions, but as soon as Detective Porezki here looked into the flights that the lady booked, we asked the same questions of the same people. Imagine our surprise to find out that she was heading back to the old country. You know, she has been in Seattle for over twenty years, yet she still speaks very fluent Farsi."

Bishop looked over at Deb. Her expression now was somewhere between furious and terrified. Another sound behind Bishop made him look. A black van, with completely dark side windows, came silently around the corner.

Deb stared at the van, her eyes getting wider as it approached. She stuck her hand out for Porezki.

"Fine. Take me to jail." She said.

Bishop looked back at her. "You'd rather go with him than with them, I guess?" He joked.

She shook her head. "There's no reason why I would kill anyone. None at all."

Bishop smiled. "I can think of twenty million reasons why you would want to kill them."

Deb shook her head. "Take me. I'll tell you everything. Just take me away."

Glass nodded at the van, and two more men came out of it. Bishop noticed that they were wearing suits, but there was the unmistakeable bulge of a shoulder holster under their jackets.

Porezki shook his head. "Sorry, boss. This is my collar. You guys are going to have to get in line."

"Not so. She was an Ensign in the Navy. She is therefore a retired military officer, and an employee of a military organization. Her employment contract states that she is subject to oversight by a military commanding officer. That's yours truly." Glass said.

Bishop touched Porezki's arm. "Sorry, Ziggy, but he's right. They've got priority over us here."

Porezki sneered and removed the handcuff. "Sounds good to me. Less paperwork for me to do. Anything I *am* allowed to do right now, then?"

Glass waved an arm casually, and the men from the van walked Deb through the open side door of the van, closed it and drove silently away.

Glass turned to look at Bishop. "Thank you for all your work, Captain. Please consider my offer. We could always use a person of your caliber in the Navy. Will you think about it and call me?"

Bishop shook his head and held his hand out. "Safe travels, Admiral. Calm seas and fair winds."

Glass chuckled. "Hoo-ah! Stay green, Captain."

He got into the back of the SUV, and the two men got in the front seats afterwards. The SUV drove down the street, following the van.

Porezki watched silently as the vehicles disappeared. He put his handcuffs away. "Well, I'd offer to buy you a beer, but is it too early for you?" He asked.

"Sorry, I'm dry. Have been for three years plus." Bishop said.

"Really? Good for you. In that case I'm going home. Can I drop you back at your house?"

Bishop sighed. "Yeah. I need some groceries. If you want to drop me near my place, I'm going to pick up some frozen lasagne."

"What are you doing after that?" Bishop asked.

"I'm going to sign up for a cooking class. Either I'll learn to cook my own meals, or I'll meet some single women. Either way, I need the distraction."

"Sounds like a plan. Let me know if you have any other dead bodies." Porezki joked.

"Don't call me, I'll call you." Bishop said.

He got out of the cruiser, watched Porezki drive off and walked up the steps to his front door.

The Flytrap papers were still on his desk, but they were now irrelevant. Bishop put some wood in the fireplace, watched the flames rise and turn from yellow to orange, then methodically burned every page of the report, followed by melting the DVD and memory stick. He watched with satisfaction as the memory stick delaminated into a plastic shell and a thin circuit board. The blue smoke from the melting plastic curled up into the chimney, taking with it the things that had made Bishop hide for several days. This time, he really had destroyed the documents.

When everything had burned or melted, Bishop doused the fire and checked his fridge for anything he needed to get.

Even doing a mundane thing like buying groceries seemed like a delight now, the freedom to come and go without fear. He called the Dean and informed him that Aunt Muriel was better, and he'd be back to work on Monday.

The Dean told him he had already heard from Admiral Glass. Life was getting back to normal.

Bishop strolled though the aisles of his local grocery store, picking up food from shelves automatically, on autopilot.

Flytrap was dead. Sparwood was dead, Carlisle was dead, Deb was in a dark hole somewhere, and he trusted that Glass would take care of the vials of yellow liquid once they got to their destination.

He stood in line at the checkout and mechanically loaded his purchases onto the conveyor belt.

The young man behind the register scanned everything, charged Bishop a quarter for a paper bag and packed the groceries into it.

He looked up at Bishop. "How would you like to pay?"

Bishop froze. The young man waited a moment then repeated the question.

"Sir, how would you like to pay for the groceries?"

"Twenty million dollars." Bishop said.

The young man screwed up his face. "Sorry? I don't understand."

Bishop smiled and shook his head. "Cash."

He pulled out a few bills for the food, carried the bag back to his Jeep and got out his phone. He wondered who he should call first, what to say, then dialed the number.

"Captain Bishop? What can I do for you?" Glass answered.

"The twenty million dollars. Who has it? Where did it go?" Bishop asked.

"You have been thinking far too hard about this, Captain. As I told you, the amount is insignificant. The important point is that we have set in motion a chain of events that will help our country stay secure."

Bishop sighed. "Yeah, yeah. God bless America, world peace, save the whales. I get it. How does that account for the twenty mill?"

Glass was silent. "What would you like me to say? That we put it back into the federal coffers, that we gave it to starving children in Zambia, or that we're using it to fund further projects?"

"It doesn't matter to me, Admiral. I just wanted to know where the money went, that's all."

"Did you want a share of it? Is that it? Do you feel you deserve a cut?" He sneered.

"Nope. I just want to know how much you're keeping for yourself, Admiral?"

There was a moment of silence. "Go to hell, Bishop." He hung up.

Chapter 15: Debriefing

It had been over four years since Bishop had submitted a report to his superiors. He thought long and hard about whether to speak up, finally deciding he should cover his ass in case anything came back to bite him. He decided he would report the incident.

The forms he used in the Army were still on his computer, the contact emails were still valid.

He composed a short, two-page review of the last few days, detailing the fact that Lieutenant Morrison had sent him, unsolicited, the Flytrap documents; that Sparwood had conspired with Carlisle to kill Morrison, Saks and Kendall; that Sparwood had stolen vials of something to sell in Cambodia, but that Deborah Bijani had tried to divert them to Iran, and that Admiral Glass had taken her into custody, but beyond that Bishop knew nothing. He fibbed and said he destroyed the documents without viewing them. After the Oslo conference happened, nobody could prove otherwise, he reasoned.

The report let the upper brass know that he had been drawn into the situation, but it also let them know he was out of it, that he had no further involvement. He never mentioned the money. Too tempting for them to pin something on him if it went sideways later, he thought.

Once he had finished the report, he printed a copy, put it in a sealed envelope he would later mail to himself, then after double-checking everything he pressed 'send'.

On Monday morning, the sky was just an ominous, dark patch of low clouds skimming below a higher level of puffy white cumulus. The wind picked up, but it wasn't biting cold, just brisk.

Bishop put on his hooded sweatshirt, longer running shorts and thick socks, then went for his usual three-mile jog. He showered, dressed, collected the briefcase with his lesson plans and drove to work.

It seemed that the last few days had been a blur, like a dream that faded as he woke up. He dropped his case on his desk at eight fifteen, put on the coffee and looked through phone message slips.

At eight twenty-seven Kelly's high-heeled shoes made a clip-clop sound as she turned the corner into the office. She stopped abruptly when she saw him.

"Bish! You're back! Everything OK?" She gasped.

He smiled. "Hi, Kelly. Good morning. Yes, you can call off the dogs, the fire is out."

She slid a chair across from his desk and rested one elbow on it, leaning forward.

"Anything you want to tell me, or is it all hush-hush?"

He shook his head. "Nothing to report, really. Someone wanted to sell something that wasn't theirs to sell, and someone else wanted to sell the same thing to somewhere that shouldn't have had it."

"When will you give me a straight answer?" She asked.

"After what happens in Oslo. Ask me then."

She tilted her head. "Oslo? What's in Oslo?" She asked.

"Damned if I know, but I'll keep you posted."

She stood up. "Either way, it's good to have you back."

"You missed my snappy repartee?"

She shook her head. "Mark can't make coffee worth shit."

At exactly eight fifty-seven, Bishop walked into his classroom. The soft chatter of his students went completely silent when he came in. He placed the manila folder containing the day's lessons on the lectern and looked out at the class.

"Good morning." He boomed.

"Thank you all for your patience with Mister Powell while I was attending to other matters. It's good to be back, and we'll carry on from the spot where Mister Powell left off."

The class stared at him, silent. One woman's hand shot up. "Yes, Jimenez?" Bishop asked.

"Sir, can you tell us where you were?" She asked.

Bishop smiled. "Not right now. But I can tell you that my experience in the Army was instrumental in permitting me to return to class."

She put her hand up again. "Are you saying you were in danger, sir?"

He thought for a moment and smiled. "Let's just say it was a roller coaster of a week."

He plugged a memory stick into the lectern and pressed the button to lower a screen behind him. "All right, open your books to chapter nine. The exercise known as 'Operation Geronimo'."

He stopped for lunch at noon, sat in his customary seat in the usual restaurant, watched the usual people file through and the occasional person nod recognition.

Kelly raced in to pick up food for the other instructors and herself, then raced back out. She nodded quickly to Bishop as she passed, and he nodded back.

Everything had gone back to normal, as though nothing had happened. That made him both pleased and sad. He had seen people die in front of him, had been placed in danger and had to hide, but he didn't feel he could tell anyone about it, and nobody here knew what he'd seen.

He walked back to class after lunch, mentally organizing the lessons for the afternoon. His cell phone rang, and he chided himself for not turning it to silent. He pulled it out and kept walking.

"Bishop." He said mechanically.

"Hey there. It's Olivia. How are you?" the voice said.

He walked slower. "Hi, I hoped I'd hear form you. How's Detroit?"

"Amazing. They love me at the station, apparently. Listen, about that. I've been given a one-year contract to do the weather here."

He stopped. "That's great, that's really great. I'm happy for you. So, are you coming back for a visit anytime soon, though? Can I see you when you're here?"

There was a pause. "Um. About that. I've asked my agent to send me my stuff. The super is buying my Saturn, but could I ask you to be a sweetheart? Give him my keys so he can let the new tenants have my place?"

Bishop sighed quietly. "Sure. Let me know if there's anything else I can do."

She yelled 'just a minute' at someone behind her. "Thanks. You're a star. Bye." She hung up.

Bishop got home at the usual time, put something frozen in the microwave and turned on his computer. He checked emails, answered the few questions from students, and waited patiently for his food to warm up.

He would drop off Olivia's keys later. Maybe he could get a hold of Jeanie and finally get that second date. Maybe. Moping around thinking about Olivia was just self-pity and sour grapes, he thought. Life goes on, shit happens, enjoy the memory. Move on, Bishop, move on.

He took his meal out of the microwave, slid it onto a plate and dumped the cardboard container into his garbage can. It hadn't been emptied in almost a week and smelled terrible.

He pulled the plastic liner out of the can, knotted it and carried it carefully outside. He walked the path beside the house, lifted the lid on the blue recycle bin and ceremoniously dropped the plastic liner in. The path was dark, but he knew every step, even in this pitch-black pathway.

He turned to go back inside. That's when he felt the gun against his spine.

"Don't turn around." A man's voice said.

The voice sounded familiar. Bishop put his hands up slowly. "Do I know you?" He asked.

The man spoke again. "You hit me, then you took my car and my gun. Remember?"

Bishop recognized him now- the thug who had followed him into the boarded-up building.

"I gave the car and gun both back, just as I told you I would." Bishop said.

"You still owe me, you owe me big time." The man said.

"Did you want me to buy you a tank of gas?" Bishop joked.

The gun pressed harder against his back. "Don't bullshit me. I heard Sparwood talking. He said you were going to get twenty million dollars. I want that money."

Bishop shook his head. "I just stole his stuff from him, that's all. He got the money, not me. I just hid his stuff from him to get to the person who killed three people, that's all I did."

The man stepped back. Bishop turned slowly around to look at the threat. He now faced the man he had smacked in the abandoned office, the one whose car he had stolen. He looked angry, desperate, probably drunk.

Bishop put his hands down. "Look, let me ask you... first, listen, tell me, what's your name?"

The man looked slightly puzzled. "Gunther."

"OK, listen, Gunther, I don't have that money. If I did, do you think I'd be sitting at home now, putting out the garbage? Don't you think I'd be flying to a tropical island somewhere?"

Gunther's finger fidgeted on the trigger guard. "I don't know. I don't believe you." He said.

Bishop sighed. He moved slightly closer to the man, but the man took a large step back. Clearly, he was not going to be easily overpowered.

The man turned red in the face. "Stop talking. Stop lying, just give me the money or I'll shoot you. Give that money to me now."

Bishop flapped his arms like a pelican. "Do you think that, even if I *had* that money, that I'd keep it on me?"

The man's eyes were red, bloodshot. He staggered slightly. Clearly, he was on something stronger than a few beers. "Stop lying. You're LYING! LYING! Give me the money now!"

Bishop sighed. "Look, Gunther, I don't know how you got the idea that I have millions of dollars. I don't. Period. Put the gun away, go home and sleep it off. You'll wake up and realize how crazy this sounded. Trust me. In a week or so we can even get together for a coffee and laugh about it. What do you say?"

The man cocked the hammer on his gun and raised it, pointing at Bishop's chest. He roared with anger, then

Bishop heard a loud gunshot. The man stared straight ahead, turned to look behind him and crumpled to the ground. He curled up and moaned, clutching his stomach.

What just happened, Bishop thought. Footsteps in the darkness came towards him, a man's footsteps. He saw the person in silhouette, half expecting this man to shoot him, too.

Out of the shadows he saw Porezki, his gun now pointed down at the ground.

"Hey, I thought I'd come by and see how you're doing." Porezki said.

Bishop sat on the short concrete wall, in delayed shock. He shivered slightly and shook his head.

"I am getting way too old for this shit. I can't take this kind of crap anymore." He said.

"Yeah, it gets boring real fast, don't it?" Porezki smiled.

Porezki bent down and took the gun away from Gunther, popped the clip out and cleared the chamber. Gunther wheezed, a pool of blood staining his jacket.

Porezki pulled out a cell phone. "Detective Porezki, badge number three-three-one-seven. I need a bus, holding a suspect with a GSW." He gave the address and put the phone away.

"Care to tell me what just happened out here?" He asked.

Bishop shook his head. "Who'd believe it besides you?"

Tuesday morning, Bishop got up at six AM, went for his three-mile run and made the effort to sprint the last quarter mile.

By seven forty-eight he was dressed, had lined up his shirt buttons with his belt buckle, and laced up his shoes.

At exactly three minutes to nine he walked into his classroom, placed the USB drive and folder with the day's lessons on his lectern and scanned the students.

"Good morning all!" He bellowed.

They responded with an unsynchronized 'morning sir' and waited for him to begin.

"Good morning." He repeated.

There was a knock at the door, likely a late student, and he turned to see who it was.

The Dean poked his head in and beckoned him over with a crooked finger.

Bishop nodded to his class and went to the door. "Dean Wilkes? Can I help you?" He asked.

The Dean motioned to him. "I just wanted to interrupt your class for a moment, if I may."

Bishop waved him in and the Dean stepped in front of the lectern.

Half the students stood at attention. The Dean waved for them to sit down.

"Good morning, class." He started.

They all said 'good morning' in unison.

"Last week, as you know, Captain Bishop was away, doing some work that will come to light in the near future. For now, let's just say that it was due to his experience, and in large part due to his experience and the skills learned in this very course twenty-five years ago, that made him essential to the successful out come of his assignment."

The Dean adjusted his glasses. "We have with us today a very special guest, a senior member of the Navy, who worked closely with Captain Bishop on the assignment. He will be glad to answer any of your questions. But please remember, he is Navy, so don't let him recruit you."

The class laughed. The Dean turned to the open door and two burly men slid silently behind the lectern. Behind them came Admiral Glass, wearing his dress uniform, with gold braid on his sleeves and rows of 'fruit salad'- ribbons and service medals in several rows over his left breast.

The class stood to attention, and Glass stayed silent for a few seconds.

He eventually nodded to the class. "Be seated." He ordered.

Everyone sat. Glass put his cap on the lectern, nodded at Bishop and turned to the class again.

"Thank you, Captain Bishop and Colonel Wilkes. My name is Admiral Hugh Glass. I am currently working in Bremerton, doing what you'll be doing in the Army, but for the Navy. Everyone thinks that what we do in the military is siloed, that is, separated by service, that Army doesn't work with Navy, and Air Force doesn't work with Coast Guard. The truth is, nobody wants to work with the Air Force."

The class laughed. Glass grinned.

"You are presently enrolled in a program that teaches you how to think, and to learn not just facts, but processes. You are being taught how to view things in ways that will help others better do their jobs. Our job in the Navy is to keep the seaways safe. Your job is to show us where to look for the bad guys. Any Questions?"

Most hands went up. Glass spent almost an hour answering questions, trying politely to suggest that some of the brighter students might want to join the Navy instead, and watching out of the corner of his eye as Dean Wilkes grimaced at the recruitment speech. After an hour, Glass put his right hand down beside him and made a fist, just for a second, a gesture only Bishop and Wilkes saw.

The two burly men moved silently out of the room. Glass thanked the class for their attention, wished them well, picked up his cap and waited for the applause to end before leaving.

Dean Wilkes touched Bishop's arm. "We'd like a brief word in my office, if we may." He said.

Bishop faced the students. "Be right back, class, read from page eighty-three, The Ghost Army."

He followed Wilkes and Glass back to Wilkes' office, down the hall from his own. The two men spoke casually, discussed golf courses and agreed to play a round over the next week.

The two burly men led the way, looking at open doors and around corners as they went. Bishop wondered if these men had ever worked in the White House.

They walked barely three steps ahead of the Admiral, unobtrusive, but silently watching everyone.

Dean Wilkes ushered Glass into his office, asked if he wanted something to drink, then buzzed for Kelly, the receptionist, and asked if she would kindly bring them some water and coffee.

Glass pulled a folded sheet of paper from his jacket and handed it to Bishop.

"What's this?" Bishop asked.

"It's your 'free pass to the Oslo summit', son." Glass said.

Bishop unfolded the paper. It had a military crest on the page above the letterhead, and in five short sentences it said that he had performed a valuable service, his efforts were acknowledged and appreciated, and that whatever information he had seen recently was no longer classified.

Bishop shook his head. "I don't understand, sir. What does this mean?"

Glass put his cap on Dean Wilke's desk. "The truth is, there are some things that are true and others that are just opinions. Is the ocean blue? Only in large quantities. A glass of it is clear. Is what I told you before true? Yes, but now it seems the Oslo minutes have been released early, so the secrecy around what you received is no longer a secret. Hell, it was on CNN last night."

"What about Flytrap? What about Deborah Bijani? What about General Sparwood? Are those people all just chaff?" Bishop asked.

Glass shot a glance at Wilkes then leaned forward. "Sparwood inadvertently did what we were going to do anyway. We were prepared to create a bogus intermediary, someone to track the product until it got to the final destination. He did the heavy lifting for us. Unfortunately, it just didn't work out well for him in the end."

"Twenty million dollars went missing." Bishop reminded him.

Glass smiled. "Now that it's over, I can tell you about that. Deborah Bijani made a deal with us. She goes to Iran, hands over the vials to the IRG, keeps the money then disappears. She knows it's just smoke and mirrors. They will think they have the real deal, but she can't let them know they've been duped or they will kill her. She can't come back to this country or she goes to jail. She's no longer our problem. The vials of liquid go where we always wanted them to go, and all is right with the world."

"Do you really expect me to believe that those vials don't actually do anything?" Bishop asked.

Glass rubbed his nose. "Do you believe in Santa Claus? Whether you do or not, he's very real to some people. Some will still believe that those vials do what they think we told them they do. They will find out that it's not the case. Let's leave it at that."

Bishop shrugged. "Fair enough. It's firing over my head, and it's out of my hair. I'm just glad that this is no longer my concern."

Glass placed his hand on the desk. "One last thing. You did the right thing- you sent a report to your old Command HQ in Washington. They liked your conclusions, by the way. I'd like to see the details of how you were able to track down the root issue, given that you had very little to work with."

"Sure. Send me an email and I'll tell you what I can." Bishop said.

Glass poked his nose at one of the burly men, and the man slipped out of the office.

"Actually, I have to catch a plane to Dallas in about an hour. Fortunately it's a military jet, so they'll hold it for me, but there are a couple of senators on the flight, so I'd rather not keep them waiting." Glass said.

He picked up his cap and stood up. Bishop stood too, an automatic response to seeing a senior officer stand.

"I'd like you to liaise with my adjutant. Lieutenant Sam Harper. Sam will have a list of questions for you. It may take you a couple of hours, so if you can arrange a convenient time after work?"

Bishop looked over at Dean Wilkes. His eyes widened slightly in a 'please do this' expression.

Bishop nodded. "I'd be happy to help, Admiral. When will he be here?"

The sound of clip-clopping heels came down the hall, the sound of Kelly with coffee, no doubt.

A very pretty woman in a blue-black dress uniform came into the room. She was tall, with blond hair tucked up into her cap, deep green eyes and a blush of red lipstick. She had a flat leather folio case tucked under her left arm and a thick black pen in her right hand.

She entered the room, transferred the pen to her left hand and saluted Glass.

"Admiral, sir." She said smartly.

"Hi, Sam. This is Captain Bishop. Can you take some time later and ask him for his thoughts on the questions we had worked up?"

She gave a sharp nod. "Happy to do so, sir."

She turned to Bishop and stuck out her hand. "Hi. Lieutenant Samantha Harper. Call me Sam."

Bishop took her hand. It was soft, and he felt a tingle as he shook it. "Pleased to meet you, Lieutenant. Good thing you're not a Captain- I'd have to salute you. A Navy Captain ranks higher." He joked.

She grinned. Bishop felt another minor rush at that small gesture.

Glass shook Dean Wilkes' hand and glanced at the young woman. "Sam, send the report to me next week. I'll be back in Baltimore then. See you soon, Colonel. Don't forget, you owe me a round of golf."

Wilkes laughed. "I remember, ten bucks a hole. You got it. Safe travels, Hugh."

Lieutenant Harper leaned over Wilkes' desk for the stapler. Bishop looked at the way her legs curved in her skirt. She was not skinny, but there was no fat, just a well-shaped curve. Her blouse, he also noted, puckered nicely when she moved.

She turned to look at Bishop. "So, would it interfere with your evening plans if we spent a few hours going over the events of the last few days?"

Bishop shook his head. She sat on the desk and stuck her long legs forward.

"Um, your wife or girlfriend won't get upset at you being away?" She asked.

Bishop grinned. "I have none at present. My evening is all yours."

Harper blushed slightly then composed herself. "Well, that sounds like a plan, then. I look forward to spending the evening with you."

"On my report." She added hurriedly.

Bishop leaned back and smiled. "Can I buy you dinner beforehand?"

She beamed. "Dinner sounds lovely. Yes, thanks."

"Do you like Mexican food?" He offered.

"Love it. I grew up in New Mexico. I miss good Mexican food."

Bishop stood up. "I'd love to hear about that. I know this great restaurant near Pike Place Market. They do terrific enchiladas."

She unzipped the leather folio and pulled out a number of papers.

"I'll work here this afternoon, then after class we can meet for dinner, Captain."

"Bish. All my friends call me Bish." He said.

"Bish." She repeated. She smiled again.

The End.

Look for the next book in the John Bishop series.

Silhouette

Sigurd Ericsson was crouched low, hiding in the clump of bushes beside a large maple tree. His weapon was empty, useless, but he still held it tightly under his right arm. The next safe spot was a second clump of bushes, just beyond a grassy area about thirty feet wide, mown low like a putting green.

If he could get to that next safe spot, he could hide until it was safe to get into the building.

The building was tantalizingly close, just forty feet past the second clump of bushes, but Ericsson waited patiently until he saw the two-man patrol walk past him, oblivious to his green camouflage uniform. He took a deep breath and sprinted across the grass to the bushes. He slid to a stop, baseball style, under a sprawling azalea bush, and waited some more.

Victory was in sight. There was no-one around, nobody to stop him from getting through the door. Ericsson made a dash for the open glass double doors. He'd gone maybe five feet, when a man in a brown camouflage uniform swung out from behind one of the maples and pointed a weapon at Ericsson. The weapon went 'putt-putt' and Ericsson's uniform splattered orange and blue from the opponent's paintball gun.

"Got you." The other man said, triumphant.

Ericsson put his hands up. "Yeah, you got me. Now let's get a beer."

The other man looked around. "Meet you later. More of the Production Department to kill yet."

He jogged away. Ericsson sauntered toward the building, disappointed that he was eliminated, but glad to be through with the silly corporate 'team activity' as they called the event.

Another man in brown camouflage jumped out and pointed a weapon at Ericsson.

Ericsson shook his head. "Save your ammo. I'm dead."

The man shook his head. "No, not yet, you're not."

He fired his weapon, with a similar 'putt-putt' sound, and the bullets entered Ericsson's forehead. He was dead before he hit the ground.

Mauro Azzano is the author of the popular **Ian McBriar Murder Mysteries** as well as this, the first in the **John Bishop Mysteries**.

Look for these Ian McBriar books, available in all popular bookstores and online.

The Dead Don't Dream

Death Works at Night

Death By Deceit

Death Never Lets Go

Dead End